Praise **Lily Everett's**

"*Sanctuary Island* is a novel to curl up with and enjoy by a crackling fire or on a sunny beach. It's a beautifully told story of hope and forgiveness, celebrating the healing power of love."

—Susan Wiggs, #1 *New York Times* bestselling author

"I didn't read this book, I inhaled it. An incredible story of love, forgiveness, healing, and joy."

—Debbie Macomber,
#1 *New York Times* bestselling author

"A heartwarming, emotional, extremely romantic story that I couldn't read fast enough! Enjoy your trip to Sanctuary Island! I guarantee you won't want to leave."

—Bella Andre, *New York Times*
bestselling author of the Sullivan series

"Well-written and emotionally satisfying. I loved it! A rare find."

—Lori Wilde, *New York Times* bestselling author

"Fall in love with Sanctuary Island. Lily Everett brings tears, laughter and a happy-ever-after smile to your face while you're experiencing her well-written, compassionate novel. I highly recommend this book, which hits home with true-to-life characters."

—*Romance Junkies*

"Redemption, reconciliation, and, of course, romance—Everett's novel has it all."   —*Booklist*

"Richly nuanced characters and able plotting . . . Everett's sweet contemporary debut illustrates the power of forgiveness and the strength of relationships that may falter but never fail."   —*Publishers Weekly*

"Lily has a talent for metaphors that make me melt . . . and I love the way she ties the story together. I'm so looking forward to the next book in the series."
                    —*USA Today*'s Happily Ever After blog

"I loved learning about Sanctuary Island and I felt as if I was there seeing and feeling everything first hand. A wonderful book to get lost in for a few hours. I definitely recommend it to other readers."   —*Night Owl Reviews*

"I couldn't help but fall in love with Sanctuary Island and want to move there myself. An enchanting romance that swept me away!"   —*Books N Kisses*

"There is little more satisfying for a fan of contemporary romance than an Everett novel."   —*RT Book Reviews*

"With strong, independent people, each with a different story to tell, Lily's smooth writing easily sucks you in to experience island life with them. I love the setting and the descriptions Lily gives us of Sanctuary Island and the people there! She makes it a place I'd love to visit."
                    —*Harlequin Junkie*

ALSO BY LILY EVERETT

Sanctuary Island
Shoreline Drive
Homecoming
Heartbreak Cove
Home for Christmas
Three Promises
Close to Home

Home at Last

A Sanctuary Island Novel

LILY EVERETT

St. Martin's Paperbacks

This is a work of fiction. All of the characters, organizations, and events portrayed in this novel are either products of the author's imagination or are used fictitiously.

HOME AT LAST

Copyright © 2017 by Lily Everett.

All rights reserved.

For information address St. Martin's Press, 175 Fifth Avenue, New York, NY 10010.

ISBN: 978-1-250-07406-5

Our books may be purchased in bulk for promotional, educational, or business use. Please contact your local bookseller or the Macmillan Corporate and Premium Sales Department at 1-800-221-7945, ext. 5442, or by e-mail at MacmillanSpecialMarkets@macmillan.com.

Printed in the United States of America

St. Martin's Paperbacks edition / March 2017

St. Martin's Paperbacks are published by St. Martin's Press, 175 Fifth Avenue, New York, NY 10010.

10 9 8 7 6 5 4 3 2 1

This one is for all my readers. Sanctuary Island wouldn't exist without you! Thank you, from the bottom of my heart.

Acknowledgments

Every book is special to me, but this one is extra special. I fell hard for bubbly Quinn and gruff Marcus as secondary characters in *Close to Home,* so I was excited to get to explore their chemistry more deeply in *Home at Last.* As always, huge thanks to my editor, Rose Hilliard, who loved these characters as much as I did and helped bring their story out.

Thank you, also, to the Writing Retreat ladies of Kiawah Island, 2016! Monica McCarty, Ally Carter, and most of all, my brainstorming muse and partner-in-crime, Sarah MacLean. You three each lent some of your magic and sparkle to the writing of this book, and I can't thank you enough. My standing stone circle wouldn't be the same without you.

And last, but not least, thank you to my husband,

Nick. The last couple of years have been such an emotional roller coaster—I couldn't have made it through without your support, encouragement, humor, and understanding. I love you.

Prologue

Quinn Harper pedaled her bike down the road, slowing the way she always did when she got to the house next door to her own. The only other house out this far on Lantern Point. The Beckett house.

His house.

When she was younger, a little kid instead of an almost teenager, she used to ring the bell attached to her handlebars in the giddy hope that Marcus might come outside and give her that friendly wave, or even better, the grin that made it seem like they were both in on a juicy secret no one else knew. Not that a grown-up college graduate like Marcus would have a secret with a twelve-year-old. Quinn wasn't delusional, but she used to ring her bell anyway.

Now she bit her lip, looking down at her silent bell. It was definitely not a day for bell ringing. Even the

gentle rustle of the candy-apple-red and white streamers sprouting from her handlebars seemed wrong
somehow—too bright, too happy, clashing with the
sadness hanging over the Beckett house.

Quinn shifted on the banana seat of her bike, pre-
paring to push off and ride back to the end of the point,
when all of a sudden the front door slammed open and
Marcus Beckett strode out.

Wobbling, Quinn stuck out a skinny leg to steady
herself against the curb as Marcus crossed the lawn
toward his waiting Camaro, black like the leather jacket
he'd slung over the shoulder of his dark suit. She'd
never seen him as dressed up as he was today. She didn't
like it. Apart from the very sad and tragic reason he was
wearing it, the suit made him look older, even more
out of reach than he already was.

Marcus tossed his jacket into the passenger seat and
shut the door with a bang before bracing his palms
against the side of the car. His head hung down, wild,
dark hair brushing his bulging biceps, and Quinn felt
the same confusing heat that had simmered in her belly
all summer whenever she'd caught a glimpse of Marcus around the neighborhood, in the park, or eating
burgers with his friends at the Firefly Café.

Now, that warmth was nearly choked off by the
awful, stomach-twisting sympathy that seized Quinn as
she watched Marcus's broad shoulders heave, once and
then again.

Realizing suddenly that he had no idea anyone was

there and that this was probably a moment he wouldn't want anyone to see, Quinn slid off her bike seat and started walking it carefully backward, trying not to make a sound.

But Marcus straightened up with a muttered word—a very bad word, Quinn recognized, simultaneously impressed and scandalized—and when he straightened to go around to the driver's side of the car, he saw her.

She held her breath, wondering if she should apologize, or if she should say she was sorry for other reasons, like everyone had been saying at the church earlier. Agonized indecision froze her tongue to the roof of her mouth.

Marcus didn't do the friendly wave, but he did smile. Small and tired, and it didn't reach his shadowed gray eyes, but Quinn smiled back anyway. She couldn't help it. She always smiled when she saw Marcus Beckett.

"Hey, Turbo," he said. "Nice dress."

Quinn glanced down at the black fabric covered in big, pink blossoms. It had been one of her favorites, but now she was afraid she'd never be able to wear it again without remembering what it felt like to wear it to Mrs. Beckett's funeral.

"I didn't have one that was all black," Quinn blurted, feeling weirdly like she should apologize for the bright blooms covering her torso. "Maybe the purple one would've been better. I didn't know."

And Quinn's mother, devastated by the loss of her

best friend and only close neighbor, hadn't been much help.

"First funeral, huh?" Marcus looked away, fingers tapping restlessly on the roof of the Camaro. "Me, too."

Whatever fleeting delight Quinn usually took in finding anything she had in common with Marcus was muted by the low, miserable sound of his voice. Her throat was full of an aching, incoherent tenderness—a need to do or say something to make things better for him—but there was nothing. Even at twelve and finding new reasons to fight with her mom almost every day, Quinn still couldn't imagine losing her.

She didn't think being older and technically a grown-up like Marcus made it that much easier.

The weight of everything she felt, everything she wanted to tell him, glued her jaws shut for an agonizingly embarrassing moment. Everyone had already told Marcus how sorry they were. It obviously hadn't helped. Maybe nothing could, but she had to say something.

"Your mom was always real nice to me," she offered. "She never minded when I asked her questions."

It didn't sound like much, but to Quinn and her insatiable curiosity, it had meant a lot. She liked to follow around the adults in her life who had interesting jobs, finding out as much as she could about what they did all day as teachers, horse trainers, veterinarians, accountants, whatever. As a nurse, Mrs. Beckett always had good stories to tell about funny things people did in the emergency room at Winter Harbor

Hospital, and she hadn't gotten frustrated or annoyed the way lots of grown-ups did at having a chattering kid hopping after them with question after question.

Marcus didn't scoff at Quinn's stupid memory, though. He looked almost as if he got it. "She liked you. And I know your family did a lot for my parents while she was sick, so thank you for that."

Quinn ducked her head, feeling awkward heat stain her checks. "Don't thank me. My dad made the casseroles and stuff."

"You visited my mother every day," Marcus countered, catching her gaze the moment she lifted her head in surprise. "Yeah, she mentioned it when I called. You came over and sat with her and distracted her from the pain by talking a mile a minute, Turbo."

A smile ghosted across his face before flickering into the grim-faced blankness he'd worn at the service. "Anyway. Since I wasn't here, I'm glad somebody was."

Without meaning to, Quinn glanced at Marcus's dark, quiet house. The house where his father would live alone, after today.

"She was glad you stayed at school," Quinn offered. "She talked about how proud of you she was. All the time."

The muscle at the back of Marcus's jaw clenched visibly. "Screw school. I should've been here. If Dad had told me when he found out how bad the cancer was—"

He cut himself off by slamming his fist into the roof of his car with a loud bang that made Quinn jump.

"I guess he wanted you to be able to graduate on time." Quinn bit her lip, wanting to defend the gray, grieving Dr. Beckett but not wanting to make Marcus think she didn't understand why he was upset. "If you're going to be a doctor, all that medical school and stuff . . . it takes forever."

Dragging his keys out of his pocket, Marcus glanced over his shoulder at his father's house. "I'm not going to medical school. I'm not going to be a doctor."

Quinn's jaw dropped. Everyone knew Marcus was going to follow both of his parents into the medical profession. He'd been working toward it his whole life. "But. You got into Stanford."

Quinn ought to know. She'd cried for a week at the thought of Marcus all the way across the country in California for years and years.

He shrugged, using the motion to slide the charcoal-gray suit jacket off his shoulders. The stark white shirt underneath stretched taut across his chest, out-lining the shape of his muscles. Quinn swallowed hard.

"Screw Stanford," Marcus said as he crumpled up the jacket and tossed it in the car with his duffel.

"What will you do instead?" Quinn asked urgently, sending up a swift, silent prayer that the answer would be "stay home on Sanctuary Island and ask you to the prom in four years."

He paused, and Quinn held her breath. Finally, with a last, hard look at the house where he grew up, Marcus said, "I'm enlisting."

"In the army?" Quinn squeaked. Oh no. No, no, no.

She'd worried about him going to Stanford for medical school and never coming back, but at least in that scenario, he'd be happy and healthy in California. Now she was going to have to worry about him coming home alive at all.

"Or the navy. I haven't decided yet." Marcus flipped his keys into the air and caught them one-handed, his gaze on the horizon. "Doesn't matter. The point is, it's my life and I'm going to do what I want."

A hard lump rose in Quinn's throat. She couldn't argue with that, and if this was what Marcus felt called to do, she could only admire him for it. But she couldn't let him leave—maybe forever!—without saying something! She had to tell him how she felt. Fear clutched at her.

Screwing up her guts, she inhaled—and then chickened out at the last second. "Just remember that there are people here on Sanctuary Island who l-love you."

Instead of softening, his expression turned flinty. "Love. That's just an excuse people give when they want to control you. People who love you think they own you, and that you owe them something, no matter what they do. Well, fu—forget that. I don't owe anyone here a damn thing."

His eyes connected with hers for a brief, stormy

moment where Quinn was mostly trying not to cry. Something about the way Marcus ground his teeth, the red rims of his eyes, told her he was in the same boat. Speechless, she watched him walk around and open the driver's side door of the Camaro. He didn't look at his house again. Instead, he lifted his head and gazed at her.

"Don't let love tie you up in knots, Turbo," he said starkly. "The world is full of people who think they know what's best for you and 'love' gives them the right to decide that. You're better off making your own choices."

With that, he slid behind the wheel and started the engine with a roar. He backed out of the driveway fast and took off down the road in a squeal of tires. He never looked back once.

Quinn knew that for sure, because the instant he drove away she pushed off from the curb and pedaled as fast as her legs could carry her, following the Camaro as far as she could with her heart pounding and eyes stinging. He outpaced her in less than a minute, leaving her struggling in his wake, sucking in exhaust fumes on every desperate, sobbing breath. Tears streaked her face, but she told herself they were from the wind in her eyes.

There was no point in her crying over Marcus Beckett. She couldn't lose something she never had to begin with.

But in a small, stubborn corner of her heart, Quinn

was very much afraid that no matter what he said or thought about love, no matter what happened or didn't happen between them . . . she'd never love anyone in her life as much as she loved Marcus Beckett.

Chapter 1

Fourteen years later . . .
Marcus Beckett passed his cloth over the top of the already gleaming surface of the zinc bar he'd carefully installed with his own hands, and wondered for the hundredth time what the hell he was doing. There was a reason he'd left Sanctuary Island in the dust all those years ago. He must've been nuts to think coming back was a good idea.

"You're going to wear a hole through that thing," observed the bird-boned, white-haired lady perched on the center bar stool.

Fist clenching, Marcus forced himself to toss the towel aside without checking the clock over the bar again. He knew what time it was. Six o'clock. Happy hour.

The saddest, most pathetic "happy hour" in the history of one-dollar beer pitchers.

He looked around his deserted bar. The paintings he'd unearthed from the attic of the building and hung on the walls. The mismatched bar stools from the flea market in Winter Harbor. The cheery blue and green plaid curtains hanging at the dark windows. The empty booths along the wall.

"I don't know what you expected." His lone customer—hell, practically his lone friend in the world—Patty Cuthbert took a dainty sip of her old-fashioned and leveled him a look over the tops of her bifocals. "You screwed and dumped Sanctuary Island's sweetheart. And this is a town that takes care of its own."

"I was born here, too," Marcus pointed out irritably. "Grew up here, graduated from Sanctuary High, the whole bit."

"But then you left. And you didn't come back, not even once, not even to visit your poor, lonely, grieving father."

Marcus's fists went white-knuckled against the edge of his bar. "Trust me. My father knew better than to expect annual visits from me."

Something flickered in Patty's bright, curious gaze, but she let it lie for the moment. "That's as may be. But not everyone in this town is as respectful of folks' privacy as yours truly. In fact, some people 'round here could be called downright gossipy. And face it, your homecoming to Sanctuary Island was one of the more exciting things to happen in these parts in quite some time. Of course people were watching to see what you'd do."

And then the first thing he'd done was to fall into bed with Quinn Harper, the literal girl next door. Ten years younger—and about ten thousand times sweeter—than anyone Marcus should even consider touching.

"I don't want to talk about Quinn," he growled.

It was unbecoming of a woman of Patty's advanced years and dignity to roll her eyes like that. Marcus frowned at her, but she didn't appear to notice.

"If you wanted to forget all about Quinn," Patty chortled, "you probably shouldn't have let her move in upstairs. Right next door to you. Again."

Frustration simmered under Marcus's skin. Patty wasn't wrong. He knew it. He just didn't seem to be able to do much about it on account of how being in the same room with Quinn Harper's sunshine smile and cute freckles made him itch to get his hands on her. So he did his best never to be in the same room with her.

Maybe it was the coward's way out to ignore the girl, but Marcus didn't give a crap. He had nothing to prove to nobody. Not anymore.

Shoving down the bitter lump of grief and regret, Marcus shrugged and waited for Patty to finish the last sip of her cocktail. He swiped the glass out of her hand, ice clinking, and nodded toward the door. "No need to stick around to keep me company. I'm going to close up early. Hit the hay."

Think about how long he was going to stubbornly keep blowing Buttercup's money on a bar with no customers.

Patty gave him a pitying look as if she'd read his mind, and Marcus gritted his teeth against the urge to snarl at her. None of this was Patty's fault. And even if Marcus was the kind of junkyard dog who snapped his teeth at kindness, he had a soft spot for steely old ladies who spoke their minds and didn't mince words.

A lady like that had changed his life, once upon a time.

"Fine, I'll go." Patty slid off her stool and gathered up her handbag. "But think about what I said. This isn't going away, boy. We have long memories here, and we know how to hold a grudge. Something is going to have to change or you're going to lose everything."

She let herself out of the bar before Marcus could come up with a nonbraggy way to explain that the situation wasn't that dire. Marcus had more money than he knew what to do with, thanks to Buttercup. Not an endless supply, but enough to keep him afloat for a while, even after the generous secret donation he'd made to the Windy Corner Therapeutic Riding Center to get Quinn her job out there.

Still. Marcus leaned his elbows on the bar and let his shoulders slump. Did he really want to gamble everything she'd left him on the chance that the people he grew up with would eventually cave and start patronizing the Buttercup Inn? Maybe he'd be better off throwing in the towel and starting over—again—someplace where no one knew him.

The thought made him scowl, determination hardening his jaw. No. He would be damned before he'd let these people run him out of town on a rail. He had as much right to be here as anyone.

An image of Quinn's pretty face, pinched with hurt, rose up in Marcus's mind's eye. Yeah, okay. He'd hurt her. But he'd done it for her own good and he had zero regrets. She was better off.

As if the thought of her had conjured her up, Quinn burst into the bar like a whirlwind made of sunshine and laughter.

Except she wasn't laughing. She didn't laugh much, these days. Marcus tried not to notice.

He tried not to notice anything about Quinn. Not the downward curve of her bow-shaped lips, not the fact that she'd lost enough weight in the last few weeks to make the collar of her shirt slide down over the cinnamon-speckled ivory smoothness of her shoulder. He clenched his jaw and glared down at the untapped keg of beer behind the bar before he could wonder if that meant she wasn't wearing a bra. Those pert, perfect breasts swaying free and unfettered under the soft, thin cotton . . .

Oh, he was doing a great job of not noticing her. Gold medal.

Marcus shook his head at himself. He could only be thankful that a few more seconds and Quinn would be past him without a word, taking the stairs up to her studio apartment two at a time as if she couldn't escape his presence fast enough.

For the best, he reminded himself. But his stoicism was tested when Quinn didn't rush through the bar without a word, the way she had every time their paths crossed since the night she showed up here and demanded a place to stay.

"Hi, Marcus."

She sounded nervous, uncertain in a way that reminded him of the awkward little girl she'd once been, all gangly limbs, skinned knees, and carroty hair. Marcus confined himself to a grunt in reply, sternly quashing any curiosity about what prompted her to approach him after weeks of the silent treatment.

There was a long pause. Marcus picked up Patty's glass and focused on polishing it dry while he waited for Quinn to get frustrated with his lack of response and give up.

He should've known better.

"The new job at Windy Corners is going well," she said abruptly. From the corner of his eye, he caught the movement of her hand propping on one cocked, rounded hip. "Thanks for asking."

Marcus steeled himself for their first real conversation since she accused him of being too big a coward to keep up their relationship.

The key was to keep it short and to the point. "I didn't ask because I don't care."

"You can be a real jerk sometimes."

Marcus said nothing. This was not news to him.

After a minute, Quinn turned on her heel and stalked away. It was a win, but Marcus couldn't dredge up much triumph. Mostly he felt tired.

Tired and angry, his default setting these days.

He was so busy brooding over his feelings like a ridiculous teenager, it took him a full ten seconds to realize that Quinn hadn't left the bar. Instead, she'd walked over to the wall switch by the door and flipped off the neon signs that proclaimed the Buttercup Inn open.

"What the hell are you doing?" Marcus demanded, conveniently ignoring the fact that he'd been about to do the exact same thing before she marched in. "It's another hour until closing time."

Quinn's stubborn little chin lifted. "No one is going to show up, no matter how long you wait. You might as well close up now. We need to talk."

We need to talk. There wasn't a man alive who could hear those words without an instinctive shudder. Marcus didn't let it show on his face, though.

"You're right. No one is going to come in if you lock the door," Marcus agreed sardonically, twisting to slide Patty's now-clean glass onto the shelf behind him with the other, untouched glasses.

"No one is going to come in here because everyone in town is mad at you."

Marcus jerked his head around to see Quinn staring him down, an unreadable expression on her pretty face. Used to be, he could translate every flicker of expression just by looking at her, but not these days.

He'd done that to her, Marcus knew. It was because of him that sunny, open, sweet-natured Quinn Harper had finally learned to put up walls around her heart.

"They're mad because you broke up with me," she pressed into the taut silence. "I'm sorry about that. I didn't ask anyone to boycott your bar."

There it was, the elephant in the room. Marcus ignored the way it felt like this elephant was poised to stomp all over his future, and walked over to the nearest table to start upending chairs. If he was closing up early, he might as well get started on cleaning.

"They'll come around," he said, sliding the heavy wooden chair onto the tabletop. He sounded more certain than he felt, so that was a plus.

"Or they won't. Or it'll take too long and you'll end up losing all your money. Face it. You're in a pickle."

He moved on to the next table and picked up a chair. "What would this town full of doting honorary aunts and uncles think if they could hear the glee in your voice when you talk about my . . . pickle."

"Don't get nasty." Quinn circled the table until she was in his line of sight, giving him a look full of injured dignity. "I'm here to help you, Marcus. Not that you deserve it."

Truer words. Marcus rolled the guilt right off his shoulders. "Don't bother. I'll get by without help. Always do."

"But you don't have to." Quinn blew out an exasperated breath that lifted strands of her red-gold hair off her forehead. "That's what I'm trying to tell you. I have a proposal."

What, a marriage proposal? Everything inside Marcus went still and quiet. He tried to tell himself it was pure terror—the fear of giving up his freedom to hitch his life forever to someone like Quinn, who was destined to leave him in the dust one way or another— but Marcus had never been good at lying to himself.

If she got down on one knee on the floor of this bar, he was going to say yes. Even knowing it would be the dumbest damn mistake of his life.

Silence stretched between them and held for a long, aching moment before Quinn's brilliant blue eyes went wide. "Oh! No, no, don't worry. Not that kind of proposal. 'Proposal' was a bad word. Proposition, maybe. Or, crap, that sounds bad, too I have a plan! That's it. A plan."

Marcus refused to acknowledge the clutch of disappointment in his guts. Of course she wasn't proposing to him. He'd ripped her heart out and thrown it away like it was garbage, and he'd done it on purpose to get her to move on with her life. Quinn might be too generous and forgiving for her own good, but she wasn't a masochist. No way she'd ever get herself mixed up with Marcus again.

His lack of response must have made her nervous, because she followed him to the next table with a jitter in her step. "Don't you want to hear my plan?"

"No." Marcus didn't want to hear anything. He

wanted to pour himself a glass of bourbon to take upstairs and nurse all night long, in the dark, by himself. That didn't seem like too much to ask.

But apparently, it was.

Quinn's gaze narrowed and her chin went up. Marcus's eyes caught on the slight dimple in that chin—the dimple he'd kissed. More than once.

"Well, you're going to hear it anyway," she said, commanding his attention the way she always had without even trying.

God help him, but Marcus loved strong women.

Straightening, he picked up another chair and tried not to picture himself holding it like a lion tamer in a circus. He couldn't afford to let Quinn get close again. "Let's get this over with. I have plans for tonight."

She arched a delicate brow in the direction of his favorite bottle of bourbon—the only bottle on the bar that was half empty after a week in business—but generously decided not to call him on his bull. Instead, she looked him square in the eye and turned his life upside down with a few little words.

"I can bring in customers for the bar—get the townspeople here to stop boycotting the Buttercup Inn. And all you have to do is pretend to be my boyfriend for the next four weeks."

Chapter 2

Quinn held her breath and laced her fingers together in front of her to hide their trembling. She couldn't wait to find out how Marcus was going to react. Although she was pretty sure he'd laugh her out of the bar, which was fine. She'd been laughed at before. She could survive that.

But if he refused to help her . . . well, she'd survive that, too. But her parents' marriage might not.

Panic compressed her ribs around her lungs, squeezing off her air supply. It happened every time she thought about the conversation she'd had with her parents that morning.

When Quinn had pulled up in front of the charming, shingled cottage where she grew up at the tip of Lantern Point, the jagged edges of her heart immediately felt smoother. Smiling at the peaked roof and the tidy shutters, it had taken her a moment to notice her mother crouched in the flower bed under the front bay window. Ingrid Harper's long, flowing skirts spread around her and a light jingle sounded from the belled anklets she wore above her rubber garden clogs.

"Pretty morning for gardening," Quinn had called, climbing out of her car and starting down the stone path she and her father had laid in by hand about ten years ago.

Ingrid knelt up with a hand to the small of her back. Her other glove-covered hand went up to shade her eyes. "I'm doing what I can, but these beds are a wreck!"

Quinn winced, guilt pricking at her skin like the thorns spiking the tangle of rosebushes. She had kind of let the flowers go while she was house-sitting. "Sorry. I didn't inherit your green thumb, I guess."

Waving away her apology, Quinn's mother gave her a vague smile as she turned back to her rosebushes. "Don't worry about it, sweetheart. I know how busy you are with all your volunteering."

Congratulating herself on having held her spaced-out mother's attention for a whole thirty seconds, Quinn stepped up onto the porch. "Is Daddy inside?"

"In the kitchen, heating up the griddle. Tell him he can start pouring batter whenever he wants. I'm just going to wash up and I'll be right behind you."

Quinn nodded and let herself into the house, breathing deeply of the mingled scents of the old books on the shelves lining the living room walls, lemony wood polish, and buttermilk pancakes.

Home.

That feeling returned even more strongly when she entered the kitchen to find her father standing over the stove, flicking droplets of water to sizzle on the cast-iron griddle. Quinn ducked under her father's arm, smiling at the familiar weight across her shoulders and the swift press of a kiss to the top of her head. "Mother's right behind me," she told him.

"Good. We're all ready to go here," Paul Harper said distractedly as he reached for the bowl and ladled out a spoonful of . . . something lumpy and grayish.

"What is that?" Quinn demanded, leaning closer to sniff at the bowl of glop, which looked nothing like the pale, foamy buttermilk pancake batter of her childhood.

"Gluten-free pancakes made with . . ." He paused and picked up a small plastic bag of meal the same iffy gray as the batter. "Rice bran? Don't get your hopes up."

Quinn gaped. Her whole life, her mother had gone through these phases, getting obsessed with one hippy-dippy idea after another. But even when she'd made the whole family go vegan, Saturday-morning butter-milk pancakes had been sacrosanct. A frisson of alarm skittered up Quinn's spine.

Sighing, she opened the fridge and grabbed the pure maple syrup—no high-fructose corn syrup colored with brown dye number four in this house—from the top shelf and popped the cap to pour it into the ceramic pitcher shaped like a curly-tailed pig. It was the one they always used for the syrup, and Quinn was unreasonably fond of the ugly little thing.

She carried it carefully to the microwave, not wanting to waste a drop of syrup. She was already planning to drown her pancakes in it. "Do you want me to do the butter? Are we allowed to have butter this week?"

"Already on the table." Her dad jerked his head toward the kitchen table snugged up against the far wall, where the funny-shaped, handleless pitcher she'd made at summer camp sat, steaming gently. The whole scene was so comforting. Even the pancake disappointment was strangely reassuring, in its own way, colored by nostalgia and fondness. Her parents were home from their travels and all was right with the world. Quinn sighed again, but this time it was a happy sigh.

"What's the matter?"

Her father's voice was sharp with concern. Quinn went back to the stove to curl her arm around his still-trim waist and lean her head on his shoulder. "Nothing's the matter. I'm glad you're done with your camper adventures for a while, that's all. It's nice to have everything back to normal."

He cleared his throat roughly, and Quinn tilted her head up to see his unhappy expression. Paul's lips thinned into a sad line under his salt-and-pepper goatee. "About that."

A nameless fear shot through Quinn's heart like an arrow. "Daddy?"

"You'll be glad to know I think I can save the roses." Quinn's mother's happy voice preceded her into the kitchen, where she stopped dead on the threshold. Ingrid's normally vague gaze narrowed on her husband and daughter at the stove. "Paul. How could you? I can't believe you would tell her without me here."

Quinn blinked at the real hurt in her mother's voice. All the warm fuzzy drained out of her body. "Tell me what?"

"I didn't say anything yet," Paul said tersely, turning his attention stubbornly to flipping the bubbling pancakes over.

Ingrid Harper took a slow, meditative breath as she slipped off her soiled gardening gloves. "Good. That's . . . good. Does anyone else want coffee? I've had a cup already, so I probably shouldn't have more unless I want to levitate to the farmer's market this afternoon, but what the hey? You only live once, as the kids say."

Quinn stared back and forth between her parents, from her father's turned back to her mother's restless flitting around the kitchen as she poured herself a mug of coffee. Something was very wrong. All the innocent gladness Quinn had taken in being back in her childhood home with the family she loved seemed to curdle like buttermilk. "Screw coffee. Someone tell me what's going on."

"Negativity!" Ingrid frowned at her daughter over

the rim of her "#1 Mom" mug. "Words matter, sweetie. They're the energy you put out into the universe."

"And they tell the universe what energy to send back," Quinn finished the familiar phrase. It took some effort not to roll her eyes like a teenager. "Mother. I know. But can I just say . . . the 'energy' you and Daddy are putting out right now is making me extremely tense. I would appreciate it if one of you would clue me in on why the two of you can't seem to even look at each other."

For the first time in Quinn's life, her mother hesitated, her gaze flicking to her husband as if looking for guidance. Nothing could have scared Quinn more than to see that uncertainty on her obliviously confident mother's face. Her father didn't turn, though. All he did was slide his spatula under the pancakes and transfer them to a platter. He didn't look at Quinn, or at his wife.

Ingrid's shoulders slumped for an instant before she shook out her long, wavy gray-streaked hair with a determined smile. She fluttered over to the table to pull out a chair. "Everything is going to be fine, sweetheart. Sit down, have some pancakes."

Quinn wanted to snap that she needed answers, not pancakes, but then her father brought the platter over to the table, and, well. She was hungry, even if the pancakes looked weird. Quinn sat and helped herself while her father went back to the stove to pour more batter out onto the griddle.

Her mother perched in the chair across from her,

long-fingered artist's hands curled around her mug as if savoring the warmth. She waited for Quinn to take a bite and make the requisite face at the slightly funky tang of the gluten-free pancakes, then dropped her first bomb.

"Your father and I are only back on Sanctuary for a few weeks. Just long enough to put the house up for sale."

Quinn's vision tunneled with anxiety. Her childhood home. The place where she'd learned to ride a bike, where she'd watched her parents dance around the kitchen, where she'd fallen in love with Marcus Beckett for the first time. That last one jerked her out of her panic enough to protest.

"You can't sell this place! It's our home!"

Paul dropped into his chair across from Quinn's, the same places they'd sat every night for dinner when Quinn was growing up. But all the fond indulgence and patience she was used to seeing on her father's face had disappeared. The laugh lines fanning out from the blue eyes she'd inherited seemed to have been written over with bitterness and defeat.

"Tell her the rest of it," he said tonelessly.

Quinn dropped her fork with a clatter. "There's more?"

Ingrid pressed her lips together, looking torn, but her husband didn't relent.

"Tell her about Ron," he said, a hint of anger creeping into his voice.

Dread filled Quinn's heart. "Who is Ron?"

But instead of looking guilty, as Quinn half expected and feared, her mother lit up. "Oh, Ron is wonderful! We met him out in Taos, and you know the energy in New Mexico, it's just amazing. So good for serenity and finding balance; it's no coincidence we found Ron there. Not that I believe in coincidence, of course, when Destiny has us all in the palm of her hand . . ."

"Mother. Please. Focus."

A frown shadowed Ingrid's expression briefly, like a cloud scudding across the face of the sun. "I'm getting to it! You and your father, always rushing me and acting like I'm too silly to notice."

Remorse curdled in Quinn's stomach. She did think her mother was silly, sometimes, with her scarves and crystals and talk about capital-D Destiny. But Quinn hadn't meant to hurt her. "I'm sorry, Mother. But you've got me pretty nervous about what else you could possibly have to say that might be worse than selling my childhood home!"

"So dramatic," Ingrid sighed, somewhat hypocritically, in Quinn's opinion. "You're not a child anymore. You need to let go of material attachments and learn to live in the now."

Quinn closed her eyes. "Mother. Tell me you're not selling the house to teach me some lesson about inner peace."

"Not everything is about you, Quinn," Ingrid said, sharply enough to make Quinn jump like she'd stepped on a bee. "Actually, selling the house was Ron's idea.

He says it will help free us from the anchor of the past, and enable us to ascend into the future unencumbered."

Speechless, Quinn looked at her father. Paul's mouth was a tight line. "Ron is your mother's new guru," he said grimly.

"Ron is *our* relationship expert," Ingrid snapped. "But the fact that you refuse to take any ownership of this process is so completely typical. Ron says that's a huge part of our problem."

"What problem?" Quinn asked, helpless tears rising up to clutch at her throat. "I didn't know y'all were having . . . marriage problems?"

"Ron says every marriage has problems. It's what you do about them that defines your relationship."

Paul's glance cut to Quinn and they shared a silent moment of complete understanding. She caught her father's slight grimace and wanted to tell him that she got it—she'd only been in her mother's presence for five minutes and she was already sick and tired of the phrase "Ron says . . ."

But Quinn also knew her mother, and if Ingrid had entered fully into a new enthusiasm, she would react badly to anything that sounded like criticism of her most recent passion.

"Mother." Quinn tried to keep the threat of tears out of her voice. "I don't understand all this. I don't think selling the house where you and Daddy have so many happy memories is going to help anything. You love this house! And what about your garden?"

"My garden." Ingrid sighed, her mouth turned down

into an unhappy curve. "I do hate to leave it. But Ron says this house is weighing all of us down, even you."

Quinn blinked. "What does Ron know about me? He's never even met me."

"Your mother has no secrets from Ron." Paul's tone was dry enough to turn an ocean into a desert.

"I told him about how you're still finding your path," Ingrid explained. "Which is exactly what you should be doing, sweetheart, no matter what your father says."

Paul frowned. "I just think Quinn would be happier if she had a goal to work toward. And maybe it's time to think about settling down to something, whether that's a family or a career. Or both!"

"Don't . . ." Quinn bit her lip, familiar frustration surging through her as her stomach twisted with guilt. They'd always been like this, her parents. So connected, even when arguing, it was like there was no one else in the room. "Please don't fight about me, and don't talk about me like I'm not here. As a matter of fact, you've been gone for a while and a few things changed while you were traveling."

"Oh?"

Two pairs of interested eyes turned her way, and Quinn swallowed hard at the sudden intensity of her parents' attention.

"I started a job—a paying job!—at the therapeutic riding center, and I love it. I could see it turning into a real career. Like, long-term." Honesty compelled her to add, "It's not full-time yet, only part-time, but . . ."

Ingrid clasped her hands to her chest with a jingle of her bangle bracelets. "But it's a start! That's wonderful, sweetie! Helping others, working outdoors in the fresh air and sunshine—it sounds perfect for you!"

Quinn beamed at her mother's enthusiasm, but it was her father's quiet smile that warmed her heart.

"I'm proud of you, honey. Real proud."

"I've been so worried," Ingrid continued, her hands fluttering like butterflies unable to land. "Ron says we've been holding you back by keeping you tied to this house where you grew up because when you come home you can be a child again instead of moving forward into your adult space—"

"Well, Ron is wrong," Quinn interrupted forcefully. She couldn't be the reason her family was falling apart. She had to do something.

"I'm an adult now," she continued, panicking a bit at the skeptical glance her parents shared. "I'm settling down, and this house is, is part of that! Because, well, you see, I have a boyfriend. A serious one. And I want you to stick around to get to know him."

"What the hell makes you think that's a good idea?"

Marcus's gruff growl snapped Quinn out of her memory of her parents' delighted surprise and back to the present, where the man she'd loved since she was a little girl looked anything *but* delighted at the prospect of dating her. Even pretend-dating.

"My parents are talking about splitting up," Quinn

told him, holding her head high. "And I can't let that happen."

A complicated expression shadowed Marcus's face before it resolved into something that looked an awful lot like pity. "That's rough. I'm sorry. But . . ."

"But people split up. I know." She raked her fingers through her hair, resisting the urge to start tearing it out in chunks. "Not my parents. Trust me on this. They're the real deal, they love each other like crazy and they'd be miserable apart. They're going through a hard time, that's all."

Marcus blew out a breath. "Maybe, but I still don't see where I come into it."

"I needed a way to stall my parents before they blew up their lives and did a bunch of things I know they'd come to regret," Quinn said carefully. "It was a spur-of-the-moment thing, I just blurted it out—but I've been thinking it over for the last couple of hours, and I know it can work. All I need is to buy some time. Time to show my parents that they don't need to worry about me or fight over me anymore, and time to help them remember how much they love each other."

"So what happens in a month?"

Quinn's heart rate spiked. He wasn't saying no. At least, not yet. "Their thirtieth wedding anniversary. I want them to renew their vows. If I can't get them to do that inside of a month, I'll . . . I'll let it go. They can get a divorce if they want."

The D-word was as bitter as grapefruit peel on the back of her tongue, but Quinn meant what she said.

She knew she couldn't ultimately control what her parents chose to do, and if this didn't work, she'd accept it.

But only after giving it her best shot. Which depended, in large part, on the man staring across an empty table at her.

Chapter 3

Marcus's mind raced in circles like a rookie doing defensive driving training on a closed course. Amid the blaring confusion of questions, one stood out from all the rest. He had to know.

"Why me?"

A sneer pulled oddly at Quinn's sweetly shaped mouth. It looked entirely wrong on her face. "Not because I'm trying to get back together with you, if that's what that worried face is all about. I may be an optimistic idiot when it comes to romance, but even I have my limits."

That's good, Marcus told himself, ignoring the pang near his midsection. *She can't have any more illusions about happily-ever-after with you.*

Still, better safe than sorry.

"Find someone else to play house with." Marcus went back to closing down the bar. There wasn't a lot to do. Without any customers to spill their drinks and drop peanut shells on the floor, the place was as clean as it had been when he opened the doors at four.

"I don't have time to audition fake boyfriends," Quinn said, impatience clipping her words short. "If there were another eligible bachelor in town, don't you think I'd be dating him for real? I grew up with these guys, my parents would never believe I'd go for any of them. You and me, though—that's believable. Everyone in town knows we were together. They won't be surprised when we get back together, and they'll confirm our story to my parents."

And if Marcus started dating Sanctuary Island's Sweetheart again, he'd be off the town's shit list. They'd finally give the Buttercup Inn a try . . . and hopefully even after this wacky scheme of Quinn's blew up in Marcus's face, the townspeople would be used to coming here.

He couldn't believe he was actually considering this ludicrous proposition.

As though sensing his weakness, Quinn pounced. "I'm not asking you to change your life in any way. We already live in the same building—no one needs to know we're not sharing your apartment. All we're talking about is a couple of dinners with my parents, maybe a picnic or something. No big-time commitment on your end. Just enough to convince them that we're . . ."

She hesitated, so Marcus supplied the obvious word. "Screwing."

Her nose crinkled. He didn't find it adorable. At all.

"That we're deeply in love," she corrected him. "Almost ready to settle down. You know, the whole basic load of crap."

Marcus frowned. It was crap. He knew it. So why did it bug him to hear Quinn talk about love and marriage as if they were things she couldn't imagine believing in?

Obviously misinterpreting his scowl as a signal he was about to turn her down, Quinn propped her hands on her slim hips and pierced Marcus with a glare. He half expected her to tell him he owed her, after the way he'd treated her. But instead, she said, "Look. Do you really think I'd come to you with this if I had any other choice? I'm desperate. My family is coming apart at the seams. You can help me stitch it back together. Please don't make me beg."

And that was it. Marcus was done. A woman like Quinn should never have to beg someone like Marcus for a damn thing that didn't involve being naked and shuddering with pleasure. He'd shot pretty wide of the mark in most areas of his life so far, but he wasn't so far gone as that.

"I'll do it." The words ripped out of him like prying a bullet out of a wound.

Quinn's eyes widened, her whole face lighting up as if someone had flipped a switch, but Marcus held

up his hands for caution before she could get too in-
candescent.

"I'll help you out, pretend to be your boyfriend for
a month—but I've got a few conditions of my own."

A wary look finally flickered to life in Quinn's eyes.
"What conditions?"

Marcus crossed to the last table and instead of picking up the chair, he pulled it out and sat in it. Gestur-
ing for Quinn to take the seat opposite, he shoved up
the sleeves of his flannel shirt and rested his crossed
arms on the rough-hewn wood of the tabletop while
his mind revved into high gear.

"First, it has to look real. I get that. But I wasn't big
into public displays of affection when we dated before,
so I don't think it'll look more real now if we're suddenly all lovey-dovey."

"But we're getting back together after breaking up.
You realized exactly what you were missing."

And he did miss it. God Almighty, did he ever. But
Marcus would be damned before he'd admit it. "I'll
hold hands in public," he compromised. "But I'm not
getting a tattoo of your name on my bicep or something. I know how your mind works. We're going to
keep it simple."

Sure enough, Quinn looked briefly disappointed before brightening again. "They make really convincing temporary tattoos these days. Anyway, we can
hammer out the details later. The important thing is,
you're in!"

"Not so fast." His stern voice dragged her pert little rear back into the seat she'd half bounced up out of. "A few details, we'll settle now. Like exactly what we're both committing to, here."

"I don't know exactly what I'll need from you," Quinn argued. "Can't we play it by ear?"

Marcus dipped his chin in a nod. "We can. Let's call it at least one get-together per week, either with your parents or somewhere public enough that people will see us and tell them about it."

"Like your bar!"

He shrugged. "Doesn't have to be. But if enough customers show up to make it worthwhile, sure."

So long as it wasn't at her parents' house, down the road from where Marcus grew up, he was fine with it.

"You're supposed to be getting something out of this, too, you know," she said earnestly, leaning over the table. "I want the Buttercup Inn to be a success. Not only because I helped build it but because there's no place else on the island where I can get a margarita! Speaking of which, how about we seal this deal with a drink? On me. I'll even do the mixing."

She was up and behind the bar before Marcus could remind her there was no mixing involved in a scotch on the rocks. But maybe putting a little distance between them wasn't a bad idea. Because Marcus still had one final condition to lay out.

He sprawled back in the chair and watched her bustle around, clinking ice into glasses and lifting bottles of liquor to sniff curiously at them. Marcus felt his gaze go heavy-lidded and intense, staring at her from the shadows, but they had to finish this conversation or he couldn't move forward with this scheme.

"Before we seal the deal, you have to make me a promise."

Quinn looked over her creamy, freckled shoulder at him, strawberry-blond hair slipping free of a braid to wisp against her cheeks. "Anything, Marcus. Seriously, I appreciate this more than I can tell you."

"I need you to promise not to get caught up in the act," he said slowly, deliberately. "Promise me you won't fall in love with me."

Quinn nearly dropped the single malt on the hardwood floor. Gripping the neck of the bottle hard enough to worry about snapping the glass with her fingers, she glared across the bar at Marcus and thought very seriously about hurling the Talisker at his head.

Only her respect for a very fine Scotch whisky stayed her hand. Well, that and an innate desire not to let Marcus see how much power he still had to affect her.

Forcing a light laugh, Quinn deliberately loosened her grasp on the bottle and set it down with care. "Oh, Marcus. You're hilarious. I'm not sure what you're afraid of exactly, but if it'll make you feel better, I think I can safely promise never, ever to fall in love with you."

And she meant it. Times had changed and Quinn

wasn't a kid anymore. She could control herself. She could keep this smart and aboveboard and completely free of all emotions except gratitude for Marcus doing her this favor.

Marcus stayed still and silent for a long moment, studying her with disconcerting intensity. She poured a couple of fingers of scotch into a glass and tried not to notice the way his long, denim-clad legs splayed slightly open from the way he leaned back in that chair. Gratitude, she reminded herself with gritted teeth. Gratitude. That's all you feel for him.

Sure, her reckless, wanton body replied. *Gratitude for the way his black T-shirt is rumpled up enough to expose that sliver of his taut, toned abs. Gratitude for broad shoulders and the way they stretch the jersey tight, and the glimpse of his strong forearms, and the shadow of stubble on a strong, angular jaw, and the glint of silver under unfairly long lashes.*

For the first time, Quinn had a moment of doubt about her ability to get through the next four weeks with her heart—and her sanity—intact. But it was too late to back out now, when Marcus was on the point of agreeing.

She'd just have to suppress the helpless longing that stirred her up like a cocktail in a shaker every time she came within ten feet of Marcus Beckett.

The man in question stood, a coiled rush of power and grace that made everything low in her body go liquid. He prowled over to lean on the bar in front of her. "You've got yourself a deal. As long as we're agreed that when the month is up, it's over—whether your parents are back together or not."

One month. It seemed like such a short amount of time to fix whatever catastrophe had gone wrong between her parents, but they'd been together and happy a lot longer than they'd been struggling. She was sure she could do it.

Quinn poured a second glass of scotch and slid the first across the bar. Clinking the glasses together, she said, "Agreed. And thank you for helping me. I know every kid thinks their parents belong together, but mine really do."

A muscle ticked behind Marcus's jaw before he tipped the glass and took a sip of scotch. "Not every kid. I'll go along with this in return for a chance to bring some paying customers into the bar, but that doesn't mean I think you're heading for anything other than disappointment."

Quinn stiffened, her glass of whisky halfway to her mouth. There it was.

Gratitude. For reminding her that Marcus Beckett might be the sexiest man she'd ever seen, but his heart was made of icy stone.

If she could keep remembering that, she'd be okay.

Paul Harper hung up the phone and pinched the bridge of his nose between his thumb and forefinger. He knew his daughter, and that was not the sound of a blissfully happy Quinn.

Something was going on with her. The only question

was whether it was Marcus Beckett's fault . . . or her parents'.

Ingrid wandered over to his desk, her journal tucked under one arm. She'd been diligently writing in it for two hours, her pen scratching out whatever thought exercises Ron had given her like a student studying for an all-important exam. Paul wondered if even Ingrid knew what a passing grade would look like.

"Was that Quinn? Are she and that nice Beckett boy coming over? I haven't seen him in years, not since my sweet Elizabeth crossed over to the other side."

Paul knew his wife's grief for her friend and neighbor was sincere, but all that stuff about the other side rubbed him the wrong way. He dropped his hand and arranged his face into something bland and pleasant. That seemed the best way to avoid yet another discussion that felt like a verbal boxing match. "They're not coming over. Quinn suggested we all meet up at the Firefly Café instead. It's Friday and she knows how much you love their fried chicken."

But Ingrid didn't look pleased. "I wanted them to come here! If Marcus is the chosen partner of Quinn's journey, we should welcome him into our home."

The fact that they'd only arrived back on the island two days ago after weeks out of town, and their kitchen wasn't exactly stocked for hosting lunch guests—that wasn't the sort of thing Ingrid Harper could be counted on to notice.

Her obliviousness had never bothered Paul. He

found it endearing, usually. But these days, it caught him on the raw.

"Our home," he repeated. "The home that up until yesterday, you couldn't wait to sell?"

"You make it sound so ugly and . . . and mercenary! It's not about the money, Paul. It's because this house is an anchor dragging us down into the past."

"Or so says Ron. You know, Ingrid, we did fine without his help for the first twenty-nine years of our marriage."

Ingrid glanced away. "Maybe for the first twenty-seven years. But the last few, since you retired . . . Paul, you can't think we've been doing fine."

The flat tone of her voice hit Paul like a dart to the heart. Bull's-eye.

"It's been an adjustment, I'll admit," he said with difficulty. "A tougher transition than I was expecting, but I thought we were getting through it. Together."

"We still are. We just have a little help now, that's all."

Paul set his jaw. The kind of help Ron Burkey had been, Paul could do without. "I don't see how it helps to add a third person standing in the middle of our marriage."

"Oh, Paul." Her fingers were white-knuckled around the spine of her journal. "You're being ridiculous. Ron is an expert at helping couples reconnect—and now he's weaving threads of communication between us, helping to translate for us."

Words stuck in Paul's throat like an unchewed bite of pancake. *We don't need a translator. We already speak the same language,* he wanted to say. *The language of our marriage, that we built together over decades of living and laughing and fighting and loving each other.*

How could anyone else, anyone outside the two of them, be more fluent in that language than they were?

But Paul didn't say it, because he didn't want another fight. So he didn't say anything at all. Instead, Ingrid drew in a breath and began to fill the silence between them with chatter about calling Ron and getting him up to speed.

Paul sat in the armchair closest to the cold fireplace and let the agitated babble wash over him. He said nothing, even when Ingrid said maybe they'd better hold on to the house for the time being, just until they could see Quinn and Marcus together and judge for themselves how serious it was. Paul was pleased that she was finally disregarding some of her guru's advice, and Paul would rather cut out his tongue than say anything that might make her change her mind.

Maybe Ron was right. Maybe there was a breakdown in communication in their marriage—that was probably true. But that didn't mean Ron Burkey, "Relationship Expert," was the one to fix it.

If there was anything left to fix, anymore.

Chapter 4

As the only restaurant on Sanctuary Island, the Firefly Café was always crowded. But every Friday, the
line of hungry customers waiting to be seated snaked
out the door and into the parking lot. Friday was the
only day they served fried chicken as a special. Apparently, that was a big deal.

Quinn's eyebrows had shot up so far, they were
practically kissing her hairline. "What do you mean,
you've never been to Fried Chicken Friday?"

Marcus shrugged. "We didn't go out to eat much as
a family, when I was a kid."

"But everyone goes to the Firefly."

She appeared sincerely confused, an adorable crin-
kle between her brows. It reminded Marcus of his
own confusion, and nameless guilt, when he asked his

mother what time Dad was coming home or whether he'd be around to throw the ball that weekend.

"My father worked a lot," Marcus said. "Both my parents did." He got that now, the way he hadn't when he was younger. All he'd understood then was that he was on his own a lot of the time while Dr. Beckett and Nurse Beckett worked their unpredictable shifts at Winter Harbor General.

They moved forward another few feet as the line finally moved. Marcus's gaze dropped to the plush softness of Quinn's lower lip where it was trapped between her teeth. "I'm sorry," she said. "I didn't mean to make it awkward."

"It's fine. I didn't miss going out with them on the weekends. My mom was usually home then, at least, and she was a great cook."

"She really was!" Quinn's face went soft and bright at the same time, like the sun coming out on a snowy day. "I remember how everyone at town potlucks would watch for her to put down her casserole or whatever she'd brought, and as soon as she moved away from the table there'd be this stampede of hungry folks ready to load up their plates."

Marcus felt a smile tug at the corner of his mouth. "I'd forgotten about that."

"And she was so modest and pleased about it. She'd blush and wave her hands and refuse to accept any compliments, but did you know—the autumn harvest festival is always in October, close to my birthday, and your mother would always be sure to bring her famous six-layer lemon cake to that one. I think she knew it was my favorite, and at that one festival every year, she'd stand by the cake and cut the slices herself. And she always gave me the first piece. It made me feel so special. I used to wonder what it would be like to have a mom like that."

The wistfulness in Quinn's eyes made Marcus frown. He hadn't paid a ton of attention to his family's only neighbors. Quinn was still a little girl when he went off to college, but he'd always had the impression they were a nice family.

Catching his frown, Quinn rushed to say, "Oh, not that my mom is bad! She's not the world's best cook, though. And I kind of doubt she knows what my favorite birthday cake is. But still. She's . . . well, she's great. And I'm sure she's going to love you."

"Hey, I never promised to make your parents love me. That's not part of the deal." Marcus frowned. "I'm not exactly most parents' dream prospect for their cherished daughter."

"You don't know my mother. She's nothing like most moms."

Marcus slanted her a sidelong look. "And your father? He's going to welcome me with open arms, I guess."

"Maybe not at first, but trust me, when it comes to my future? The bar is set low. Like barely an inch above the ground. At this point, Daddy would be

willing to throw a parade in honor of anyone who
could get me to settle down and fulfill my true po-
tential. Whatever that means. Mother, on the other
hand . . ."

Quinn sighed, and Marcus started to get the feeling that he knew at least one thing her parents fought
about. Their daughter.

It was a heavy burden to put on anyone, the knowledge that your choices had strained your parents' relationship. Marcus knew that better than most. But he
also knew that whatever lay at the heart of Quinn's
parents' troubles, it wasn't Quinn's fault. There had
to be more to it than a disagreement over how their
daughter should live her life.

He supposed he'd find out soon enough. Years of
training and experience in reading people ought to help
him get the lay of the land fairly quickly. If they ever
made it inside.

Just as his stomach grumbled at the delay, several
families in a row left the restaurant looking blissfully
full of fried chicken, and the line finally moved forward. Marcus and Quinn were almost at the door when
he caught a sudden movement out of the corner of
his eye.

Someone was approaching Quinn, coming up on
her from behind, and Marcus didn't stop to think.
Training kicked in, and before he knew it, he had her
tucked behind him with one arm held back to make
her stay put while he squared off with the threat.

The threat . . . who turned out to be a slim, tanned

woman in her early sixties with flowing wavy, gray-streaked hair artfully woven with feathers.

Damn.

"Mrs. Harper?" Marcus said resignedly, dropping his arm to let Quinn move.

She shoved her way past him. "What was that all about, you maniac? Mother, you look nice."

Mrs. Harper laughed like bells tinkling, her wide eyes fixed on Marcus. "Oh, call me Ingrid. So good to see you again after all these years, Marcus. How is your father? We haven't seen much of him since we got home, but it's only been a few days."

"Welcome back to Sanctuary Island," Marcus said, smoothly sidestepping the issue of his father. "It's a nice place to come home to. At least, it has been for me."

Mrs. Harper—Ingrid—cast her eyes down, the smile slipping sideways into a grimace. "I've always loved Sanctuary Island. Paul grew up here, you know, and when we got married I couldn't wait to start our life here in this beautiful place. I can't imagine leaving."

"Then why are you even considering selling the house?" Quinn asked, throwing her hands up. "Mother, I just don't get it."

Instead of snapping back, Ingrid shook her head sadly. "I know you don't, sweetie. But it wouldn't be the same for me here, if your father and I . . ."

She trailed off and the silence that followed was full of a gut-twisting tension until Quinn broke it.

"There's Daddy!" She waved at her father with false

cheer. "Hey! We're up here. Did you find the best parking spot? Daddy's superpower is finding the best parking spot, no matter how crowded it is."

"Not much of a superpower," the trim, graying man said mildly as he held out his hand for Marcus to shake. "You certainly have grown up."

Marcus was careful not to grip Paul Harper's hand too hard. He had nothing to prove here. "Time will do that. But somehow Mrs. Harper looks exactly the same. Is that your superpower, ma'am?"

"Oh, go on." Ingrid flushed with pleasure, but it was the expression on her husband's face that interested Marcus.

Paul looked at his wife and said quietly, "It sure is her superpower. She's as beautiful as the day I married her."

If Ingrid glowed any brighter, she was going to start attracting moths. At Marcus's side, Quinn slid a slender arm around his waist and murmured, "Who knew you could be such a charmer?"

He glanced down at her warningly at the touch, which wasn't exactly PDA—but his involuntary reaction to Quinn's nearness threatened to turn an innocent embrace into something a lot more X-rated.

Quinn gazed back at him with one brow arched, a blend of surprise, gratitude, and challenge on her pretty face. She hadn't been sure he would really play along, Marcus realized. She thought he'd sabotage her somehow, or maybe just grunt antisocially at her parents until they stopped asking him questions. The thought stung, even as he admitted to himself that it wasn't completely off base.

But Marcus could put on a show with the best of them. He didn't like it, but he knew how to do it.

"I charmed you, didn't I?" he murmured, unwinding her arm from his waist and bringing her hand to his lips. They tingled where they brushed her warm, soft skin. His tongue darted out automatically to catch the trace of her flavor, salt and honey, still clinging to his mouth. He dropped her hand and took a half step back, suddenly desperate for a little distance.

"You sure did." Her breathy voice helped to sell the moment, Marcus thought, and Ingrid confirmed it with a happy sigh.

The screen door at the front of the restaurant banged open and a woman with a face like a crinkled paperback and a towering gray beehive stuck her head out. "Are there four of you? Come on in."

"Thanks," Paul Harper said, hurrying up the steps as if he were in a rush to get away from the sexual tension crackling between his daughter and Marcus. Ingrid followed him more slowly, waving at friends and stopping now and then to dispense patchouli-scented hugs to people she hadn't seen in a few months. Marcus was starting to see where Quinn got her social nature, and the effortless sweetness that made her such a favorite in town.

"What are you doing flirting with my mother?"

Quinn demanded in a playful hissed whisper as they
lagged a few steps behind. The clink and clatter of
dinnerware combined with the chatter of happily eating
customers to mask their conversation from her parents.
Still, Marcus wasn't about to drop character. Never let
down your guard. That's how things turn to crap in the
blink of an eye.

Besides, it wasn't only her parents they were trying
to convince. It was the whole town. And in his peripheral vision, Marcus could see several familiar faces
turned in their direction, interested eyes tracking how
close they were standing and the obvious intimacy of
their whispered conversation. Marcus put on a smile
that felt like it showed more teeth than was strictly
necessary.

"I'm being a good boyfriend. Isn't that what you
wanted? For your parents to like me and be glad we're
dating?"

Quinn's mouth twisted ruefully. Her gaze was self-
aware and steady. "I guess I should have expected it.
You have such a thing for older women! First Miss
Patty, now my mother. What's that all about, anyway?"

Inescapably, Marcus thought of the woman she
hadn't named because Quinn didn't know anything
about her.

Buttercup.

Grief was a funny thing, he'd found. After the first
raw wound of it scabbed over, he could go days without thinking of his ex-boss. Weeks, sometimes. But
then it would hit him out of the blue, a sucker punch

from an unseen assailant, and he'd be right back in the first crushing grasp of it.

Quinn was staring at him expectantly. Marcus's first instinct was to shut her down, hard enough to make sure she never asked about this again. But they were in the middle of a crowded restaurant. The people at the tables closest to them were starting to look up curiously, wondering why they'd paused. Marcus gritted his teeth.

"My last boss was . . ." Damn, how could he describe Buttercup? To the world, she'd been a charming, charismatic warrior for justice. She'd certainly dedicated her life to public service, to helping the most vulnerable and disadvantaged parts of society.

But to Marcus, she'd been a firecracker. A pain in the ass with no regard for her own safety. And later, a true friend.

"She was a complicated woman," he finally settled on. "About Miss Patty's age, or a little younger."

Quinn's round eyes were fixed on him now, every part of her straining closer. He was uncomfortably aware that this was the most he'd ever said about his life after leaving Sanctuary Island all those years ago. "And you respected her. Loved her?"

He shrugged, the question striking too close to the scabbed-over spot on his heart. "She used to say that after a certain age, women became invisible. People smiled, they said hello, but they kept their distance like they were afraid getting old was contagious. I don't think that's right—I mean, that's not how it should be."

"Everybody deserves to be seen," Quinn agreed softly, staring up at him as if she were seeing *him* for the very first time.

"Maybe so." He rolled the tension out of his shoulders and started moving again, leaving Quinn—and this too intense conversation—lagging behind. "But you might not always like what you see."

Marcus Beckett had to be the most frustrating man who ever lived. Quinn fumed, her legs sticking to the vinyl bench of the booth seat. His thigh was a rock-hard length of heated muscle pressed against her and she couldn't make herself unaware of it.

Every time she was ready to write him off as a cranky loner who hated all people, everywhere, he did something like this. He turned out to be besties with Miss Patty, or he made Quinn's mother feel beautiful with a few well-chosen words.

When he let Quinn catch a glimpse of the man behind the scowling mask, it reminded her of that teenaged boy she'd idolized and dreamed about for so many years.

Of course, the mask dropped back down again almost instantly, leaving her feeling cold and alone on the other side—but with the tantalizing memory of having come close to touching the real Marcus Beckett.

"So you own a bar?" her father asked, politely enough, but the sharp glitter of his gray eyes warned Quinn that an interrogation was on its way.

"It's more of a gathering place," she interposed

smoothly. "A place for folks to meet up, build community, share a few laughs . . ."

"And a few beers." Daddy raised his bushy brows as if daring Marcus to contradict him.

"I serve beer, yes." Marcus took a sip of his water, his eyes never leaving her father's. "Also wine and liquor. It's a bar."

Biting her lip, Quinn shot a glance at her teetotaler dad, but instead of looking disapproving, there was a satisfied curl to his mouth as if he liked Marcus better for not backing down. Her mother, however, was another story.

"We don't drink much. All those terrible toxins," she was saying with no irony whatsoever, between bites of fried chicken and sips of intensely sugary sweet tea.

Personally, Quinn didn't think there was anything better in the world than a lunch of fried chicken and sweet tea, but no one could argue that they were perfectly pure and healthy.

Blissfully unaware of her daughter's judgment, Ingrid went on. "And alcohol leads to so many terrible things. Violence and bad decisions and people staggering drunkenly through the streets . . ."

"One bar isn't going to turn Sanctuary Island into Bourbon Street," Quinn said, rolling her eyes. "It's a nice place, Mother. You should come see it sometime. I'll make you a mocktail."

"What's that? It sounds strong," Ingrid said worriedly.

"It's not. It's the weakest thing there is. It's a cocktail with no alcohol. You'll be fine. I used to make them for my friends in college, to keep them from doing something stupid at a frat party."

"So that's what you were doing when you should have been studying," her father observed.

Quinn's shoulders wanted to hunch, but she forced herself to smile brightly at him instead. "That's right. And it turned out to be a very marketable skill, so maybe I was using my time better than you thought."

Paul's eyes narrowed. "A marketable skill—don't tell me you're working at this bar."

Ouch. That was a bit of a sore spot, considering Marcus had fired her before she ever had a chance to start working. And dumped her at the same time.

"Quinn's work with the therapeutic riding center doesn't leave her a lot of time for being a cocktail waitress," Marcus said, unexpectedly.

She shot him a look, but the expression on his face was blander than milk.

"Really? I thought it wasn't a full-time job," Dad said, brows lifting in that skeptical way that made Quinn feel about three inches tall.

"It's not exactly full-time," she admitted, looking down at her plate where her fingers were shredding her biscuit into flaky pieces. "But I really like it."

"It's not full-time because the rest of the hours are spent on the certification course," Marcus put in, as if he were reminding her, and Quinn glanced up at him from beneath her lashes. She was grateful for the support. And she couldn't help noticing that Marcus seemed to know an awful lot about this job, considering she hadn't started it until after they'd broken up.

"Oh, another class." Daddy was nodding as if everything made sense now, disappointment stirring in his gaze. Quinn's stomach dropped.

"I don't know why you say it like that. Quinn loves to learn, don't you, sweetie?" Her mother's mouth had tightened and now she put down her piece of fried chicken to cross her arms over her chest as she glared at Paul. "There's nothing wrong with a young woman pursuing an education."

"Of course there isn't," Dad said wearily, "so long as that young woman ever plans to use all these classes she's taken over the years for more than just a hobby."

"Hobbies aren't such terrible things to have," Mom said. "You could stand to look into getting a hobby yourself, now that you're retired."

"That's probably true, but I'm not a young woman starting out in life," Dad pointed out. "And our daughter needs to learn to commit to something. We won't be around forever. She needs to be able to build a life for herself so we know she'll be okay without us."

The words landed in the middle of lunch like a giant spoonful of mashed potatoes plopped right onto the table. Quinn, who had slowly slid lower and lower in her seat as her parents volleyed back and forth, shut her eyes and wished for the floor to open up and swallow her.

When she felt Marcus shift next to her, his large,

superheated presence at her side moving away as he stood up, she tried to feel surprised. But she couldn't. How could she expect him to stick it out through this unpleasantness? If it were an option, Quinn would run away, too.

But Marcus wasn't running away.

Quinn opened her eyes to a world gone bonkers. Marcus wasn't running away—he wasn't even standing up.

He was kneeling down.

Chapter 5

Marcus ignored the gasps of shock and excitement from all around the restaurant. He stubbornly kept his eyes fixed on Quinn's reddening cheeks and slightly parted lips peeking out from between the fingers she'd brought up to cover her mouth.

This was the stupidest thing he'd ever done. And he'd once run straight at a man holding a gun.

But just like that day, the day he'd caught Buttercup's eye and gotten assigned to her detail permanently, Marcus was committed now. There was no turning back.

The thought reminded him of why he was doing this. He turned to lock eyes with Quinn's father and said, "You don't know me well—but you don't know your daughter well, either, if you think her life is only about messing around with unimportant hobbies. She *can* commit to things. When she wants them bad enough. And she's fully capable of standing on her own. But she doesn't have to, when I'm here."

Acknowledgment and a complicated mixture of respect and chagrin darkened Paul Harper's eyes.

"Marcus, what are you doing?" Quinn said, her voice a low thread of husky sound.

He looked back at her. "I guess I'm hoping I'm one of those things you want bad enough."

"You mean . . . ?"

He reached for her hand, feeling like a total idiot still propped up on one knee on the sticky diner floor. Her fingers were cold and a little shaky in his. He gave them a reassuring squeeze and allowed the thrill that went through him every time they touched to show in his smile.

"Quinn Rosalie Harper. Will you marry me?"

She nearly fell out of the booth. Marcus managed to catch her handily, hauling her wriggling warmth in to his chest and smelling the sweet sunshine scent of her hair. He wasn't expecting the roar of happiness that swept through the restaurant, people cheering and clapping and banging their empty plastic cups on their tables.

Over Quinn's shoulder, Marcus saw her father's jaw clench while her mother squealed in unrestrained delight, the feathers in her hair quivering with joy. Quinn had thrown her arms around his neck and buried her face in his shoulder, but she lifted her head to press her lips to his ear and say, "I can't believe you did this. You're insane."

Marcus cupped the back of her head in his broad palm and nuzzled her temple. To anyone watching, it would look as if the couple were exchanging blissful coos of mutual adoration. No one could hear them over the din of congratulations.

"You want to prove to your parents that you can commit? This is how we do it. You're welcome."

Before she could reply, Marcus rolled to his feet in a single motion, heaving Quinn up with him in a princess carry. Turning to face the crowd of well-wishers and fried-chicken enthusiasts, he shouted, "She said yes!"

"Put me down," Quinn demanded, wriggling like a hooked fish. Every move seemed to press her gently rounded curves up against him in new places, electrifying him with memories and desires that he had no business thinking about in public.

Or anywhere. That part of their relationship was over, Marcus reminded himself sternly. Unfortunately, it was going to take more than a stern mental talking-to before his entire body got the message, but removing temptation would help.

He loosened his hold and let Quinn's toes kiss the worn linoleum of the café floor. Their gazes caught and clung for a brief, electric moment. It felt as if the raucous celebration of all the people around them faded away and suddenly Marcus and Quinn were the only people in the restaurant. Marcus's hands tightened on her shoulders, his palms shaping the warm, slim roundness of her and aching to pull her closer. To kiss the soft, shocked mouth and hear her throat-deep whimpers of pleasure. Her eyes darkened to cobalt, lashes sliding low, and he knew she was thinking about it, too.

How good they were together. How they'd made each other moan.

He bent down slowly, fighting the magnetic pull of her lips as they parted temptingly—and jolted upright as a pair of bangle-braceleted arms encircled them both with startling strength.

"Congratulations!" Quinn's mother said, all but vibrating in place. "Oh, my dears, my very, very dears! You're going to be so happy together."

Quinn pulled back, a tremulous smile surfacing as she tucked her hair nervously behind her ears. "Thanks, Mother. I don't know how you can be so sure, since you've spent about ten minutes watching us together, but I'm glad you approve."

"It only took me ten seconds to see how melded and complementary your auras are," Ingrid informed them airily. "To the experienced eye, your compatibility as a couple is completely obvious."

Wry amusement dimpled Quinn's cheek, but she didn't let it into her tone. "Well, that's nice to hear. Now can we sit back down and eat our fried chicken before Marcus is overwhelmed by all this excitement?"

Ingrid laughed and sat, but as Marcus stood aside

to let Quinn climb into the booth across from her, Paul said, "I'm sure he can handle it. He's a grown man. Very grown."

"Dad, don't start," Quinn begged, her eyes flicking to Marcus, who gave an easy shrug.

"He's not wrong, Quinn. I'm older than you. By a lot."

"Ten years isn't that much," she argued, casting a glare at her father. "Not in the grand scheme of life. Besides, if we're okay with it, there's nothing more to say. It's no one else's business but ours."

She said it as if she thought that should be the end of it, but it was one of those moments that reminded Marcus painfully of just how young and inexperienced Quinn was. Marcus sat down and met Paul's eyes across the table. Paul raised his brows slightly and Marcus dipped his chin in a reluctant nod of acknowledgment. That was going to be a fun conversation.

He hadn't thought this through—hadn't had time to think about more than the fact that he hated the way Quinn's parents were hurting her without meaning to. And he could stop it.

Maybe it was true that she was young—inexperienced, and innocent, and too damn sweet for her own good. But in that moment, all Marcus could think about was shielding Quinn from pain.

At least for a while. When they broke off their engagement, it was unlikely to be simple, but they'd figure out how to cross that bridge when the time came. And

Marcus would make sure her parents would see that she'd be better off living life without a man as broken down and damaged as Marcus Beckett.

"Let's see the ring," Paul said with forced cheer. It was an obvious effort to change the subject, but it was doomed to failure because Marcus didn't have one.

"Oh, yeah." Quinn laughed, a little shrill with nerves. "A ring."

"You do have a ring for her." Paul frowned. "Don't you?"

"Ugh, do you have to be such a traditionalist, Paul? The kids are in love, isn't that enough?"

Quinn's parents had turned toward each other, another argument in the works. Beside him, Quinn tensed unhappily. Before Paul and Ingrid could get going, Marcus said, "I thought we could shop for the ring together. So Quinn can get exactly what she likes."

That was a thing people did, right? Marcus thought it sounded okay. Plausible.

It shut Quinn's parents up, at least. Even Paul softened visibly, the worried lines smoothing from his forehead. Marcus had hoped for that. What he hadn't prepared for was the way Quinn turned to him, eyes shining, and said, "That's perfect! You're perfect."

For the space of a heartbeat, Marcus wanted this moment to be real so badly that if he'd had his mother's engagement ring in his pocket, he would have handed it over.

But in the next breath, Quinn leaned over to kiss his

cheek and took the opportunity to whisper, "Very smooth, mister. Where did you learn to be such a good liar?" in his ear. And that brought Marcus back to reality with the unpleasant thud of his dumb, daydreaming ass hitting the floor.

Get your act together, he told himself harshly. *This is a harebrained scheme, not a real engagement. And you wouldn't want it to be real, anyway.*

He pulled away from Quinn with what he hoped was a neutral smile, and tried not to think about how much that felt like a lie.

Quinn was so impressed by all this quick thinking Marcus was doing. Right around the time their food arrived, she'd started to realize that maybe she was out of her depth when it came to running a con on her own parents.

If Marcus hadn't been at her side, ready with a believable answer to every question, she probably would have given up and blurted out the truth already.

Maybe if she treated it like a game, it would be easier. But the shock of Marcus's proposal had thrown her off course and it was hard to get back on track. So when her beaming mother picked up her biscuit to slather it with honey butter and asked, "How did y'all reconnect, anyway? I can't believe we haven't heard this story yet," Quinn blurted out the first thing that came into her head.

Well, the first thing that wasn't the truth. She

obviously couldn't tell her mother that she'd jumped Marcus's bones with a box of "Welcome Home" cupcakes.

"Marcus is a client out at the therapeutic riding center," Quinn said without thinking. "I mean, not one of my clients, obviously. That would be unethical. Because I don't have my equine-assisted therapy license yet. And also because we're dating. Engaged. And it would be a conflict of interest."

Below the table, where her parents couldn't see, Marcus laid his hand on her nervously jittering knee to stop its bouncing. Above the table, Mom's entire expression melted like warm wax. "Oh, Marcus. We heard you went into the military, and then another dangerous job—wasn't it the Secret Service? So impressive. Were you wounded at some point?"

Marcus went still at her side while Quinn fought not to let her surprise show. Her fake boyfriend—ahem, fiancé!—used to be a Secret Service agent. She felt like she probably should have known that.

Of course, back when he was her real boyfriend, they hadn't spent a lot of time talking. Not that Quinn hadn't wanted to, but Marcus was so closed off. Like a fortress with extremely high, thick stone walls. She'd been working on chipping away at those walls through a combination of strictly enforced cuddling and determined pillow talk, but evidently she hadn't even scratched the surface.

Questions swirled through her like petals blown from the trees outside, blanketing every memory of their time together. Who had he guarded? What had it been like? She made a silent vow to find out more about that time in his life, the minute they were alone together.

Marcus coughed. "No, I was one of the lucky ones. I left the army on my own terms, under my own steam, barely a scratch on me."

Quinn noticed he didn't mention leaving the Secret Service unscathed.

"Oh." Mom glanced at Quinn with the bright, embarrassment-proof curiosity of a bird. "I thought Quinn mentioned that the therapeutic riding center works with physical disabilities and rehab."

"Mostly, but we have some PTSD cases, too," Quinn said, then snapped her jaws shut on the realization of what she'd implied about Marcus. "Sorry, I probably shouldn't have said that."

But instead of getting angry or denying anything, Marcus gazed at her parents with that steady, implacable stare he'd probably perfected in basic training. And Quinn could've leaped over the table and planted a kiss on her father for saying, gruffly, "No need to apologize, Quinn. There's no shame in a PTSD diagnosis. Especially for a man who worked to defend our freedom."

"Certainly there's no shame," Quinn's mother exclaimed, rearing back. Ingrid's hair beads clattered with her agitated head shaking. "When I think of what you men and women go through in the armed forces, and how badly we as a society care for you when you

come home . . . well, I'm just glad you've found a place
to get the care you need."

"I think we should change the subject," said Quinn.
"This is a very personal topic and Marcus doesn't need
to explain himself to us."

Marcus's jaw hardened. "It's fine. What do you want
to know?"

Quinn's heart sank. She should've known he couldn't
stand for her to try to protect him. Sometimes he was
such a guy, it made her want to scream.

And sometimes it made her want to climb him like
a tree. What? She never said she was well adjusted.

Across the table, her father pushed his nearly un-
touched plate away and leaned his elbows on the table.
"So tell me, Marcus. How does a man go from the
Secret Service to working as a bartender?"

"There were a few steps in between. And I'm not a
bartender. I'm a bar owner. There's a difference."

"I didn't mean that the way it came out. It would
probably be a lot easier to tend bar for someone else.
Take it from someone who owned his own business for
thirty-five years. It's no walk in the park."

There was a brief pause, then Marcus smiled
slightly. "You miss it."

"I miss it like hell," Paul sighed. "Every damn
day."

"Daddy!" Quinn blinked. "I thought you were looking forward to being retired."

Paul shifted in his seat. Beside him, Ingrid stared
down at her plate with an unhappy curve to her mouth.

"It's been a bigger adjustment than either of us anticipated."

Obviously sensing the tension, Marcus said, "The bookstore is still open, though. I was in there the other day."

"I sold it," Paul confirmed. "To a young lady from Quinn's high school class, actually. Very impressive, to be ready to own and operate your own business at that age. She has her MBA and everything."

"Please, no more about Perfect Poppy Pringle." Quinn groaned, sucking up the last of her sweet tea with a loud crack of the straw. "It was bad enough when we were in school and she beat me in every subject, and got elected class president and landed the lead in the school play."

"Don't be bitter, sweetheart," Ingrid advised, amusement lightening her tone. "Bitterness is a poison. And Poppy is a lovely person."

"I know," Quinn said glumly. "She's wonderful. Smart and funny and thoughtful and kind. I was sure once we graduated, I'd be rid of her. But no, you had to go and sell the bookstore to her."

"Well, I had to leave it in good hands, didn't I? Of course, I always pictured passing the family business on to my daughter, but as I recall, you were planning to go back to school at that time. Art school, wasn't it?"

Marcus turned to her. "I didn't know you were an artist."

Embarrassment heated the back of Quinn's neck, but it was Ingrid who jumped in and said, "Oh, Quinn is very talented. She has an eye for beauty—she always has."

"I was interested in curating, actually. It's a fascinating field, when you dig into it—how museums and galleries choose what pieces to feature, how they arrange them and how they put them in context for the viewer."

"So why didn't you pursue it?" Marcus asked.

"Why doesn't she pursue anything?" Daddy shook his head in fond exasperation. "She moved on to the next thing."

Quinn resisted the urge to squirm in her seat. "I realized that all the real opportunities for a career in curatorship were in New York, Chicago—big cities. And I didn't want to leave Sanctuary Island. I love it here. This is my home."

"You could've opened an art gallery on the island," her father pointed out, doggedly rehashing the same argument they'd had at the time. "Owning your own business is very rewarding. It would have been a good experience for you."

Quinn bit her lip, not sure how to say that the life her father had chosen and loved wasn't what she wanted for herself. She didn't have to figure it out, because her mother jumped in with, "Oh, Paul. Let it go. So Quinn didn't want to stay up nights balancing her books and worrying about how to give her employees benefits and I don't know what all. It's not a crime for her to want to have a life."

"I had a life," Daddy protested. "The store was closed every Sunday."

Ingrid snorted. "One day a week when we had you home—and even then, you were usually thinking about the store. I thought once you retired, you'd be happy. We both could be happy and together."

The raw hurt in her mother's voice shocked Quinn to her core. For the first time, she considered that maybe the rift between her parents went a lot deeper than she'd thought.

After a short, tense pause, Daddy's quiet voice broke the silence. "I'm sorry you were unhappy with our life, Ingrid. I tried the best I could to provide a good life for our family. If I could have been around more—"

"Well, now both of you can slack off." Quinn jumped in. "Retirement should be when you get to relax finally, and enjoy the fruits of all your years of hard work. I thought that was why you bought the camper, to travel around and see the country and have new experiences together."

Ingrid looked away, biting her lip. Her husband looked at her still profile for a long moment before saying, "I'm afraid I've never been very good at relaxing. Retirement—it hasn't come as easily to me as I was hoping for. But the best part of it has been spending more time with your mother."

His voice rang with sincerity, with love, and Quinn's heart lifted. Ingrid's face brightened, too, her mouth widening into a brilliant smile—as the tinny strains of an Enya ring tone filled the air. In the next instant, she'd snatched up the cell phone lying beside her plate and stood up from the booth to answer it.

The sight of her father's face closing off, the shutters slamming closed and all the hopeful light going out of his eyes, filled Quinn with pain. Oblivious, Ingrid hurried away from the booth, weaving through the tables to find some privacy for her conversation outside the café.

"Who's on the phone?" Quinn asked with a sinking feeling in her stomach.

Her father mustered up a grim smile. "Oh, that's just Ron Burkey. The man who's trying to convince your mother to divorce me."

Chapter 6

Marcus gauged the distance to the door of the jewelry store. If he put on a burst of speed, he could make it before anyone noticed his escape.

"This one's real pretty, Quinn," the shop owner was saying. "Kind of like your mom's ring, with the center stone and the side stones like petals."

Quinn, who had been admiring the ring sparkling on her left hand, made a face and immediately tugged off the gold band.

"Don't you like it?" The jewelry store owner looked crestfallen.

"Oh, Carol Ann, of course I do! It's beautiful. But it's not really me, if you know what I mean."

The petite blond woman brightened determinedly. "No problem at all! I'm sure I have something that will suit you. Maybe if you gave me some idea of what you're looking for . . ."

She trailed off expectantly, and Quinn immediately raised her eyebrows in Marcus's direction. "What do you say, honey? This ring-shopping expedition was your idea."

Marcus hoped Carol Ann hadn't noticed the sarcastic emphasis Quinn placed on the word "honey." He'd gone to school with Carol Ann, and unless she'd had a personality transplant sometime in the last twenty years, he knew she'd love nothing more than to spread a rumor that Sanctuary Island's new favorite couple were already fighting.

In an effort to hold back the tide of gossip, Marcus looped his arm around Quinn's shoulders and tugged her close to his side. He hoped the move looked natural and full of ease, instead of full of the tension that beat between them like a pulse.

"I'll like whatever you like," he said with a flash of a smile in Carol Ann's direction.

"That's so sweet." He wondered if he was the only one who could hear the gritted teeth behind Quinn's smile. "But not all that helpful."

Carol Ann whisked the flower-shaped ring back under the glass counter and replaced it in the display. "I tell you what. I've got a few things I'm working on in the back that aren't quite ready to be put out in the storefront yet, but you could get an idea if maybe one of them . . ."

"Oh, that would be so wonderful! Carol Ann, we appreciate this so much."

"Nonsense!" Color filled Carol Ann's round cheeks. "As if I wouldn't do whatever I can to help you find your perfect engagement ring, after all the help you gave me when I was setting this place up. I'm just flattered you might want to wear one of my creations."

"I love your jewelry," Quinn said, as sincerely as if this weren't the one and only jewelry store in town. "And you don't owe me anything. I was happy to help."

With a parting smile, Carol Ann bustled into the back of her shop. As soon as she was gone, Quinn stepped out from under Marcus's arm. Bending over to stare down at the glass-topped display case, she gave a convincing impression of someone entranced by the silver bangle bracelet decorated with a giant dragonfly made of shimmery green stones.

She'd been standoffish all morning, ever since Marcus knocked on the door across the hall from his to tell her he was ready to go ring shopping. Come to think of it, she'd been pretty quiet and aloof on the car ride home from the Firefly Café the previous afternoon.

He'd attributed it to Quinn's being upset over the abrupt end to their fried-chicken lunch. Her mother's phone call from their marriage guru had effectively thrown a bucket of ice water over the proceedings. Her father had gone silent and aloof while her mother seemed distracted by whatever she and Ron had discussed. Marcus had never been so glad to pay a check and get back to his dark, empty bar.

Friday night's happy hour had seen a few people poke their heads into the bar. He'd sold a couple of beers to the local veterinarian and a guy who was familiar to Marcus, like he'd spent time on the island as a kid but hadn't grown up there. The two men hadn't stayed long, but they'd both complimented the beer selection before they left.

It wasn't much, but it was better than the tumbleweeds that were all Marcus'd had in there before. He'd woken up feeling like this crazy plan of Quinn's might actually work.

Until now, as he stood alone with her in front of a case of handmade silver jewelry and wondered if he could even get her to look at him.

"What's wrong?" he demanded bluntly, unwilling to beat around the bush.

"Nothing. Everything is fine. This ring shopping was a good idea. Gotta have the right props for the act."

He frowned, eyes flicking to the doorway behind the jewelry counter to make sure they were still alone. "You make it sound like I'm the one who convinced you to lie about our relationship."

She straightened up as if he'd pinched her. For a moment there was a mulish set to her pretty mouth, but as Marcus watched, it melted into something softer. Softer, but not necessarily happier. "I'm sorry. You're right, and I'm grateful. I am. But I mean—isn't it already getting out of hand? Now you're not just my fake boyfriend, you're my fake fiancé! Maybe we should quit before it goes any further. I mean, how are we going to pull this off when I didn't even know you'd been in the Secret Service?"

The pitch of her whisper got steadily higher and more distressed. Marcus winced. Shit, he knew that was going to come back to bite him.

"It's not a big deal," he tried. "You covered fine last night."

"It's not about whether or not I can convincingly cover the fact that we hardly know each other," Quinn muttered, then bit her lip.

Marcus couldn't afford to be soft here. "Sure it is. Because nothing else matters."

She shook her head, the honeyed red of her hair swinging forward to hide her face. "I don't think I can do this."

Cursing silently, Marcus wrestled with himself for a long moment before saying, "Look, if it's that important to you, ask me what you want to know."

"Anything?" She perked up, slanting him a glance from underneath her lashes. "And you swear you'll tell me?"

He gave her his how-dumb-do-I-look face. "No. I'm not making any promises. But you can ask, and I'll tell you if I can."

Quinn didn't waste any more time. "Were you in the Secret Service?"

"Yes."

"Were you assigned to the White House?"

"For a while."

"Why did you leave?"

"Got reassigned."

She huffed in frustration. "Were you ever on a protection detail or were you part of the advance team that goes in to secure locations, or what?"

Marcus paused. "You did some research."

"I may have spent a little time last night Googling, yes. Come on, answer the question."

Marcus considered reminding her he hadn't promised he'd answer every question, but there was no real reason not to answer this one. No reason except that he was pretty sure he knew what the next one would be.

"I did some of everything in my time with the bureau."

"Well, did you ever protect anybody famous? Like the president?"

This was the moment where Marcus would either stonewall, or tell Quinn the truth and watch her realize exactly what he'd been through. He had zero interest in rehashing the whole thing with her. God knew, it would be easier to shut this conversation down. But now that he came right down to it, that felt like the coward's way out.

He could just imagine what Buttercup would've had to say about that.

With "In my day, men were men and women knew how to keep them in line," ringing in his head, Marcus found himself suppressing a smile. "Yeah. After an attempt was made on her life, I was permanently assigned to Mrs. Colleen McCarty's protection detail."

Quinn's jaw dropped. "Colleen McCarty. The ex-First Lady."

"Once a First Lady, always a First Lady," Marcus corrected, "in Mrs. McCarty's own words."

"But she—"

Quinn cut herself off and Marcus could see it, the exact moment when she remembered what happened to Colleen McCarty, beloved national icon . . . and the best woman Marcus had known since he lost his own mother.

He didn't shy away from it. "She died. And I retired and came home."

He said it with finality, to end the questions. There was nothing more to be said on the subject, or at least, nothing more Marcus intended to say. Poor Quinn was practically buzzing with curiosity, but after the weeks they'd spent together, she knew when to push and when to back off. It was something he'd always grudgingly appreciated about her.

This was definitely a time to back off.

Except . . . it was possible that Quinn cared less, these days, about pissing Marcus off. In the instant before she opened her mouth, he knew she wasn't going to let it drop.

"What was she like? I mean, other than the most beloved First Lady since Eleanor Roosevelt and Jackie rolled into one."

Marcus blinked. It wasn't the question he'd expected

and dreaded, about his feelings when she was killed or whatever. Startled, his guard dropped enough that he said without thinking, "Buttercup would've liked that comparison."

"Buttercup?"

Crap. Reluctantly, Marcus explained. "The Secret Service gives code names to high-level targets. JFK was Lancer; Jackie was Lace. Eisenhower was Scorecard; Mamie was Springtime. Like that, usually with families' code names starting with the same letter. President McCarty was Boomer. His wife was Buttercup."

Quinn melted right before his eyes. "You named your bar after her, didn't you?"

It was obvious enough at this point that Marcus didn't feel the need to answer. He'd already said more than he wanted to.

"Come on, don't clam up on me now! Tell me about her. Was she as cool as she always seemed in interviews? I used to love when they'd bring her out for inaugurations and stuff, she'd look so elegant and classy, and when they asked about her clothes, she'd smack them with some off-the-cuff statement that was so smart and insightful about a real issue of the day, like child hunger or poverty, and they'd all be scrambling! She was amazing. I was so sad when she died—hey, wait! Marcus!"

Marcus glanced down. His feet were moving without his making a conscious decision, carrying him out of the store and onto the sidewalk that ringed the town square. The spring sunshine woke him up, piercing through the dark fog of grief and regret that threatened to overwhelm him. He breathed in deep, forcing air into his constricted lungs and tasting the salt tang of the ocean on the breeze.

Quinn caught up to him a moment later, freckles standing out on her pale cheeks like fresh nutmeg in a bowl of cream. She was so achingly beautiful, it closed Marcus's throat.

"Where are you going? We haven't got the ring yet!"

He kept moving, shoving his hands in his pockets and walking as if he had a destination in mind. Quinn hurried along at his side, practically emanating a worried distress that Marcus wasn't ready to deal with.

"Okay, fine," she tried. "We can go back to the shop another time, I guess. Although, gosh, poor Carol Ann isn't going to know what's going on—she's going to think we just ditched her! Which we did, actually. Marcus, can't you stop for a second and tell me what's going on?"

"Nothing is going on," he ground out, eyes forward. "I don't have time for any more of this crap today. I have work."

"You invited me," Quinn pointed out reasonably, "so I assumed this was a good time for you."

Something mean and ugly rose up in his chest to snarl at Quinn's patient concern. "If you think anything about this screwed-up situation is a good time, you need to get out more, sweetheart."

Quinn stopped in her tracks and forced Marcus still

with a hand on his elbow. The muscles of his forearm hardened to granite under her touch. "Let's get something straight here, Marcus. I know you're running away because, somehow, talking about your ex-boss means I got too close. I get it. And if you don't want to talk about your life before you came back to Sanctuary Island, that's your prerogative. If you want to stay shut down and closed off from anyone who ever tries to get close to you, that's your business. But regardless of what act we're putting on for my parents, I don't have to take that tone from you. Not ever. I'd rather call the whole thing off right now than stand here and take this."

Her tone was firm, uncompromising, but the tremor at the corners of her lips told Marcus how hard this was for her to say. Shame washed over him in a sickening tide, but at the same time, he was proud of her for standing up for herself.

The point was, she shouldn't have to. Not with him.

"You're right." He forced the words out roughly, his throat clenching down on them like a fist. "You shouldn't put up with me. You deserve a hell of a lot better than I can give you."

The words hit Quinn like a dart between the eyes.

You shouldn't put up with me. You deserve a hell of a lot better than I can give you.

Is that why he broke up with her? The question burned in her mouth, but she swallowed it down. Even as her memories of their relationship reshuffled and rearranged themselves like a deck of cards, she knew better than to make a big deal out of this moment. Marcus was this close to bolting again. She was like a *National Geographic* photographer in the wild or something—she didn't want to spook him.

"I appreciate the apology—well, the sort-of apology," she amended with a determinedly light tone and a lift of one brow. "But I'd appreciate it even more if you'd leave it to me to decide what I deserve."

Marcus's eyes narrowed to slits as he stared stoically into the distance. "No promises. But I'll work on it. Good enough?"

"Good enough," Quinn agreed, trying not to sound too eager. Trying and failing, but come on! This was easily the most real conversation she'd ever had with Marcus Beckett, maybe since the day of his mother's funeral. She was going to have to take her time figuring out how all this new information fit into the picture of Marcus she carried around in her heart, but in the meantime, she felt good about the way she'd spoken up. Because there were still four weeks of this crazy farce to go, and it would never work if she kept to the same sort of meek reluctance to rock the boat that she'd stuck to when they were sleeping together.

She realized now that she'd spent those weeks just waiting for the other shoe to drop, always sure that the wrong word or question at the wrong moment would mean Marcus kicking her out of his bed and out of his life with no warning.

And she reminded herself that, as it happened, she'd

been right. The difference now was that they weren't sleeping together, and he wasn't in her life. Not really, not for good. So she didn't have to tiptoe around him anymore.

She'd already lost him in every way that mattered.

Now they needed each other, but it was mutual. Equal. They both had something to lose.

Speaking of what Quinn stood to lose . . .

"Quick, give me your hand," she muttered, lacing their fingers together and waving with her free hand. "That's my mom's car."

His palm was warm and broad, interestingly callused and rough in places, reminding her of the sweet rasp of those fingertips over her body. Quinn shoved down the heat that quivered to life in her belly and leaned down to peer into the blue hybrid hatchback that pulled over to the curb beside them.

"Hi, Mother! What are you doing out . . . and . . . about . . ."

Quinn's voice withered in her chest as she took in the overly tanned older man sitting smugly in her mother's passenger seat. Quinn didn't even know how she knew the guy was smug just from the way he sat, but somehow, it was glaringly obvious. As glaring as the sheen of his improbably black hair and his large, perfectly square teeth.

"Oh, sweetie." Ingrid Harper leaned her head out of her open window and beckoned them closer. "How amazing to run into the two of you right now— although, of course, it's not a coincidence. It's Fate!

Anyway, come here, I want you to meet someone very special."

Quinn's feet suddenly felt as if they were made of lead and weighed about twenty pounds each. Marcus had to tug her forward, already plastering on the fake smile that had so charmed her mother the day before.

I don't want to, she thought nonsensically, even as her feet finally shifted and her mother turned the car off.

"This can't be good," Marcus murmured in an undertone as Ingrid and her passenger climbed from the car.

"Darling," Ingrid said breathlessly, rounding the front of the car to grab her guest by the elbow. "This is Ron Burkey. He's a miracle worker, well versed in intuitive healing, relationship coaching, aura work, breath work—you name it, he's an expert in it."

Oh, Lord. Quinn mustered up a smile but she was afraid she couldn't do much about the hard stare she directed at the great Ron Burkey as she held out her hand. "So, you're a psychiatrist? Should I call you Dr. Burkey?"

"That's not necessary," he said with a wide smile. "And spiritual psychologist is the more accurate term."

He slipped his smooth, plump hand into hers and Quinn had to hold back a shudder of revulsion at the touch. Disentangling herself half a second before it was truly polite, she said, "Nice to meet you. I didn't realize you made house calls."

"Well, when your mother told me the happy news

last night, I hopped the first flight out of New Mexico! And here I am. So interested to meet you both." The somewhat portly man ran surprisingly shrewd eyes over Quinn before moving on to Marcus, who crossed his arms over his broad chest in a way that made Quinn notice the sinewy strength of his forearms.

Oh, good, she thought a little hysterically. *He was in the Secret Service. He has ways of intimidating bad guys.*

Part of her felt guilty for immediately and automatically assuming Ron Burkey was evil. She might not buy into any of the New Age stuff her mother liked. And she might even be pretty sure that most of the people who claimed they could see auras or do astral projection or whatever were total imposters—but there were probably plenty who had convinced themselves as thoroughly as they'd ever convinced anyone else. Quinn knew she should give Ron Burkey the benefit of the doubt.

She just didn't want to. And from the steely glint in Marcus's gaze as he stared down the shorter man, he didn't want to, either. Which only made it harder for Quinn to be generous.

Especially when she glanced at her mother and saw the starry look in her eyes. That look used to be reserved for Quinn's father. To see it now when her mother gazed at this man who was supposed to be fixing her marriage—but who was actively trying to wreck it, if Daddy was right—made Quinn's blood overheat with a restless, incoherent anger.

"Well, now you've met us," she said abruptly. "So you can head on back to New Mexico, Mr. Burkey."

"Quinn Rosalie Harper!" her mother gasped, but Ron held up a pale hand peaceably.

"Now, now, Ing. Your daughter is entitled to her opinions, and besides, I see by her aura that she's in some genuine pain and confusion about the situation with you and Paul. Let me handle this. Quinn, I prefer Dr. Ron," he countered. His smile was like a shark's, wide and pointed below a flat stare. "And I'm not going anywhere. In fact, I'm delighted by your engagement and your parents' decision to keep their house, and I think I have a way to use the flames of new love to help rekindle the dying embers of your parents' marriage."

Dying embers? Quinn saw red. "Listen here, you—"

"We should all commit to staying there," Ron interrupted with an expansive wave of his arms that made the shiny gray fabric of his sport coat shimmer. "At the house where you grew up. We will all live there together, nonstop, for the next two weeks. Myself, your parents, you, and your charming fiancé. What do you say?"

Chapter 7

"Hell, no. That's what I say." Marcus slammed the door of the Buttercup Inn behind him, startling Quinn into whirling around to face him.

They'd left Ingrid and her bronzed, Botoxed guru on the street with some vague promises of thinking it over, while Ingrid clasped her hands and looked nervous for the first time in Marcus's memory. He couldn't imagine how Paul Harper was going to react to this new development, and he was willing to bet Ingrid was having a hard time imagining it, too.

Not that it mattered, because Marcus wasn't moving in with Quinn's parents. End of story.

Lantern Point, where Quinn's parents' house was situated, was a tiny spit of land sticking out of the southwest corner of Sanctuary Island. To get to it from the main town square, you had to drive all the way out to the farthest edge of the island, around Lantern Lake, through the wildest and most undeveloped land Sanctuary had to offer. The only other house within a mile of Quinn's parents' place was the house where Marcus grew up.

The house he'd vowed never to return to.

As if she could read his mind, Quinn turned big, pleading eyes on him. "What if I promised you'd never have to see your dad? I can count on the fingers of one hand the number of times he's come into town in the last few years. My parents haven't laid eyes on him once since they've been home."

Marcus stiffened, feeling uncomfortably exposed. He hadn't talked to Quinn about his father, although he had vague memories of seeing her right after that final fight, before he took off for good. Or what he thought was for good, at the time.

It probably wasn't that hard for her to guess the source of his reluctance to go back to Lantern Point, but that didn't mean he had to like it.

"That's beside the point," he said stubbornly. "The real issue is that this isn't what we agreed on. This whole idea was brainless from the start, but at least it had a shot at working when it was just a couple of dinners out with your parents per week. You honestly think we can keep up this charade twenty-four-seven, with your folks and 'Dr. Ron' watching our every move?"

"It's not ideal, I admit. They think we're engaged, and that you have PTSD—and now there's a guru involved. My God, what a mess."

"You're not exactly selling me on this, Turbo."

Quinn sucked in a breath. "Turbo. You haven't called me that in years."

"The prospect of moving back to Lantern Point makes me think of you zooming down the street on your ten-speed, with those glittery streamers blowing in the breeze."

Cringing and laughing, Quinn brought a hand up to partially cover her face. "Oh my gosh . . . don't remind me. I was such a little pest. You must have hated the way I tagged after you and your friends all the time."

He hadn't, actually, but he'd been a different person back then. Just a kid, as young and soft as Quinn was now. Marcus remembered mostly feeling flattered and pleased at the attention.

Which would be the exact wrong thing to tell Quinn now.

"You were okay," he said instead, gruff enough to cover the tidal rush of memory that swept over him as he ducked behind the bar and started clearing out the taps.

"Golly, you'd better quit gushing. I'm all aflutter." But she was grinning a little as she went around to the two-top and four-top tables to pull the chairs down and arrange them across from each other. "So, about moving in with my parents. Look, I know it's a lot to ask, but they're my parents and I want to help them any way

I can—and this way, we can keep an eye on Dr. Ron. As my fake fiancé, can I count you in?"

He groaned aloud. "Give it a rest, Quinn. I said I'd think about it, and I will."

He didn't imagine for a second that she'd be able to let it go, but to his surprise, they fell into a comfortable silence as they worked together to get the bar ready to open. And when the clock ticked down to four o'clock, they were set almost before Marcus knew what was happening.

"Ready for the rush," he said sardonically, bracing himself for disappointment as he went to flip the switch on the OPEN sign.

"Tonight should be better," Quinn said with a cryptic smile. "At least, I hope so. Fingers and toes crossed!"

Marcus narrowed his eyes in suspicion but before he could ask her what she'd done, the bell over the bar door tinkled and Miss Patty Cuthbert swanned in, trailing a trio of tittering older ladies like ducklings all in a row. All four ladies were dressed in their Sunday best, hats and all, and Marcus put on his best smile for them.

"Ladies! Welcome to the Buttercup Inn. Would you like to sit at the bar, or there's a nice table by the window."

Miss Patty, the obvious de facto leader of the group, nodded decisively in the direction of the four-top in the corner. "You know I like to sit at the bar and flirt with you, young man, but we have serious business to handle. We'll take the table."

"That sounds ominous," he said with a grin as he led the way to the table. "Can I get you ladies started with anything to drink?"

"We'll take a pitcher of martinis." Patty seated herself with a flourish. "Not too dry, plenty of olives, stirred and not shaken. Unlike that James Bond wimp, we like our martinis strong enough to dissolve paint."

Marcus felt his eyebrows climbing toward his hairline. "Martinis. This *is* serious. Okay, coming right up."

He ducked behind the bar and grabbed the gin, bypassing the well bottles and going straight for top shelf. Nothing too good for Miss Patty, who'd finally managed to bring some friends along with her to the Buttercup.

"She got them to come!" Quinn perched on the corner bar stool and rubbed her hands in undisguised glee. "I thought maybe she'd be able to, now."

Marcus scooped four martini glasses full of ice to chill them down while he mixed the drinks. "Who are they?"

"Let's see. Mrs. Crump was my kindergarten teacher, Mrs. Ellery runs the local flower shop, and Miss Ruth makes the best homemade ice cream in the state. I worked at her ice-cream stand one summer during high school, selling peach ice-cream cones to kids."

"Every one of those women loves you like a grand-daughter." Marcus wasn't asking—he knew it was true.

"They've all known me since I was a baby." Quinn shrugged, cheerfully unconcerned with her popularity.

Marcus didn't point out that most of them had known him, too, or at least had known his family. He actually recognized all three of Patty's friends, although he wouldn't have been able to call up their names. But that wasn't exactly what he'd been asking, anyway.

"Do you have any idea what this serious business is that they're here to discuss?" He made it a point not to get involved in his customers' private lives, but if Miss Patty was in some kind of trouble, Marcus wanted to know about it.

But Quinn laughed. "Oh, it's deadly serious, all right. This is Miss Patty's bridge club. There's a big tournament coming up next Sunday night in the Methodist church basement, and I think she's got them practicing their bidding conventions around the clock."

And indeed, when Marcus carried the tray over to the table and set down the four martini glasses, fogged with chill and each bearing a toothpick laden with four green olives, Miss Patty's gnarled hands were shuffling cards with the dexterity and grace of a riverboat gambler.

"Here you are, ladies." Marcus poured them each a martini from the glass pitcher, then set it down to one side of the table to leave the center open for their card playing. "Good luck in the tournament."

"Bridge isn't a game of luck," Miss Patty said, a

dangerous gleam in her faded blue eyes. "It's about skill and nerve. And the ability to count cards."

"Oooh," said a wizened lady even older than Miss Patty. She was the one Marcus remembered the most clearly, and in his memory she was associated with summertime and milk shakes. Miss Ruth, he decided. "This martini ought to help our nerves, at least. Liquid courage never tasted so good."

"Too bad we can't take flasks of this stuff into the tournament," lamented the woman across from Miss Ruth, the purple turban wrapped around her henna-red hair nodding as she took another sip. "You Methodists. You don't want anyone to have any fun."

"Get over it, Alice Ellery," the oldest woman said bluntly. "You're not bringing spirits into my church and that's final."

"Jesus made wine out of water, you know," Mrs. Ellery grumbled.

"Well, gin is a little different from wine. And anyhow, it's the church's policy, not Miss Ruth's," the last woman pointed out gently before turning her soft smile up at Marcus. Unused to having such sweetness and light beamed in his direction, Marcus nearly took a step back, but he forced himself to hold his ground.

"Thank you for the drinks, young man," she said, with the kind of soothing voice he expected a kindergarten teacher to have. The way she'd shut down the bickering between Miss Ruth and Mrs. Ellery was another telltale clue. "This seems to be a very nice place you've built here."

A warm glow of pride suffused Marcus's chest. "Thank you for giving it a try."

She exchanged glances with Miss Ruth across the table, before twinkling back up at Marcus. "We're only sorry it took us so long. But we just weren't sure, you see."

"I grew up on the island," Marcus said diplomatically. "I know how long it can take folks here to make up their minds about something new. Sanctuary Island has never had a bar before."

"Oh, it wasn't the bar we weren't sure about," said Miss Ruth, her dark eyes glinting shrewd as a fox's.

"But I was at the Firefly yesterday," said the lady with the turban, who had to be Mrs. Ellery. "So I saw the whole thing. Congratulations on getting Quinn to forgive you, by the way. And then when Quinn came to us and told us how much she hoped this place would be a success, well, we realized that supporting the bar was really a way of supporting our dear Quinn's future. So here we are!"

Of course Quinn talked to them. Marcus fought the urge to glare over his shoulder. When they eventually "broke up," all this was probably going to explode in his face like a cartoon birthday cake. But in the meantime, he had the chance to make a good impression on these women.

And if Marcus remembered how this small town worked, it was women like these four who truly ruled the roost. The rest of the community would follow their lead.

"Well, whatever the reason, I'm glad you decided to allow me a chance to give you a fun night out. To show my appreciation, the next round is on me."

The ladies fluttered gratefully, thanking him and picking up their cards. While they were busy arranging their hands, Patty sent Marcus a wink and an approving nod to send him back over to Quinn.

Who was watching with open delight, and more than a hint of satisfaction. "Nicely done," she said, leaning up on both elbows and craning forward to speak quietly across the zinc-topped bar separating them. "Miss Ruth is on the town council, the vestry at the church, and she heads up the festival committee. If you can get her on your side, no one in town will dare to say a word against you."

"This would have been good information to have a few weeks ago," Marcus grumbled. "You could have talked her into stopping by anytime."

"Maybe I could have, although Miss Ruth has a mind of her own. I'm persuasive, but even I can't convince a woman of principle to go against those principles."

"Believe me, I know how persuasive you can be," Marcus said without thinking, and just like that, the air between them went heavy and humid with desire. His gaze dropped to her light pink lips, parted softly and damp where the tip of her tongue had darted out to wet them.

She was so close. She'd shifted at some point to kneel on the bar stool so that her whole torso was propped on the bar, putting her face mere inches from his. Marcus fought the gravitational pull, but it was hard to fight when most of him wanted nothing more than to grab the back of her neck and haul her over the bar, to take her mouth and get her under him and wreck them both with pleasure.

"I persuaded you a few times right here on this bar, as I recall," she said, her voice no more than a husky wisp of breath that reminded Marcus viscerally of the rasp of her sighs in his ear when he'd pushed her up against the wall and wrapped her legs around his hips to get their bodies as close as two people could possibly be.

His gaze moved from her plump, succulent, bitable mouth to the helpless heat of her eyes. In them, he saw the same memories flickering through her mind that were playing on an endless reel in his brain, taunting him with how good they'd been together.

She breathed in and he felt like she'd hooked him by the collar and reeled him in. Marcus's head dipped and Quinn stretched up, and their lips met.

Marcus had an instant, a heartbeat, to register the honey-salt taste of her mouth, the coy stroke of her pointed tongue teasing at his lower lip, before a round of sighs and applause jolted them apart. Over her shoulder, the bridge-club ladies were shamelessly catcalling and clinking their glasses together merrily.

Pulling back with a flush across her cheekbones, Quinn swallowed hard and ducked her head. When she peeked up at him from beneath her lashes, the clear question in her gaze nailed Marcus to the wall.

What the hell was he doing? This couldn't happen. He couldn't be this big of an asshole. It wasn't possible that he could let Quinn Harper think even for a second that they might get back together.

From the deepest part of whatever remained of his soul, Marcus dug up a slow, conspiratorial grin. With calculated precision, he lowered his head to whisper in Quinn's ear, in a move he knew would look like loving teasing to the old ladies who were avidly watching.

And he said, "Nice moves, Turbo. I think they bought it."

Chapter 8

Quinn held very still, as if the pain of Marcus's words were a stalking animal that would pounce the instant she moved. But there was no escaping this hurt, because she'd brought it on herself. It was her fault, and no one else's.

You came to him. You practically begged for his help, she reminded herself brutally. *You thought you were safe after the way he hurt you before. You thought it would be easy to keep your distance.*

Well, now she knew. It wasn't easy. Even now, even knowing that Marcus had kissed her as nothing more than a show for his first few customers, her body wanted to sway back toward him and melt against the hard plane of his chest.

Instead, she carefully shifted her weight away from

him. Uncurling her legs, she sat on the stool the normal way, letting the process of finding her balance restore her balance in other ways, too. "Told you I could be persuasive."

Quinn was impressed with the lightness of her tone. She sounded almost normal. She couldn't quite bring herself to meet Marcus's watchful gaze to see if he was convinced. Luckily, in that exact moment, the bell over the bar door rang to signal another new customer, and Quinn felt her phone start to vibrate in her back pocket.

With a tilt of her head toward the stairs at the back of the bar, Quinn waved her phone in Marcus's direction before answering it and hurrying up to her tiny, one-room studio across the hall from Marcus's apartment. She needed to get herself together.

Half an hour later, Quinn trooped back downstairs feeling more wrung out and stressed than she had been when she went up.

She paused on the threshold, though, and the sight that greeted her did more to lift her spirits than anything else could have. The Buttercup Inn wasn't filled to capacity, but it was busy enough to buzz with the energy of a vibrant, energetic place. Miss Patty's bridge club was on their second round, if the increasingly raucous sound of their laughter was any indication.

Of course, Miss Patty had been in before. But tonight, she wasn't the only customer. A couple of farmers were propped up at the bar, nursing beers, and there was a table of six teachers from the high school earnestly debating something academic over two bottles of wine.

Behind the bar, Marcus was in his element, mixing drinks and pulling glasses of draft beer as if he'd been born to do it. He didn't look obviously overjoyed at the bar's sudden popularity—he wasn't the sort of man to openly grin and joke around with his customers—but Quinn was surprised to realize she knew him well enough to be able to tell.

Marcus was happy.

At least, he was until he caught sight of her hovering in the doorway. Whatever he saw on her face had a shadow lowering Marcus's brow like a thundercloud. Throwing down the white cotton towel he'd been using to wipe glasses, he rounded the corner of the bar and headed straight for her like a heat-seeking missile.

It's a show, Quinn told herself firmly as all that concentrated intensity and attention sent a shiver over her skin. *He doesn't mean anything by it. At least, not what you want him to mean.*

"What's wrong?" he demanded as soon as he was within arm's length of her.

Ignoring the way he loomed, all big and muscley and ready to beat down anybody that looked at Quinn funny, she said, "Nothing, really."

She tried to laugh it off, but it stuck in her throat. Marcus crossed his arms over his chest like he intended to intimidate the truth out of her. "Really."

"That was my dad on the phone."

His brow cleared a bit. "Ah."

"Yeah." She wrapped her arms around her torso, feeling suddenly cold. "To say my father is unhappy that Mother invited Ron Burkey to stay with them indefinitely—well, 'unhappy' would be a major understatement."

"Understandable. I'm not all that thrilled at the prospect, either."

"I know. Believe me, there are people I'd rather be locked in a house with. Satan springs to mind. But my father . . . I don't know how well you remember my parents, from growing up down the lane."

He shrugged, massive shoulders bunching. "Not that well."

"I've never heard my dad sound like that," she explained haltingly. "Like he didn't see the point of anything, like he might be ready to just give up."

Marcus didn't say anything, but his intent gray eyes never left her face. Quinn knew he was hearing her, and it gave her the courage to keep going. "I feel like a stupid kid for being so thrown by it, but my father has always been the strong one in our family. The steady one. My mother—I mean, you met her. She's lovely. I love her. But I can't count on her, not the way I count on Daddy. Sorry, I know that sounds childish . . ."

"No," he surprised her by saying. Marcus glanced away, back toward the bar, but Quinn thought it was more to hide his eyes than to check whether the guys were done with their beers yet. "I get it. When the person you rely on falters, when you lose them, it changes everything."

All of a sudden, Quinn remembered how the young Marcus had looked on the day his mother died, as if the bottom had dropped out of his world.

Her father wasn't dead, but for Quinn, the solidity of her parents' marriage had always been a touchstone. If it fell apart, she'd lose some essential faith in things turning out the way they were supposed to. Maybe that's what it meant to grow up.

She set her jaw. If that's what growing up was, she wanted no part of it.

"Did your father agree to let Burkey stay at the house?"

"I guess so." Quinn pinched the bridge of her nose between her thumb and forefinger, trying to stave off a headache. "Again, you met my mother. She might seem wispy and vague, but she knows how to get her own way."

A wry twist tugged at Marcus's mouth. "Hmm. Who else do I know who's good at getting her way?"

Quinn slapped the side of his arm, trying not to shiver at the hard bulge of his bicep. She couldn't help it if her hand lingered a bit. "Shut up! Or wait, does that mean you plan to give in and spend the next two weeks at my parents' house, sharing the misery with me?"

Their eyes locked for a long moment, during which Quinn felt the muscle under her lightly resting fingertips tense into solid steel. For the space of a heartbeat, she had the wild fantasy that it was taking everything he had to restrain himself from reaching for her. Tension ratcheted up and up and up while Quinn held her breath and waited to see what Marcus would do or say.

The moment broke with an almost painful snap when a smooth masculine voice behind her said, "Yes, Mr. Beckett. Do tell us if you'll be joining in our grand treatment plan at the Harpers' house."

Quinn stiffened in dismay. She couldn't help pleading up at Marcus with her eyes, ignoring the surprise presence of her mother's guru behind her.

Unruffled, Marcus said, "I haven't decided yet."

Her heart sank even as Ron Burkey hummed thoughtfully. She stepped aside to turn their twosome into a three-way conversation, taking in the calculating sharpness of the marriage guru's gaze.

"I have to wonder why you would refuse." Ron placed a short, stubby finger to his chin in a contemplative pose. "Surely you want to help your future in-laws repair the energy disharmony that's causing their marital issues."

"Of course he does," Quinn said, darting a gaze at Marcus, who was staring stone-faced at Ron Burkey. Stone-faced and silent, of course. Quinn clenched her jaw in frustration.

"Unless . . ." Ron stroked his bronzed chin. "Unless you two are experiencing some energy disharmony of your own."

"We're not! We're perfectly happy!" Quinn hastily looped her arm through Marcus's, trying to behave as though she felt one hundred percent comfortable putting her hands on him.

"I wonder. Because I have to tell you, I'm quite sensitive to aura imbalance, and your two auras are in direct conflict. The kind of conflict I'd expect to see with a couple in an advanced phase of their breakup."

Quinn's blood ran cold. How could he know they'd broken up? Before she could panic, Marcus's hand came up to cover hers where it wrapped around the inside of his crooked elbow. "Our auras are just fine," he said with a sardonic curl of his lips. "Thanks for the concern."

Ron shook his head sadly. "A skeptic. I sensed that about you. But you know, auras don't lie. I'd encourage you to accept Ing's invitation—if we had two weeks to do some breath work and a little body whispering, I'd feel comfortable attempting astral healing on you. That's like psychic surgery for your aura. It could be very beneficial. Not just for your *relationship,* but for your life."

From the way Marcus's muscles twitched under her hand, she knew he'd caught it, too—the slightly mocking emphasis Ron placed on the word "relationship."

"It's kind of you to take an interest in our relationship," Quinn said cautiously. "Considering that you already have your hands full with my parents.'"

"Well, you really made it impossible for me to ignore you when you cited your relationship as a reason your parents should ignore my professional advice. Of course I'm delighted that one of the major blockages stifling open energy pathways between your parents is resolving itself—that would be you, my dear," Ron said kindly. "And your parents' worries over your aimless, directionless life."

Quinn sucked in a breath as that jab socked her square in the eye, but Ron wasn't done.

"I've read your parents' star charts backward and forward. I've studied the gestalt of their marriage, holistically and exhaustively, and it's my considered opinion that the house on Lantern Point is so layered with years of bad energy that it's become a psychic scar that will be quite difficult to heal. I feel so strongly about it, I even offered my wife's services to help them offload the house—she's a very successful real estate broker in Santa Fe, but she has connections on the East Coast as well. I'm sure we could have put together a deal that would allow your parents the freedom to paint a portrait of retirement that allows them to soar into the future . . . but if you're determined not to allow that, who am I to oppose you?"

Quinn's heart was pounding so loudly in her ears, she had to focus hard to take in the last part of Ron's speech. She had no doubt this guy was bad news, but at the same time, the idea that she was selfishly keeping her parents from doing something that would help their marriage was so painful that for a moment, she wondered if it was true. Maybe she was a spoiled brat, a whiny baby who couldn't bear the thought of not having the house of her childhood to run home to when being a grown-up got too hard. Maybe she needed to take her own wants out of the equation and only consider what was best for them.

Honing in on her soft underbelly, Ron said silkily, "I sense that you don't entirely disagree with me. Or maybe you're rethinking your stance, now that you've seen their energy disharmony for yourself."

Marcus uncrossed his arms, making Quinn drop hers to hang at her side, empty and adrift. Until he lifted the arm she'd been holding and curved it around her shoulders. The warm weight of it anchored her in place, solid and steadying, and she gave him a grateful smile.

After a moment of silent study of her face, Marcus looked back at Ron Burkey's waiting, smug smile and said, "The only thing we're rethinking is how soon we can move into the house with Paul and Ingrid."

Disappointed anger flashed through Ron's eyes for an instant before he pulled the gentle Zen veil back over his face. "And me. We'll be very cozy; it's not a huge house. Snug as five little bugs in a rug, all getting to know each other's secrets and learning so much about ourselves. Wonderful. I'll be looking forward to watching the two of you interact as a couple."

With that, Ron Burkey turned on his heeled, pointy-toed boots and walked out of the bar. Quinn gazed after him. "I have the awful feeling that all we've done is delay the inevitable. Still, a stay of execution is better than a beheading, any day."

"The next two weeks are going to suck."

Quinn melted a little at the reminder of how relieved

she'd been when Marcus spoke up and shut Ron down before she could waffle. "It *will* suck. But you're going to do it anyway, because you're my hero."

He hated that, she could tell. "I'm nobody's hero."

"If you want me to buy that," she told him, "you're going to have to stop being there for me when I need you the most."

Hoping if they showed up late, it might be less awkward, Marcus threw a random selection of shirts and pants into a backpack and clomped down the stairs to meet Quinn by his truck for the drive to her parents' house.

Marcus was in too deep. He knew it. The worst part was that he was afraid Quinn was starting to get the idea, too.

She had him wrapped around her little finger. It was embarrassing and idiotic, but true.

His goal for the next two weeks was to get through it without sinking any lower than he already had. He'd played off that kiss okay, but it hadn't done a damn thing to release the sexual tension between them. If anything, it had torqued it tighter, twisting the coil of hunger around his guts until he could barely breathe for wanting her.

And the way he reacted when anyone came after her? From her own parents to the slick bastard who'd tried to make her feel like her parents' divorce was her fault . . . Marcus would happily burn them all right down to the ground if it would keep that shattered look off Quinn's face.

He was in trouble. But at least he knew it. His only hope lay in the fact that Quinn currently believed that he didn't want her anymore.

Now all he had to do was keep up that pretense for two weeks of being in her presence pretty much non-stop, and he'd be fi— Oh crap.

Marcus paused at the foot of the stairs, one hand on the door to the outside, and cursed with the silent viciousness he'd learned to employ around a former First Lady who hated foul language.

Sighing, he pushed open the door and saw Quinn waiting for him, her hands snugged up under her armpits to combat the chill of the spring evening. "How many bedrooms does your parents' house have?" Marcus asked, tossing his backpack into the bed of the truck.

"Three," she said, frowning. "Why?"

He didn't even flinch. That was the value of bracing for the hit. "No reason."

Quinn's mouth dropped open and her eyebrows crinkled together in consternation. "Oh! Oh. I guess . . . you and I will be sharing a bedroom for the next two weeks."

"I guess we will. Unless you'd prefer to share with Dr. Ron."

She snorted. "See above, re: preferring the actual devil to that shiny-suited, shellacked, fake-baked jerk."

"I don't think I've ever heard you say anything so mean about anyone," Marcus marveled. "Not that I disagree."

Climbing into the cab, Quinn slammed the door grumpily while Marcus started the engine with the well-oiled growl that gave him a deep-down satisfaction every time. "It's fine. I'll sleep on the floor."

"Is that really necessary? We've shared a bed before."

She said it lightly, easily, as if they'd been platonic roommates in college or something. But the words—and the image they conjured—sparked a flame of lust in Marcus's belly that he had to grimly snuff out.

"Not up for discussion," he clipped out, flipping the truck into reverse and taking off down Main Street.

Silence reigned in the cab as they passed into the darker reaches of the island, away from the street lamps and cozily lit houses of the town center. The warm glow of lights from houses came along more and more infrequently until it had been five minutes since they passed a single other car on the road and Marcus had the brights on nonstop to illuminate the narrow road that skirted Lantern Lake.

There was a house out there now, just one, right on the edge of the lake. And after they passed it, the road stretched out, black and empty for several miles. Marcus didn't speed. The wild horses who made Sanctuary Island their home were too smart to wander carelessly into the road, but this far out from town, the lines between civilization and wilderness were blurred.

It was more likely to see wild horses grazing right along the roadside out here than anywhere else on the island.

As they made the final, familiar turn that would take them out onto the slender jut of Lantern Point, Marcus felt his pulse rocket into overdrive.

He was going home.

Chapter 9

"Is this the first time you've been out this way since you got back?" Quinn asked, skirting the subject of his father with surprising delicacy. Quinn was many things, but subtle wasn't usually one of them. It was something Marcus treasured about her.

"Yes," he said shortly.

"That's got to be weird."

The tentative sympathy in her voice made him feel like crap. Was he really such a bear that she hesitated even to express . . . actually, yeah. He definitely was. And she'd known that going in.

"I'm fine."

Out of the corner of his peripheral vision, he noted the compression of her lips. She didn't believe it. But she didn't push. "Okay."

Marcus risked a glance away from the winding road

to see her staring out the passenger window. Her strawberry-blond hair looked wine dark in the shadows, the messy braid lying over her shoulder a stark contrast to the graceful turn of her pale, freckled cheek. She said nothing more, and he tried to believe he wasn't disappointed.

This was what he'd wanted. For Quinn to stop trying to save him, and to quit believing he'd save her. She could do better than a broken-down old man like him, and Marcus, well . . . he was beyond saving.

The sight of his father's darkened house looming on the right-hand side of the road drove that home to Marcus like nothing else. It was late, but every single window was black and not a single porch light was lit to push back the night.

Marcus's foot lifted off the gas without him intending it, slowing the truck as they passed by the two-story seaside cottage. There were his mother's prize azalea bushes, overgrown into a tangle of bare, dead branches that nearly overran the front porch railing. The porch steps sagged on the left and one of the window shutters upstairs had come loose and hung at a disreputable angle. He wondered if the curtains his mother had hand sewn and put up by herself while Dad was at the hospital were still there. The paint was peeling in patches, he could see, and the whole house had an air of neglect that was hard to look at.

"I tried to offer to help him paint," she said guiltily. "Last year."

"But he wouldn't accept help," Marcus finished,

determinedly focusing his eyes forward again and stepping on the gas.

"Actually, I couldn't even get him to come to the door. He yelled at me to go away, so I did." She huffed a short laugh that sounded like it hurt. "Like father, like son, I guess."

Marcus's knee-jerk response was to deny that he was anything like his father, but he couldn't form the words to protest. Quinn wasn't wrong in this case, and no matter what Marcus felt or wanted, underneath it all was the lingering fear that he was, in fact, exactly like his father.

As they left the grim shell of his childhood home behind them, another house came into view. Farther down the road, almost to the tip of Lantern Point, the Harper house shone like a beacon in the darkness. Golden light spilled over the wraparound porch, inviting and welcoming, beckoning them closer.

Even with the upstairs windows mostly dark—it was going on midnight, after all—the house felt inhabited. Alive.

Marcus pulled into the driveway and cut the engine. Beside him, Quinn blew out a breath.

"Here we go. Are you ready for this?"

He quirked a brow at her. "Are you?"

The quick flash of her irrepressible grin lit the darkness inside the truck cab brighter than the overhead lights. "Heck, yeah. This is going to work, Marcus. It's all going to be worth it."

Her blind optimism should've been annoying. He

ought to want to give her a reality check, make her admit that this ridiculous scheme had zero chance of success. But instead, Marcus felt his own mood lifting to mirror hers.

Not that he could ever, on the best day of his life, match Quinn Harper's sunny cheer. He wasn't built for happiness. But when he was with her, he came close enough to get an idea of what it felt like.

Before he could go any further down that soppy path, Marcus shoved out of the truck and grabbed both their bags. He followed as Quinn tripped up the porch steps and flipped over the corner of the welcome mat with the toe of her sneaker to reveal a house key. The ex-Secret Service agent in Marcus cringed at the abysmal security, but it wasn't his business to assess locations for safety any longer.

And it was a good thing, too, because when a figure loomed out of the darkness at them, Marcus startled so badly that if he'd had a gun in his hand he would've taken the shot. Maybe winging Quinn's father would be a way to get out of this crazy mess she'd landed them in, he thought as his heart rate spiked and adrenaline gushed through him in a useless flood, but Marcus couldn't imagine it ending well for him.

"Hi, Daddy," Quinn said softly, throwing her arms around him for one of her no-holds-barred hugs. Marcus told himself he didn't miss them. And he definitely wasn't envious.

"We weren't expecting you until the morning," Paul

said, hugging his daughter back and staring at Marcus over the top of her head as if contemplating how to dispose of the body.

Marcus understood. If he had a daughter, he wouldn't appreciate coming face-to-face with the idea that she was spending her nights with a man like Marcus, either. But since he couldn't lay the man's fears to rest and tell Paul that he didn't intend to touch Quinn that night or any other night in the future, Marcus made do with an apologetic grimace. "Sorry to show up so late. The bar just closed."

"It's fine," Paul said, lips thinning briefly. Marcus couldn't help but notice that he looked worn down, the lines on his face deepened to grooves and the line of his shoulders slumped. "I was up anyway. Your mother will be happy to see you at breakfast, Quinn. I think she made up your room already, so come on up. Marcus, you need a hand with those bags?"

"Got them handled, sir."

Quinn shot him a glare over her shoulder like she thought he was overplaying it or something. But Marcus didn't see how it could hurt to be respectful. He was a guest in the man's house, and as far as Paul knew, Marcus was regularly looking at his daughter naked. The least he could do was keep a civil tongue in his head.

The stairs creaked under their quiet tread, and the staircase was gently lit with wall sconces that cast a warm gleam over the rogue's gallery of framed family photos. Marcus gazed from side to side, seeing Quinn in the pigtails he remembered while riding her bike, Quinn holding a bouquet of roses out to her mother, Quinn graduating from high school in a black robe that made her hair look like a living flame. Interspersed with those pictures was the evidence of Paul and Ingrid's decades of happy marriage—because if those two were faking it in these shots, Marcus would eat his backpack.

Paul and Ingrid laughing in the backseat of a VW bug, Paul and Ingrid slow dancing at their wedding, with Paul in a wide-lapeled suit and Ingrid in a white macramé dress with a wreath of flowers crowning her flowing blond hair.

Marcus knew better than most that a happy family could turn into an unhappy one, in almost the blink of an eye. But looking at these pictures, Marcus understood for the first time exactly why Quinn was so certain her parents' marriage could and should be saved.

The Harpers were the real deal. A real family who stuck it out and worked through it and made the best of things together.

The kind of family Marcus always thought he had . . . until his mother got sick.

He clenched his jaw until it hurt, using the pain to drive away the memories stirred up by seeing this old street again. His old house. The house where his mother died.

Paul led them to the first door on the right of the upstairs landing and held the door open. Quinn trooped in confidently, as if she'd never left home, but Marcus couldn't help hesitating on the threshold.

Partly because he could see the cozy bower of a room from the doorway and was already calculating how impossible it would be to get a minute's privacy for the next two weeks while sharing that tiny, pink space with Quinn. And partly, he paused because Paul Harper grabbed him discreetly by the strap of his backpack and held on.

"I'm allowing this because you're engaged," Paul said in an undertone so low, it didn't reach Quinn where she'd wandered into the en suite bathroom to wash her hands. "And because Quinn and her mother have me backed into a corner. No other reason. Please don't imagine for an instant that this means I accept you sharing a room with my daughter. Please remember that, and be respectful of the fact that you're staying under my roof."

Marcus cleared his throat. He wasn't a man accustomed to embarrassment, but damn if he didn't feel awkward as hell just then.

"Understood, sir."

Paul held his gaze for the length of a heartbeat, and Marcus didn't know exactly what his own face was doing, but whatever Paul saw there made his eyes widen a fraction. Damn it. Marcus was shooting for sincere and upstanding, not lovesick idiot.

Things just got a little too real.

The light clicked off in the bathroom and Quinn came out, drying her hands. She paused when she saw them hovering in the doorway and her eyes slitted in suspicion. "What are you two talking about over there?"

Paul dropped his hand quickly, with a guilty twitch that Marcus covered by stepping smoothly into the room and answering, "Your dad wanted to know if I'm a breakfast eater. I told him not to go to any trouble, but he's pretty insistent."

"What can I say? We like breakfast in this house," Paul said, a little too heartily, but it was enough to make Quinn relax and regard them both with fondness.

"I just hope Mother is over her gluten-free thing soon. In the meantime, maybe omelets, Daddy?"

"You got it, sweetheart." Paul stepped into the room far enough to scruff a kiss over the crown of Quinn's head. "Good night, you two. Sleep well."

The door closed behind him with a gentle click, leaving Marcus and Quinn staring at each other over the narrow queen-sized bed she'd slept in as a little girl. The light pink walls felt as if they were closing in on Marcus, the sloped roof caving down on his head. They were standing too close together. He wanted to back up, get some distance between their bodies, but there was simply nowhere to go.

Every breath he took was filled with Quinn.

The old house creaked as it settled around them, her father's footsteps fading and the low murmur of voices from down the hall tapering off into silence. Or as silent as it ever got way out here at the edge of Sanctuary Island.

As Marcus and Quinn stood, caught in each other's eyes, he could hear the slow, steady crash of the waves against the rocks that tipped Lantern Point. Wind rustled through the maritime pines and the first, brave crickets set up their early summer song.

"People who say it's too quiet in the country are obviously not listening very closely," Quinn said, doing that uncanny thing where she almost read Marcus's mind.

Clearing his throat, Marcus attempted to ignore the curves and lines of Quinn's firm, athletic body mere inches from his own, much larger form. She was smaller, more slender, but she wasn't fragile. Quinn could hold her own.

Danger. Redirect.

"Do you have an extra pillow?" He dumped their bags on the floor and kicked them off to the side of the rose-patterned rug. "And maybe a quilt."

She frowned. "Don't be ridiculous. There's plenty of room in the bed."

Marcus looked at the bed in question. It was less queen-sized and more full-sized. Every tiny motion, every shift of weight, every breath Quinn took . . . he'd feel it. He deliberately blanked his expression.

"I'll sleep better on the floor."

"Oh for the love of . . . Fine." Marching over to the foot of the bed, Quinn snatched up the comforter that was folded at the end and flung it around her own shoulders like a superhero's cape. She snagged a pillow and dropped it on the far side of the bed from the door, where the hardwood floor was mostly covered by the plush wool rug.

And then she plunked herself down by the pillow and stared mulishly up at the ceiling.

"What are you doing?" Marcus leaned over the bed to glare down at her.

"I'm sleeping on the floor," she replied loftily. "Since you think we can't be trusted to keep our hands to ourselves for two, tiny little weeks."

"You're not sleeping on the floor." It was a struggle to keep his voice low when frustrated irritation wanted him to yell. "I said I'd sleep down there."

"Well, now I'm sleeping down here. Get used to it."

"Quinn. Get in the bed."

Her eyes flashed dangerously. "Make me."

Grinding his back teeth, Marcus studiously did not imagine scooping her up and tossing her over his shoulder, caveman style. If he did that, and threw her on the bed the way he wanted to . . . neither of them would be sleeping on the floor.

Neither of them would be sleeping much at all, in fact.

"I don't get it," he finally said.

She eyed him warily. "What?"

"I don't get why you have to make things so much harder than they have to be."

The words came out weary, and Quinn had the grace to wince. "Sorry. But I'm the hostess. You're already doing me a huge favor. I'm absolutely not making you sleep on the floor too, on top of everything else."

"You know what?" Marcus shrugged and turned away. "Fine. You win. I don't know why I'm even arguing with you."

It wasn't as if Marcus were some stereotypical Southern gentleman or something, determined to lay his coat across a puddle rather than let a lady get her shoes wet. Quinn was a grown woman, not some delicate flower. If she wanted to sleep on the floor, let her.

"There's not usually much of a point to arguing with me." Quinn was cheerful again, now that she was getting her way.

He shucked his jeans in silence, shrugging out of the flannel shirt he'd been wearing and leaving him in just his boxer briefs and a T-shirt. Hesitating for a moment, Marcus fingered the hem of the shirt.

Usually, he slept in the buff. A fact that Quinn was all too familiar with. Rolling his eyes at his own belated sense of propriety, Marcus tugged off the T-shirt and slipped between the covers. He'd leave his underwear on as some kind of nod to decency. But Quinn said she wanted him to be comfortable, so he'd take her at her word.

Reaching over to turn the old-fashioned knob on the multicolored stained-glass bedside lamp, Marcus plunged the room into darkness.

The sounds of the spring night swirled up around

them again, filling his ears. But in addition to the beat of the surf and the chirrup of the crickets, if Marcus concentrated, he could hear the soft in and out of Quinn's breath.

It was those near-silent inhalations and exhalations that lulled him to sleep.

Quinn rolled onto her side, biting back a whimper as her hip bone banged the floor in the spot where it already felt bruised from the first hour of tossing and turning.

Flopping onto her back, she blew out a breath. She was almost surprised it didn't fog the air, it was so cold down there on the floor. The blanket she'd pulled from the bed had long ago been wrapped around her like a cocoon, but it didn't seem to do much to keep her warm.

All it did was make it nearly impossible to sit up, but by inch-worming herself along, she managed it. Quinn popped her head up by the bedside to stare at Marcus.

He slept on his back, exactly the way she remembered, with his face turned away from her and one arm thrown over his head. His sheets had slipped down, revealing the tender underside of his arm with its tuft of silky dark hair, and the broad planes of his chest. From where she knelt, she could just make out the shadow of one dusky nipple.

Her heart picked up speed, blood whooshing through her veins and throbbing in her ears, just from the sight of Marcus Beckett half naked in her child-hood bed.

He might've been right to worry about her ability to keep her hands to herself.

Quinn had taken the floor for exactly the reasons she'd said, in addition to the knowledge that however little she liked to think it mattered, Marcus was ten years older than she was. And he was a secret stress case who carried all his tension in his back and shoulders. She should know, since she'd nearly sprained her thumbs trying to dig the knots out during a massage that had started out sexy and turned into a to-the-death battle between Quinn and the long muscles lining Marcus's spine.

Marcus didn't need to screw up his back by lying on the floor for eight hours, was her point. Not that she would ever say that to him. She didn't have a death wish.

But as it turned out, the floor was more uncomfort-able than Quinn had anticipated. And as the hours wore down, so did her resistance to the temptation of the warm, soft bed mere inches from her stiff, aching body.

She stared at Marcus's sleeping form and wondered if she dared.

Then she wondered what the hell was the matter with her. It was a bed. They were adults. Sleeping next to each other didn't mean they were automatically going to cross some invisible, arbitrary line. She wasn't going to roll over in her sleep and accidentally impale herself on his penis. They'd be fine.

This is fine, she told herself, getting up off her shaky knees and creeping around to the other side of the bed. The way her knees popped when she stood up was a deciding factor. Quinn carefully peeled back the covers and slid into the bed beside Marcus.

Quinn held her breath, but he didn't move. His broad chest rose and fell with his deep, even breaths. He threw off heat like a roaring bonfire; Quinn went from chilled to toasty in seconds.

Letting her body relax into the softness of the mattress, she drifted peacefully into sleep.

Quinn's dreams were chaotic, flashes of memories mixed with totally random people from her past and present. She was aware they were dreams, in that vague way that happens sometimes, even when the dreamer is deeply asleep.

In the dream, she and Marcus were walking through the woods behind her parents' house, holding hands. Even Dream Quinn couldn't suspend disbelief quite enough for that. Marcus wasn't a hand-holding kind of guy. So she knew it was a dream, even as he led her deeper into the pine copse, their footfalls muffled by layers and layers of dried pine needles that released their evergreen scent as they were crushed.

Come here, said Dream Marcus, giving Quinn the smile she'd only glimpsed once or twice—the small, private, completely unguarded smile that made

Marcus look like the carefree boy Quinn had first fallen for.

She could never resist that particular smile. Not that she wanted to resist. This was only a dream. She could have whatever she wanted, with no consequences.

Emboldened by her freedom, Quinn followed Marcus down to lie on a bed of springy green moss. He lay back, arms crossed behind his head and more relaxed than she'd ever seen him in real life. Sunlight dappled his handsome face, patterns of light and shadow that shivered over his cheekbones when wind fluttered through the branches overhead.

Her heart swelled with all the feelings she'd been stuffing down and denying since the day Marcus unceremoniously ended their relationship. It wasn't smart to care about him. She knew that, and Quinn wanted to be smart, she really did.

The trouble was that she'd never learned how to stop caring about someone. Her poor, bruised heart was as optimistic and stubborn as her hungry body was when it came to Marcus Beckett.

Despair teased at Quinn's mind, but she pushed it away. *This is a dream,* she said aloud to remind them both. *Only a dream.*

Beneath her, Marcus smiled again, the smile that promised things like love and forever and the kind of pleasure she could live on. Thighs tensing with need where she was suddenly straddling his hips, Quinn felt the low-down clench of her body around the emptiness only Marcus could fill.

A shudder racked her, sweeping up her frame in a rush that tightened the peaks of her breasts and forced her mouth open on a gasp.

Yes, like that, Marcus murmured, his eyes going hot and feral the way she remembered from their first nights of passion. The grip of his hands at her hips excited Quinn. She squirmed a little, wanting to feel it, hoping it bruised so she could look in the mirror later and see the evidence of Marcus's desire for her.

With a smooth twist of his massive torso, he flipped them so that Quinn's back was arching off the cool moss and Marcus was covering her with his body. Her legs fell open, wanton and wanting, and she relished the stretch of her thighs as he fit himself into the cradle of her hips.

His hardness slotted against her softness with a series of rhythmic nudges that stoked the fire inside Quinn higher and higher. In the dream, her panties melted away like fog, and he was naked too, and they were pressed together so intimately and perfectly and yet, somehow, there was still something in the way, a barrier to Quinn getting what she really wanted. Frustration mounting, she reached down between their hot, straining bodies and felt . . . cotton?

Quinn blinked and suddenly, instead of staring up at the waving pine needles of the Lantern Point woods, she was looking at the familiar starburst pattern of the plaster ceiling in her girlhood bedroom.

Her immediate thought was a dismayed *No, let me go back to the dream!* But in the next instant, she realized Marcus was still on top of her, his hard chest and strong arms caging her in. Their legs were tangled hopelessly in the sheets and they were both still wearing what they'd gone to bed in, but other than that?

The dream was real.

Eyes still closed, Marcus twisted his hips, grinding wickedly against Quinn's most sensitive spot and scattering her thoughts like dried pine needles before she could figure out what to do. She reacted mindlessly, her body taking over and bowing up hard, her arms going around Marcus's neck.

Through her haze of heated lust, Quinn saw the exact moment Marcus woke up.

Chapter 10

Marcus catapulted straight from one of his favorite dreams—Quinn laid out like a feast on top of his bar—and into a reality where he was sprawled over her and thrusting against her in her parents' house with her mother and father right down the hall.

Or maybe they were downstairs, he realized distractedly as he noticed the soft morning light washing over Quinn's face. Her skin was pearly and clear, gleaming with youth and vitality. The hectic red flush of passion across her cheekbones only made her more irresistible.

She was everything soft and welcoming, even in this moment where both of them were frozen into stillness, waiting to see what the other would do.

Marcus knew exactly what he should do. He should make a joke or make her mad, get himself away from the silky, lithe temptation of her body twined with his in innocent pink cotton sheets.

He drew in a breath to gather himself to move off her, but they were so close together that the inhalation made his chest brush the very tips of her breasts, and Quinn convulsed under him with a soft cry. The feel of her hard nipples, even through her thin tank top, lit a flash fire in Marcus's belly that obliterated all higher reasoning.

Dragging his chest against her breasts, he savored the shivery moan of Quinn's breaths and the spasmodic clutch of her fingers at the nape of his neck. His cock was iron hard and aching, trapped in his underwear and pounding with need.

He propped himself on one elbow and dragged the opposite hand down the center line of Quinn's beautiful body. Between her taut breasts and over the jumpy muscles of her stomach to gently cup his palm against the soft liquid heat between her thighs. He wanted in. Wanted to be as close to Quinn as he could get, to put himself inside her and live there forever.

She writhed against him, agile as a cat, and Marcus snuck a finger under the elastic of the lace panties he remembered with painful clarity. He could tell by touch that they were the black ones with the little satin rosette at the back, right above the shadowed cleft of her bottom.

Burying his face in her sweet-smelling neck, Marcus set his open mouth against her collarbone and fought back a primal shout of triumph at the slick of her silken folds around his fingertip. Quinn's chest heaved enough to press his teeth gently into her skin, which she seemed to like, going by the way her fist clenched in his hair. Marcus got it. He'd never gotten off on a woman pulling his hair before, but with Quinn, sometimes the feelings racing through him were too big, too wild for gentleness.

With Quinn, every sensation was magnified and twisted into pleasure. It was a strange alchemy Marcus didn't understand. All he knew was that it had been far too many days since he'd experienced the special magic he and Quinn created together.

"Stop teasing me." Quinn trapped his hand between her thighs and tugged his head back by the hair, far enough that she could stare into his eyes. Her gaze was direct, hot, a little desperate. He rewarded her with another rub of his fingers, right where she wanted them most. "Oh! I missed you, Marcus."

She whispered it like a confession, like an admission of guilt, and it made Marcus pause. The moment he stopped moving his fingers, a tragic look crossed Quinn's face. "Don't . . ."

Marcus hung over her, poised on the point of no return, but he never found out whether Quinn was saying "Don't stop," or "Don't keep going," because at that moment a knock rapped against the bedroom door.

"Rise and shine, you two," caroled Mrs. Harper's chipper voice. "Breakfast is ready!"

Quinn, who'd twitched at the sound of her mother's voice, dropped her hands from Marcus's neck to throw an arm over her eyes and hide her red face. "Coming, Mother."

Some devil prompted Marcus to lean down and whisper, "We could be, if she'd waited five minutes."

Quinn convulsed in shocked giggles under him, which made Marcus grin instead of grimacing while trying to smoothly remove his hand from her underwear. His dick, like most dicks, had no sense of time or place or the inherent unsexiness of nearly getting caught in the act by his girlfriend's mom like a couple of teenagers.

No, his dick still thought the original morning plan was A-OK, ready for action, go go go. But Marcus was in charge, so instead of following orders from below the belt, he swung off of Quinn.

The physical pain he felt was simple sexual frustration, he told himself. Reality had intruded on their stolen moment of passion. Now that they were fully awake, he couldn't shut his eyes and ignore the fact that sleeping with Quinn now would make it that much harder to disentangle himself at the end of the month.

But unless his position had changed when it came to whether or not he and Quinn could be together long-term, he had no business touching her. He wasn't some undisciplined raw recruit with no handle on the consequences of his actions. He was a grown-ass man. He had more respect for himself, and certainly for Quinn, than to think he could screw her casually and have it mean nothing.

He wouldn't apologize for this morning, he decided,

staring down at his hands where they lay on his knees. It had been mutual. Mutual pleasure. Mutual mistake. There was no need to belabor the point, since it wouldn't be happening again.

Resolved, Marcus stood up and crossed the room to dig through his backpack for his toothbrush and a change of clothes.

"Can you toss my bag over here?" Quinn asked.

He picked it up and turned to hand it over. The sight that greeted him immediately tested his resolve not to touch Quinn.

She stood on the other side of the bed, hair tousled into strawberry-blond waves over one bare shoulder. All she wore was a tank top with tiny straps that seemed too delicate to contain the bounty of her breasts, which were clearly outlined under the thin material. On the bottom . . . the black lace panties were every bit as sinfully tempting as he remembered.

Quinn held out an expectant hand, her brows lifting in question at his pause. But she wasn't impatient or embarrassed or anything like that. No, she was as near to naked as made no difference, in front of the ex she'd convinced to pose as her fiancé, and she met his gaze as directly as if she'd never heard of the idea of shame. Instead, she smiled at him.

"Everything okay? We need to get moving. Breakfast is kind of a thing in this house."

In that moment, Marcus knew he loved her. He handed over her bag wordlessly and held himself very still as she brushed past him and into the bathroom.

Once the door between them closed, he allowed himself to sink back to sit on the edge of the bed and drop his head into his hands.

He was in love with Quinn Harper. And he was pretty sure she loved him, too.

The bitch of it was, it changed nothing. He was still no good for her. She was young, and as much as he hated it when her parents dismissed her commitment to the Windy Corner Therapeutic Riding Center, there was some truth behind their skepticism.

One day, Quinn would wake up and move on from Marcus, and that would be the best day of her life. He believed that with his whole heart. She deserved better. That hadn't changed. Nothing had changed.

Except how bad Marcus was going to hurt when this was all over.

No matter what was going on in your life, no matter how messy things got, you could still take pleasure in the little things. Paul looked over his bowls of crumbled goat cheese, sautéed mushrooms, caramelized chopped onions, and lightly beaten eggs with satisfaction.

Like life, omelets moved fast. He liked to get all his fillings ready ahead of time so when the eggs were just barely set in the pan, he wouldn't overcook them while he got the other ingredients together.

No surprise, his wife was more of a fly-by-the-seat-of-her-pants type of cook. Paul carefully regulated the heat under his nonstick skillet. Too high, and the butter would scorch; too low, and the eggs would absorb too much of the butter before they set enough to add the fillings. Omelets were a tricky, delicate business, which was why they were more his province than Ingrid's.

Ingrid didn't cook much, in general. She didn't mind throwing things together, like a stir-fry of leftovers and whatever random things she could scavenge from the fridge, but she didn't like following a recipe. If a technique caught her interest, she would be relentless about practicing it until she had it down—she beat the egg whites into meringue for Paul's lemon meringue pie, for instance. Insisted on doing it by hand, always getting them to the perfect stage of glossy, stiff peaks. But ask her to follow the exact proportions for the lemon custard filling, and she'd get bored and distracted halfway through, and wander off to another project.

It felt like an uncomfortably apt metaphor for their marriage. Paul stared glumly down at the melting butter and wondered if this was how the lemon custard felt when she left it to curdle on the stovetop.

They'd fought the night before, when Ron went out to drive around the island. Paul couldn't believe she'd invited "Dr. Ron" to stay with them. Two full weeks, never able to get away from the man. Paul had lost it, in a way he rarely had with Ingrid.

But unlike the few other times Paul put his foot down about something, this time, Ingrid hadn't immediately backed off.

No. This time, with tears standing in her beautiful,

cornflower-blue eyes, she'd pressed her lips together and stubbornly refused to call Ron and rescind her invitation. At first he believed her when she argued that it would be rude—Ingrid hadn't been raised on Sanctuary Island, but she'd wholeheartedly embraced the island's signature warmth and open-arms welcome of visitors.

The longer they wrangled around about the visit, however, the more Paul became convinced that there was more to it. Finally, after an hour of long, cold silences punctuated by angry words, Ingrid had said, "He's staying. Don't you see, Paul? This is our last chance."

As she'd no doubt intended, that ended the argument. Paul's blood still ran cold when he remembered the serious look on Ingrid's face. It wasn't a look he'd seen often, in the decades of their marriage. Not that Ingrid was frivolous—on the contrary, she took everything seriously, things no one else cared about, like saving a perfect spiderweb glittering with dew, or the importance of eating a strawberry within fifteen seconds of picking it, for the best flavor.

But when it came to interpersonal relationships? Ingrid tended to go a little hazy. People bewildered her, because they so often cared a great deal about the things she found unimportant, and seemed to not even notice the things that were central to Ingrid's life.

Paul had always appreciated her, even if he didn't understand her. He'd marveled at her ability to float through life, focusing only on what brought her joy.

Since the moment they met, he'd been the person who was on the inside of Ingrid's bubble, borne aloft on the breeze with her.

Last night, for the first time, he'd been forced to accept that he was on the outside of the bubble. And he had no idea how to get back in.

"They're coming down," Ingrid announced, wafting back into the kitchen.

Paul jumped, startled. Looking down at his pan, he saw that he'd managed to burn the butter after all. Grabbing a paper towel, he wiped out the pan and started over with fresh butter.

"It's lovely to have a full house," Ingrid tried, bustling around to get a fresh pot of coffee started and put water on for tea.

Paul concentrated on pouring the beaten eggs into the pan and swirling them around evenly.

When he didn't respond, Ingrid sighed. "Should I wake Ron up for breakfast, do you think?"

The eggs were setting up nicely, pulling away from the edges of the pan but still creamy in the middle. Paul reached for his bowls of fillings and started sprinkling them carefully along the center line of the pan. "I don't think Dr. Ron seems like the breakfast type. He seems more like someone who's used to sleeping in."

"Who's sleeping in?" Quinn asked as she trooped into the kitchen, followed by Marcus Beckett.

"Ron," her mother said. "Coffee?"

"Yes, please."

In spite of the tensions of the morning, Paul had to grin at the fervor of Marcus's answer. "First omelet's up in thirty seconds. Who wants it?"

Never shy, Quinn piped up, "I'll take it! Unless you want it, Mother. Don't worry about Marcus, he'll be communing with his coffee for the next ten minutes before he's ready for anything more challenging, like conversation. Or food."

With a practiced flick of his wrist, Paul released the egg from the pan and folded it over on itself. He tipped it onto a plate and turned to hand it to his daughter in time to see the glare Marcus sent her over the top of his mug. Paul also saw Quinn's totally unrepentant smirk before she thanked him for the omelet and sat down to dig in.

Paul hurried through the rest of the omelets and joined his family at the table. Quinn was nearly done with hers, and she was sitting shoulder to shoulder with Marcus and talking a mile a minute about her new job. Every now and then, she'd say something to distract Marcus so she could try to filch a stray mushroom from his plate. Marcus caught her every time, but all he did was narrow his eyes as she plucked up the mushroom and popped it in her mouth with a smug smile.

"If you're still hungry, I can make you some toast," Paul told her.

He wasn't surprised when she shook her head. "No, thanks, this is more fun."

"Fun for who?" Marcus grumbled, but Paul didn't miss the way his daughter's fiancé followed her with his gaze when she hopped up from the table to pour herself another glass of orange juice.

And for a moment, when Quinn's back was turned, Paul caught the strangest expression of longing on Marcus's face. As if he were looking at something he wanted desperately that was forever out of his reach.

Then Quinn came back to the table, offering juice to anyone who wanted it, and the fleeting expression was gone. But the memory of it stuck with Paul, even as he watched Quinn and Marcus jostle each other at the sink like kids while they did the dishes, flicking soap bubbles at each other and getting water all over the place.

Well, Quinn flicked soap bubbles. Marcus endured it stoically until all the plates and glasses were clean and in the drying rack, and then he turned the detachable spray faucet on her.

Quinn shrieked, Ingrid laughed, and Marcus went brick red like he'd forgotten they weren't alone. Paul waved away his promises to clean up the mess.

"Don't worry about it," he told Marcus. "It's only a little water on the floor. Small price to pay to see my only daughter so happy."

"Happy!" Quinn twisted her hair to wring water out of the ends. "I'm soaked!"

"Soaked in love," Ingrid said, clasping her hands under her chin. Her eyes shone as she stared back and forth between Quinn and Marcus. "Oh, I think Ron was so right to suggest that y'all stay with us for a little bit. It's doing me a lot of good to have this youthful, happy energy in the house. I can tell a difference already."

Quinn wrinkled her nose. Paul was willing to bet she was thinking that Ron's "suggestion" was more of an ultimatum. But instead of immediately blurting that out, she very diplomatically said, "I'm happy if we're helping you, Mother. Truly."

Maybe his little girl was finally growing up, after all. And maybe Marcus Beckett was ten years older and about a hundred times rougher around the edges than anyone Paul would've picked for his daughter, but maybe he also had something to do with Quinn's newfound maturity.

Not that he thought Marcus could make Quinn behave a certain way, or that it would even be healthy if he could. But Paul, of all people, knew that part of being in a great relationship was bringing out the best in each other. He didn't know Marcus well enough to be able to tell, but he wondered if the taciturn, grim-eyed ex-soldier might be a bit lighter and easier when Quinn was around. It wouldn't surprise Paul to find out he was right about that.

He had no intention of admitting it to Ingrid, much less to Dr. Ron, but Paul could admit privately that he was glad to have this time with Quinn and her fiancé. There was nothing like living cheek by jowl, all cozied into one house, for getting to know someone. This up-close-and-personal view of his daughter's relationship was doing a lot to ease Paul's mind.

Now if it just lasted longer than a few weeks, he

might start to believe Quinn was finally ready to settle down.

Maybe if he and Ingrid could stop worrying about Quinn, they'd have time to work on their marriage. Paul looked across the kitchen to where Ingrid was sipping her second cup of green tea and laughing at something their daughter had said. His heart clenched.

Paul got up to find the mop to clean up the spilled water. Hopefully that would distract him from the fear that if he and Ingrid no longer had to worry about Quinn, they'd lose their last real connection to one another.

Chapter 11

When Dr. Ron finally wandered downstairs at the crack of ten, Quinn took malicious delight in informing him that breakfast was over and cleaned up. "There's still coffee in the pot, though," she told him with exaggerated solicitousness. "I'd be happy to pop it in the microwave for you to warm it up."

As she'd expected, Ron turned up his nose at microwaved coffee. He pursed his lips briefly and said, "Don't trouble yourself. I never normally eat breakfast anyway. I don't like to pollute my body the moment I wake up."

"I'm sure that's wise," Dad said calmly from behind his spread-open copy of the *Sanctuary Gazette*. "My apologies for the omelet I polluted you with this morning, honey."

"No apologies necessary, as far as I'm concerned,"

Marcus said. He raised his coffee mug in an ironic sa-
lute. "Personally, I'm all about polluting my body."

Ron ignored the byplay the way a king ignored his
subjects' ill-bred demands for better working conditions. "We have much to accomplish, and only a short
time in which to accomplish it. Ingrid, as you've ex-
pressed it to me, your garden is your pride and joy."

"Not more than my family is," she half protested,
eyes darting around the kitchen. "But . . . I have worked
hard on the garden, yes."

"And it's time your family joined you in that work."
Dr. Ron patted Ingrid on the hand in a way that made
Quinn want to slap his plump, pale fingers away from
her mother.

"Oh. Is it?" Ingrid bit her lip, and Quinn fought a
smile.

Her mother wasn't particular about very many
things, but her garden was one area where she went
from wispy to waspish. From the soil composition
to the plant food to the organization of the beds,
she planned every detail and controlled for every
variable—and heaven help anyone who suggested a
variation.

In fact, Quinn reflected as all urge to smile faded,
forcing Ingrid to accept interference in her precious
garden was one of the fastest ways Quinn could think
of to put an incredible amount of stress on her already
fractured family. Which left her with only one real
question.

Was Ron, the "Relationship Expert," an idiot? Or

was he actively trying to sabotage her parents' marriage? And if so, why would he? Surely his reputation, if not whatever fee he charged, was based on how many couples he'd helped to stay together.

"Don't worry, Ing, I'm sure everyone in the family will be extremely respectful of your feelings about the garden, and work together to create something new that will reflect the whole family's place in the garden, which is really a metaphor for your heart."

Ugh. Quinn caught Marcus's eyes and tried to convey silently how sorry she was about all this. Meanwhile, Ron went relentlessly on.

"The idea is to build something within the garden, using only your own hands, which will stand as a monument to your commitment to one another."

"With our own hands." Quinn's father dropped the pretense of reading the paper, folding it and placing it to one side of his empty plate. "Won't we need . . . I don't know, nails? A hammer? If we're going to do a gazebo or, honey, you've always talked about a trellis, haven't you?"

Ingrid nodded, starting to perk up a bit, but her face fell when she caught the slow shake of Ron's head.

"No, I've got something much better in mind than a trellis." Ron paused dramatically, waiting until all eyes were on him before he lifted his arms with a flourish like a magician pulling a rabbit out of his hat. "You're going to build . . . a standing stone circle!"

Marcus blinked. "Like . . . Stonehenge?"

"Exactly like Stonehenge," Ron enthused. "But on a slightly smaller scale, of course. Ha ha!"

On any scale, it sounded like a very weird idea to Quinn. "So basically, you want us to lug a lot of big rocks out to the backyard and set them up in a circle."

Even from across the kitchen, Quinn could see the clench of Ron's jaw. When he spoke, his tone was tight with forced patience. "You don't have much magic in your soul, I'm sensing. Maybe if you opened up your aura a bit, enough to let the light in . . . but we can work on that. In the meantime, yes. That is the basic process for making a stone circle."

"I don't get it," Dad said bluntly. "Why would we do such a thing?"

"And what will it look like when it's finished?" Mother fretted.

Ron held up a placating hand. "As I was saying, when one goes beyond the basics, there are many reasons to build a standing stone circle. It can be a very meditative process. When I've suggested it to my other soul travelers—that's the term I use instead of 'clients', I hate that awful, clinical word—well, in the past, people have found it very meaningful. Almost cleansing, really. In fact, that's part of the point. The center of the stone circle will be a fire pit. And when the circle is complete, we'll build a big fire and each of you will toss into it something that reminds you of an aspect of a family member that makes you unhappy—something you want to let go of. Symbolically, of course. I'm not suggesting you throw in your old handbag or a pair of high heels you no longer want, ha ha!"

Hmph. As if all women thought of was purses and stilettos. Ingrid wore garden clogs or sandals every day of her life, and Quinn was more likely to be in sneakers or flip-flops than anything else. So far, Quinn couldn't say she was impressed with Ron's powers of perception, but maybe he did better on the astral plane.

"Building the stone circle will be the perfect way to spend the next two weeks together," Ron was saying firmly. "Clear your schedules. This is going to be a big project."

Marcus looked at Quinn across the table. His face was perfectly expressionless, but she didn't need to read his aura to be able to tell what he was thinking. "That's just fine," she told Ron hastily, "but don't forget that Marcus and I both have to go to work. So we can't clear our schedules completely."

When he was thwarted, Ron Burkey looked exactly like a toddler whose favorite toy was taken away. "Fine," he pouted. "But it's not ideal. There's a certain way I like to do things, and I can't be held responsible for the lack of commitment shown by some of the travelers on this soul journey."

Despite herself, Quinn felt a surge of guilt. Was she truly endangering her family's chances of surviving intact? Should she quit her job and devote herself to this thing full-time?

She bit her lip, but before she could say a word, her father snorted. "If your treatment doesn't work out,

Dr. Ron, I'm sure it won't be because my daughter and future son-in-law honored their commitments to others outside the home. Surely you believe in honoring all types of commitment. As a marriage guru."

"Please, relationship expert," Ron corrected him, smoothing his hands over his already smooth hair. "And of course I respect their professional obligations. I'm simply saying . . ."

"We understand," Ingrid jumped in, all fluttering hands and soothing voice. "No one will blame you for anything, Ron. We know you're only here to help."

That was debatable, Quinn thought, but she didn't have time to actually debate it. "Great. Since that's all settled, I've got to get to my shift out at the barn."

"On a Sunday?" Ingrid asked, surprised. "Whatever happened to a day of rest?"

"Not to worry, I'm in no danger of getting over-loaded with my busy schedule of working twenty hours a week." Quinn laughed it off, pushing back from the table and taking her coffee cup to the sink.

"Don't act like it's not a real job. You're doing good work out there."

Marcus's gruff voice from behind her made Quinn pause with the water from the kitchen sink running over her hands. He sounded as if he knew what he was talking about—as if he knew anything about the work she'd been doing at Windy Corner. But he couldn't. He'd never been out there.

Although her parents and Ron weren't supposed to know that, Quinn reminded herself, shutting off the water with a quick flick of her wrist. Probably Marcus was only doing his part to shore up their story, which he was so much better at than she was. He probably didn't even think she was doing a real job. He was probably just saying that to seem like a supportive fiancé.

"Thank you," Quinn said finally, turning back to face the table where her father was eyeing Marcus speculatively. Marcus was giving him nothing, muscle-corded arms crossed over his chest and a blank look on his face, although when he slanted a look in her direction, Quinn thought she read a certain discomfort in his eyes. Nothing made him more uncomfortable than saying something true out loud, she knew.

Maybe not everything he'd said was a lie.

The thought warmed her all the way through, better than the cup of coffee had done. Which made it easy to beam at Marcus as she rescued him from a day of hauling stone around the backyard.

"Actually, darling," she said, "don't forget you've got your session this afternoon, too. So we might as well drive into town together. Sorry we won't be around to help pick out the stones, but Daddy, you let those Hackley boys do the heavy lifting when you get to the hardware store, okay? You don't need to strain your back."

"Don't worry, I'll keep an eye on him," her mother said, with a tentative smile at Paul, who scowled.

"I'm not a child," he grumbled, "I know my own limits."

"Then why did you spend three weeks last year, laid up on the couch?" Ingrid pointed out tartly. Before he could refute it, she turned back to Quinn and said, "Don't worry about a thing, sweetheart. You two go on and have a good time. We'll get the building supplies together and be ready to get started on construction next week."

Quinn bit back the urge to point out that she wasn't off on some pleasure cruise, she was going to work— the point was not to have a good time. But her mother was trying, both her parents were. And if they couldn't take her seriously after years of waffling around about her career, whose fault was that?

That very reasonable thought sucked away some of the warmth and optimism Quinn had been floating on, leaving her to thud back down to earth. And as she left the kitchen to head upstairs to get ready for work, she realized, *Oh crap. I just invited Marcus to spend the afternoon at work with me.*

What if I mess up? What if this job I love seems like an idiotic waste of time to him?

And the most troubling questions of all . . . if she was really as done with this relationship as she claimed, why did she care so deeply about Marcus's good opinion? And why was she already looking forward to waking up beside him for the next two weeks?

When they reached the second landing, Marcus nearly walked into Quinn because she stopped in her tracks on the stair ahead of him.

"You don't have to actually come to Windy Corner with me," she whispered, with a shifty glance over her shoulder. "You know that, right? I just thought you'd rather get out of the house than spend the day alone with Ron and my parents."

Marcus paused to study her carefully. "Do you not want me to come to the barn with you?"

She bit her lip. He tried not to imagine biting it for her. "Noooo, I mean. I do. If you want. But it'll probably be super boring for you. I'd totally understand if you wanted to do something else."

He wasn't sure what exactly was going on here, but Marcus had to admit to himself that he was curious about the results of his secret donation to the barn. He wanted to see what Quinn was up to out there. So he said, "The bar is closed on Sundays," and left it at that.

Quinn's shoulders slumped a little in defeat, but she nodded glumly and trudged up the last few stairs to her room. The moment they were closed in, alone together for the first time since they'd woken up already locked in a heated haze of passion that morning, Marcus felt his pulse skyrocket. But he knew how to keep an impassive expression through pretty much anything, so he gestured to the bathroom and said, "You take the first shower. It'll take me less time to get ready."

"I'm not some girly girl who puts on a ton of war paint and perfume and jewelry before leaving the house," Quinn said sharply.

"I know that," Marcus said slowly. "But you have all that hair, and I have this."

He gestured at his close-cropped head and watched the fight go out of Quinn. Grimacing slightly, she said, "Sorry to jump down your throat like that. Being home . . . I love it, but I guess it makes me a little overly sensitive. Anyway, I'll go shower."

Shit. This felt so far outside Marcus's skill set, it might as well have been basket weaving, but he had to say something here. "Look. Don't get down on yourself. Making the jump from being your parents' little baby to having an adult relationship is hard for most people, I bet. There's bound to be some growing pains."

To his relief, Quinn perked up and gave him a grateful smile as she slipped away into the bathroom. The shower started.

Marcus distracted himself from imagining steam billowing around Quinn's naked body by walking over to stare out her bedroom window. Filmy curtains with pastel balloons printed on them fluttered against his arm as he braced it on the wall by the window.

The view across Lantern Point spread out below him, long tangles of cord grass rippling in the breeze alongside the winding road that led back toward town. The same road that led past the house where Marcus grew up. Quinn had grown up staring out her window at his house, Marcus realized. They'd been the only two kids on the block, but with ten years between them, Marcus hadn't taken much notice of the little girl who'd dogged his heels and tried to tag along when his friends came over.

He'd never thought about how lonely she must have been.

"The bathroom's all yours," she said from the other side of the bedroom.

That was fast, even for Quinn, who was definitely not a girly girl. Marcus looked over to find her still squeezing water from her long tail of hair, which was much darker red than usual. The contrast with her fair skin, and the way the droplets dampened the thin, light blue cotton of her T-shirt, made Marcus's mouth go dry.

Without a word, he snagged his clothes from the bed and brushed past her to get to the shower. He shucked his boxers and flipped the shower knob all the way to cold. If he didn't get his unruly body under control, it was going to be an unbearably long day.

By the time he and Quinn were both climbing out of his truck in the parking area behind the Windy Corner Therapeutic Riding Center, Marcus wished he'd had time for an even longer cold shower. It was ridiculous at his age—he wasn't some randy teenager—but when Quinn was around, his body didn't seem to remember its advanced years or the strict discipline and training he'd imposed on it since he was even younger than Quinn was now.

No, instead, the mere scent of her hair drying in the sea air blown in through the open window made Marcus hard. The thought that this explained why her hair always smelled like salt and honey made his heart race. The silence between them as they drove, a silence that could have been fraught with tension but somehow wasn't . . . even that made the fabric of his jeans stretch uncomfortably.

This being-in-love stuff wasn't for weaklings, Marcus reflected as Quinn bounded ahead of him to greet her friends and coworkers in the barn office.

Marcus hung back, not wanting to insert himself into her business too much. He left her leaning in the office doorway, situated halfway down the wide corridor separating the barn stalls, and wandered over to check out the horses.

The barn smelled pleasant, like cedar shavings and sweet oats and large, warm-blooded animals with big, gentle eyes. The horse in the nearest stall hung his head over the low stall door to gaze curiously at Marcus.

"Hey, big guy," he said, coming closer and lifting a cautious hand, fingers curled under, to be snuffled at by the velvety, whiskery muzzle.

"Hey yourself," said an amused masculine voice from the other side of the hall.

Marcus pivoted, fast enough that he startled the horse, who backed away with a nervous snort. Eyes searching the darkness of the stall across the hall, it took Marcus a tense, hypervigilant moment to recognize the dark hair, wide grin, and easy movements of Johnny Alexander.

Marcus's shoulders relaxed, his body falling automatically out of battle stance. "You're back. Since when?"

Johnny and his wife, Tessa, had reconnected on

Sanctuary Island a few weeks ago after spending a year and a half apart while Johnny worked undercover for the ATF. The time apart had wreaked havoc on an already fragile relationship, but from what Marcus understood, Johnny and Tessa had found their way back to each other and were stronger than ever now. They'd gone on a short trip to close up the town house they'd shared in D.C., in preparation for Johnny joining his wife on Sanctuary Island permanently.

"We got in last night," Johnny said, giving a fond scrub of his fingers through the black mane of the horse he'd been grooming. "Tessa's checking in at the bakery."

"I'm surprised you're not with her. Before you left, you were having a hard time letting her out of your sight." Marcus crossed the hall to shake Johnny's hand. He was glad to have the man back in town. Along with Miss Patty, Tessa's boss at the bakery, Johnny Alexander was Marcus's only real friend on Sanctuary. The two men weren't much alike even though they shared surprisingly similar backgrounds in the military, which had led to careers in other areas of law enforcement. But Johnny had a charm about him, an ever-present wide grin that made him easy to be around.

Which was why Marcus was a little surprised when Johnny grimaced and averted his gaze, dropping Marcus's hand to go back to combing through his horse's mane. "Yeah, well. It turns out that's not exactly normal or healthy behavior. Tessa put up with it as long as she could, but it all came to a head when we were packing up the town house. I had kind of an . . . episode, I guess."

For the first time, Marcus considered that Johnny's bright smile might be a mask to hide the darkness inside. "I'm sorry to hear that," he said seriously. "I don't know what happened with you, but I have bad days, too."

When Johnny met his gaze again, his eyes were weary and knowing. "Yeah. Or bad minutes, like when I startled you. I thought for a second you were going to come at me, fists up."

Marcus rolled his tight shoulders. "Yeah. Sorry about that."

"You don't have to apologize to me. Trust me, I get it. All too well."

"There are days when it's hard to leave the past in the past," Marcus said slowly, choosing his words with care. "And there are days when you think you're fine, but the smallest thing can set you off and you find yourself right back there again."

Johnny nodded. "Toward the end of our trip, I was having more bad days than good. Tessa made me promise when we got home, I'd get serious about my sessions out at the barn. So here I am."

He bent down to the plastic-handled tub at his feet and pulled out an oval brush with soft-looking bristles. With gentle, rhythmic motions, Johnny started running the brush over the horse's hide. Obviously blissed out, the horse braced its long legs and hung its massive head with a shudder of pleasure.

"I see they've got you doing hard labor," Marcus observed, glancing up and down the halls. If this was a therapeutic riding session, shouldn't there be more actual riding involved? And where was Johnny's therapist, anyway?

"We start and end every session like this," Johnny explained. "Just me and Impromptu, here. I groom him by myself, and it's my chance to say anything I didn't get out in the session."

"You tell the horse?" Marcus didn't mean to sound skeptical, but it was a little weird, right?

"Sure." Johnny shrugged. "Impromptu never judges me, do you, boy? He never makes me feel like I need to suck it up and be a man about it, or some bull like that. It's more relaxing than you might think."

The words struck a chord deep in Marcus's chest. They also made him feel like he was accidentally intruding on an important part of his friend's therapy. "I get that. I'll leave you to it. I need to go find Quinn, anyway."

Interest flared bright in Johnny's dark eyes. "Oh? Is that back on?"

Marcus resisted the urge to palm the back of his neck or shift his weight uncomfortably. "For now. We'll see how it goes."

He didn't like lying to Johnny, but the worst part was how it didn't feel like a lie. Not exactly.

"Congrats, man." Johnny smiled with genuine happiness. "I always thought you two were kind of perfect for each other."

"Yeah, well. We're giving it another try." Marcus left it at that. Lying to Quinn's parents and his prospective customers was one thing. It was a whole other thing to lie to one of his few friends. "It was good seeing you. Come by the bar sometime. Bring that pretty wife of yours."

"Oh, right, you're open now! I'm sorry we missed the opening. How's it going?"

"Business was slow at first, but it's picking up." Now that everyone in town thought Marcus was making Quinn happy. If they only knew. He put on a smirk to cover the ache of that thought. "Anyway. I'll let you get back to your chat with your horse."

"Don't knock it until you've tried it, man." Johnny laughed fondly. "There's something about being around horses. I never thought it would work for me, but I have to admit—I'm glad to be back here. It's hard work, digging into all the stuff that messed me up over time. But it's work that's worth doing."

There was something almost defiant about the way Johnny said it, like he didn't expect Marcus to agree, or like he thought Marcus looked down on him for being in therapy, when in fact the exact opposite was true.

"You're a better man than I am." Marcus realized his fist was white-knuckled on the edge of the stall door and consciously loosened his grip. "I respect the hell out of you for doing this."

Johnny relaxed and gave that blinding grin. "Thanks, Beckett. That's good to hear. But you know, there's basically nothing I wouldn't do to become the man Tessa already thinks I am. The man she deserves. This is hard, but it's worth it. Because at the end of the day, I go home to her and I can look her in the eye, knowing I'm giving this everything I've got. If I weren't doing this . . . man, I don't know if I ever could have believed I was good enough for Tessa."

The conversation stuck with Marcus long after he walked away and left his friend to his meditation with curry comb and gelding. Johnny was a good man. Marcus knew that the moment he met him. Tessa obviously knew it, too. Johnny was the only one who needed to be convinced.

And maybe he never would be. But clearly, the knowledge that he was trying his best was almost as good.

Marcus envied him.

Chapter 12

Quinn found her wayward fiancé with one boot propped on the bottom rung of the outdoor paddock fence, watching Jo Ellen Hollister putting a new mare through her paces.

Quinn joined him at the fence line. The sun beamed down on them, warmer than it had been all year yet, probably coaxing even more of Quinn's freckles out of their winter hibernation.

"Jo does all the training with the new horses," she said, enjoying the sight of her boss's elegant grace atop the chestnut mare. "She's amazing. It's like she and the horse can read each other's minds."

They watched in silence for a moment, but all of Quinn's attention was focused on the man at her side.

"Johnny and Tessa are home," he said abruptly,

without taking his eyes off the horse training happening in the middle of the sawdust-floored ring. "I saw him inside."

"That's great! I missed them. Did they get the house all packed up? I know it must have been emotional going through all those memories of their life together, before they figured things out."

"We didn't talk about that."

Quinn hid a smile. Of course they hadn't mentioned anything messy and deeply emotional. Johnny and Marcus were such guys sometimes. But then Marcus surprised her by adding, "We talked about his therapy, though. I mean, the sessions he's doing out here. Like the ones I'm pretending to do, I guess."

For some reason, Quinn's heart started to race. "Oh? That's good. I'm glad he feels he can share that with you. Some of our clients, especially the ex-military ones . . . well, when they first come here, it's like they think there's some sort of shame in needing help to process what's happened to them. Which of course there isn't. Everyone needs help sometimes. I'm glad Johnny can be open about it."

"He seems to think it's doing some good. Or that it will, if he works at it."

"That's the idea." Quinn was struggling to keep her tone light. It felt as if something momentous were about to happen. "I've seen people here make amazing strides."

She held her breath, not even sure what she was hoping for—but Marcus dropped his boot off the fence and said, "I'm sure you have better things to do than stand around here talking to me. Don't let me keep you from your work."

Quinn wanted to protest that there was nothing more important to her than Marcus, ever, but that wasn't how she was supposed to feel anymore. She was supposed to be smarter than that. Stronger than that.

And anyway, she did have to work.

"Okay," she said, feeling a little shy all of a sudden. "Well, I've got a few calls to make. Jo's daughter, Ella, just put me in charge of wrangling donations for the charity auction at the Spring Blooms Festival. It's a great opportunity for me, but it's scary, too! There's a lot riding on the money the auction brings in, so the donation items need to be really good."

"You're the perfect person for the job." Marcus gave her a slight smile that lit up her nerve endings like a field full of fireflies. "Everyone in town loves you. You can call anyone on Sanctuary Island out of the blue and get whatever you ask for."

Quinn fought the urge to squirm with embarrassed pleasure. "That's not entirely true, but I appreciate the vote of confidence. Are you going to hang out here, or should I give you a call at the Buttercup when I'm ready to head back to my parents' house?"

Marcus glanced back into the ring, where Jo Ellen was reining her horse in ever smaller and tighter circles. Her salt-and-pepper hair was in a long braid down her back, her tanned face set in lines of concentration. "I think I'll see if I can make myself useful here. Now that their best volunteer got a real job, they can probably use some help."

Flushing at the pride in his voice, Quinn stuck her hands in the back pockets of her jeans and rocked on her heels. "Sounds like a plan. I . . . you know, I don't have to start making those calls right this minute. If you wanted a tour of the facilities, I could do that instead."

Marcus studied her for a long moment before saying, "Johnny was grooming a horse. As part of his therapy. I could try something like that. Or you could show me some of the other exercises you do with the clients."

Once again, Quinn was poised on the edge of a cliff, unsure what lay below. She wanted to jump, but this felt too important to leap into without looking first. "Marcus, I can't be your therapist. Besides the fact that I'm not fully trained or licensed yet, we just have too much history for it to be ethical."

To her relief, surprise widened Marcus's gray eyes briefly. "Oh, hell no. I'm not looking to hire you to be my shrink or something. That would be way too weird. I was only thinking . . . no, forget about it. It's not important."

Quinn had never heard strong, silent Marcus Beckett sound so unsure of anything in his life. Clearly, whatever this was, it *was* important to him. "No, it's fine! If you're curious, I can definitely go over some of the simpler things I've been learning about. I mean, if you're really interested."

Stepping back from the fence, Marcus said, "Show me."

Which was how they ended up in a field behind the barn, staring across the pasture at a dappled gray gelding calmly cropping grass along the far fence.

Marcus looked down at his empty hands, then over at Quinn with a skeptically raised brow. "You expect me to catch that horse with no bridle or halter or rope of any kind. Do I at least get a handful of hay to bribe him over here?"

"Nope!" Quinn leaned against the pasture gate, the rusted metal warm under the early afternoon sun. "Use your words."

He pressed his lips together, probably to keep from complaining that he never used words if he could help it. Quinn took pity. "Just talk to him, Marcus. About anything. It doesn't have to be your innermost fears and feelings—although if that's what comes out, that's okay. It's the sound of your voice that matters."

"This is pointless," Marcus growled. His hands were fisted inside his pockets, Quinn could see. Luckily, she'd observed this exercise many times before, and there was often a lot of resistance at first. A sense of calm washed over her as she realized she knew exactly what to say.

"It's not pointless. The point is to make a bond between the client and the horse he'll be working with, going forward."

The other point, which she wouldn't mention because she knew it would make Marcus self-conscious and ruin any chance of it working, was to lay the foundation for him to understand that talking got results. Lots of the ex-military men and women who came through Windy Corner seeking help with PTSD and other trauma-related issues had a hard time opening up. It was perfectly understandable—they lived in a culture that told men they had to be strong at all times and never admit to emotion. Or for the female soldiers, that they had to be twice as tough as any man to make it in the military. Those attitudes didn't exactly make it easy for them to open up and share.

Hence this exercise, which gave the client some distance from the therapist, who would wait at the gate while the client tried to persuade the horse to follow him with only his voice as a lure.

Not that Marcus was her client, Quinn repeated silently to herself. He was just . . . interested in what she did all day.

Which was pretty lovely in and of itself, she mused, watching Marcus's long, denim-clad legs stride across the pasture toward Captain. She'd noticed that people tended to tune her out when she talked about her various jobs. They were always nice about it, but she was more likely to get the verbal equivalent of a pat on the head than a series of probing questions.

Of course, it was her fault for never sticking with anything long enough to give people time to trust it was an actual career and not a passing fancy. She was the girl who'd cried "I want to be this when I grow up!" too many times to be easily believed now.

But her work at Windy Corner was different. And it fed something deep in her soul to believe that Marcus could sense that difference, and honored it.

She crossed her arms on the top rung of the gate and laid her cheek on them. With a sigh, she gave herself permission to enjoy the way the wind off the ocean molded Marcus's cotton T-shirt to his body and outlined his broad, hard shoulders and back.

Between the shivery possibilities of this moment and the memory of his hands skimming her waist as he devoured her mouth this morning, Quinn was starting to wonder if she'd repeated her worst pattern of behavior with Marcus. Like every job she'd ever tried and quit, had she given up on Marcus when things got rough?

It doesn't get much rougher than a guy telling you that he's through with you and you need to move on, the scared, hurt part of Quinn's heart reminded her.

But maybe there had been more to Marcus's devastating words that day than she knew. Marcus had always been a volcano of emotion waiting to erupt—it's what had drawn her to him when they were kids, and it was one of the things she found most compelling about him now. His heart was a mystery, a puzzle, an unexplored land waiting to be discovered.

Was it possible that Quinn was the right woman to conquer that uncharted land after all?

This is ridiculous. The words repeated in Marcus's head like a mantra as he slowed his steps the closer he got to the placidly grazing horse.

He felt like an idiot, hands spread wide as if he were bracing for the horse to try to tackle him. As if he'd be able to stay on his feet if the horse charged him anyway.

The horse—Captain, Marcus remembered—casually shifted his impressive weight until his dark gray dappled hindquarters were facing Marcus. Captain's tale swished once, lazy and unconcerned with whatever the human behind him was doing.

"I get it. I'm not as interesting as that patch of clover," Marcus tried. Captain glanced at him, then went back to his lunch. Marcus frowned. The sound of his own voice was loud in the otherwise quiet pasture. He shut his mouth and listened to the buzzing of insects through the tall grass, the rhythmic munch of the horse's teeth, the shriek of seagulls wheeling high overhead.

All those sounds were natural. They made sense here. Unlike Marcus babbling nonsense to an animal that couldn't understand him.

Gritting his teeth, Marcus reached a slow, cautious hand toward Captain's side. The horse's short-haired hide twitched, as if he were shaking off a fly. Captain took a step away from Marcus before going back to snuffling through the grass for sweet, tender clover.

Come on, Marcus thought, setting his jaw. Keeping his movements smooth and steady, he tried to approach Captain again, this time from the front instead of the side. But again, Captain merely turned his ample backside to Marcus and kept on eating.

They repeated the dance a few more times, and every time, Marcus felt his frustration grow, until finally, he turned on his heel and shouted across the field to Quinn standing outside the gate. "Look, this isn't working."

From dozens of feet away, he was still nearly bowled over by the brilliance of Quinn's smile. "Isn't it?"

She gestured behind him, to where Captain had paused in his scavenging to crane his head around and look at Marcus.

Man and horse blinked at one another, unmoving.

"Keep talking," Quinn shouted encouragingly.

Still feeling like an idiot, but more willing to suck it up if it meant getting this over with, Marcus cleared his throat. "Ah. Hey. Nice horse. So . . . you want to come with me to the barn? It's where all the cool horses are hanging out."

Captain didn't look convinced by this blatant peer pressuring, but he didn't go back to eating and ignoring Marcus, either.

"Come on," Marcus tried. "Make me look good in front of that girl with the red hair, and there might be a carrot in it for you later. Oh, that got your attention, did it? You're a little food-obsessed, Cap. Although I know how it is when you work hard and burn through calories like a bonfire made of dead leaves."

Marcus thought back to basic, to days of ten-mile runs in full gear with packs on, obstacle courses in the rain and mud, push-ups in the dirt for any infraction. He was a big guy and his metabolism had always been

high—his mother used to ruffle his hair and complain
he was eating her out of house and home—but in the
army, he could eat six hamburgers in a row and still
feel hungry.

"That's one thing about getting older," he told Captain, daring to lay a hand on the horse's sun-warmed
neck. "I can't eat like that anymore. Not that I really
want to. I wonder how Dad gets by, without Mom to
cook for him. Used to be, he'd forget to eat if she
worked a double shift. But I guess he's survived without her."

For the first time, Captain took a step closer to
Marcus and lowered his head as if investigating his
pockets for treats. The big body knocked into Marcus, giving him something to brace against.

"The last few weeks, before Quinn came to me with
her crazy scheme, that was me," Marcus said, low and
muffled against the horse's neck. "I was just surviving.
Not really living. I guess that's been me for a long time.
Maybe since my mom died—or maybe it got worse
when Buttercup died. But now . . ."

Captain nudged at Marcus with his muscled shoulder, gently bumping him back a step in the direction
of the gate. Marcus laughed a little, lifting his head to
find Quinn watching them with that happy smile still
lighting up her face.

Hell, that smile could light up the whole world.

"Now I'm alive again," Marcus muttered as emotion rushed through him, painful and aching and in-

tense and invigorating. "And it's all her fault. Come on, let's go kick her in the shins."

But of course, nobody kicked anyone. Instead, Captain followed along behind Marcus as docile as a dog on a leash, and waited patiently while Quinn exclaimed over how well they'd done. Captain knew the drill.

Sure enough, once Quinn was done praising Marcus, she reached into her jeans pocket and pulled out a plastic baggie full of irregularly shaped white lumps. "The horse gets sugar," Marcus said, crossing his arms over his chest as Quinn held her flat palm over the gate for the treat to be licked up by the long, rough tongue. "What do I get?"

Quinn unconcernedly wiped her hand on her hip and gave Marcus a flirty look. "You can have some sugar, too, if you want."

Just to be a dick, Marcus held out his hand. But instead of dropping a sugar cube into his palm, Quinn stepped up onto the lowest rung of the gate and leaned over it to plant a kiss on the corner of Marcus's mouth.

"There's your sugar," she said, in a throaty voice that went straight to Marcus's groin. "And there's more where that came from. Unless you're going to tell me this morning was a mistake."

Marcus felt his throat tighten up, but he shoved the words out anyway. "It might be a mistake. But I want you."

For as long as I can have you, he amended silently

while Quinn threw her arms around his neck and hung on tight.

I know it won't be forever. But I'll take what I can get. And deal with the pain when it comes.

In the meantime, he'd have this. Quinn in his arms, her soft, lush mouth against his, her agile fingers flexing in his hair.

This is worth a lot of pain, he mused as he sealed their lips together in a fiery kiss.

Chapter 13

Paul didn't know what changed between his daughter and her fiancé that day she took him with her to the barn, but something definitely had. They were . . . easier with one another, somehow, and yet at the same time, the air between them crackled with a kind of electricity that made Paul clear his throat and hide behind his newspaper.

He wanted that happiness for his daughter. Of course he did. He just didn't want to think too hard about what all those smoldering stares and glancing touches were leading up to.

And if he were honest, it all reminded him too much of the heat he missed between himself and Ingrid.

It had been years since they couldn't bear to be out of arm's reach. It was natural that time would mellow the intensity of that first flush of passion, but Paul still missed it sometimes.

These days, the closest he and Ingrid came to matching the heat of their early relationship was when they argued over Dr. Ron's ridiculous stone circle. Should they do it at all, and if so, where would it go and what kind of stone would it be made of? How big would it be?

"I just think, if we're going to do it we might as well go all the way," Ingrid argued. "And yes, we're going to do it, you already agreed. I don't want to have that fight all over again."

"I agreed under duress," Paul grumbled, staring up at the stacks of stone samples out back of Hackley's Hardware on Main Street. It was where he and Quinn had bought the paving stones they'd used for the front walkway, and the Hackley brothers had agreed they could source the larger stones Ingrid had in mind. They'd barely even smirked, in spite of their reputation as the town pranksters and resident bad boys.

His wife tended to have that effect on people, Paul thought. She was so earnest, even in her goofiest beliefs, that it took all the fun out of mocking her. Not that Ingrid ever seemed to notice. She tended to assume everyone agreed with her wacky outlook on life.

Paul had always admired that ironclad sense of self, but these days, he envied it, too. Ingrid knew exactly who she was and she never faltered from that vision of herself and her life. Nothing seemed to shake it.

He flipped over the price tag taped to the wall above a stack of slate in varying shades of blue and gray, shaking his head. "I just can't believe we're spending money on this."

"It's not about the money. Why does everything come back to money with you?" Ingrid wrung her hands together in distress. "You worked long hours for years and years so we wouldn't have to worry or be a burden to Quinn when we got older, but now here you are, still worrying! Can't you enjoy the moment?"

Paul manfully didn't point out how little there was to enjoy in a moment spent standing in the packed-dirt yard behind Hackley's Hardware, contemplating hunks of rock. At least they'd managed to ditch Guru Ron and come alone.

Instead, he said, "We have enough savings to keep us comfortable for whatever time we have left, but not enough to throw money away on senseless extravagance. We have to be sensible."

Glowering, Ingrid said, "I hate that word. Sensible. It exists solely to suck all the joy out of life. You didn't used to be so sensible all the time. So staid and conventional."

"I was, though." Paul looked away, his jaw hardening. "I really was. Maybe you didn't want to see it, but I was always the sensible one. Somebody had to be."

The bitter little sentence hung in the air between them, poisoning every breath, until Ingrid finally choked out, "Oh? And how's that working for you? Are you happy?"

"Happiness isn't all that matters in life."

"You couldn't be more wrong. It's the only thing that matters."

They stared at each other, lost in the moment. Ingrid looked at him like she either wanted to shake him or kiss him, and Paul heard the blood pounding in his ears. He'd always loved the way she went toe-to-toe with him over the things she wanted. Right now, it felt as if she were fighting for him, for them, for their life together.

Paul's gaze dropped to her mouth, those lips he knew so well. He'd be able to tell her kiss in the dark, distinct from hundreds of other women. He'd kissed her so many times, the act had all but lost its meaning.

Right then, standing under the open sky and surrounded by slabs of cold, featureless stone, Paul remembered exactly what it meant to need to kiss his wife.

He leaned in, savoring the way Ingrid's eyes widened then creased with delight as she moved closer to meet him. But before their mouths could touch, Luther Hackley called from inside the store, "Hey, how are y'all making out? See anything you like?"

Ingrid jolted back a step, a pretty pink flush heating up her cheeks. Gritting his teeth, Paul held back a comment on exactly how he and his wife had been about to make out before they were so rudely interrupted. But it was for the best, probably, Paul rationalized with a sinking heart. They weren't kids. They couldn't solve all their problems by falling into bed.

"We'll take the limestone," he said, looking away from his wife's bright blue eyes to dig through his pockets. "I've got a page with the measurements we need. Here."

"And we'll need help loading it into the truck," Ingrid put in, raising her chin defiantly at him as if she expected Paul to argue the point.

But he wasn't stupid. He knew he wasn't a young man anymore. He was old and past it—past everything.

He handed the paper with the stone measurements to Luther, his fingers gnarled and skinny next to the strapping younger man's broad, work-callused hands. Shoulders hunching, Paul turned away from his wife and headed back through to the cash register inside the store to fork over hundreds of dollars for the chance to make his backyard the laughingstock of the island.

Not that he cared. What did it matter if people thought they were nuts for building a standing stone circle in their garden? If Ingrid actually went ahead and left him, they'd give the town something a lot juicier to talk about.

The breakup of a marriage after thirty years.

Over the next few days, things at the Harper house settled into a comfortable, if unconventional, routine. Quinn's father made breakfast every morning, then he and her mother went outside to argue over the placement of the stones while Ron looked on with an anticipatory gleam in his flat, shark's eyes. On the days when Marcus didn't tag along to Windy Corner with Quinn, he served as the muscle for the stone circle project, digging foundations and heaving waist-high rocks around.

It was a good outlet for his excess energy, which tended to build up over a night of sleeping with Quinn in his arms. By mutual, unspoken agreement, they were taking things slower this time around. Which meant plenty of heavy petting, kissing until her mouth was swollen and red, but that was it.

They'd done everything backward so far, Marcus thought. They started sleeping together before they really knew each other, then they broke up before getting engaged, and now here they were. Not engaged for real, but together for real, even if everyone around them thought Marcus was her fiancé and not her boyfriend.

It seemed like getting together for real should have made their lives less complicated, but it hadn't. At least they weren't talking about it all the time. They were letting things be, and planning to reassess their relationship on her parents' anniversary, the original end date for their fake engagement. Which either wasn't fake, or wasn't an engagement.

Complicated.

Marcus sighed and squinted his tired eyes against the late afternoon sun. Mrs. Harper's garden was a riot of spring color: cheerful scarlet and gold striped tulips waved their heavy heads in the salt breeze, shaded by flowering lilac bushes. The air was sweet with the scent of everything in full bloom, the tender, green smell of grass mingling with the mineral tang of limestone dust and sandy dirt.

For once, he was alone in the garden. Paul and Ingrid had gotten increasingly icy with each other over the angle of the northernmost stone, until finally they'd retreated to their separate corners. Paul was in the kitchen, and Ingrid had closeted herself in their room with Dr. Ron for some kind of psychodrama gestalt aura work.

Marcus leaned on his long-handled shovel and scrubbed the back of his wrist over his sweaty brow. It came away gritty with rock dust that he wiped on his jeans.

He was fantasizing about the giant glass of lemonade he planned to guzzle as soon as this final rock was set in the ground when he heard Quinn's car pull up in front of the house. Without meaning to, Marcus felt his lips curl upward in a smile.

Sue him, he was happy she was home.

Reminding himself it was okay to enjoy this while it lasted, he waved at Quinn when she stuck her head around the side of the house to see who was still at work in the garden.

The way her eyes lit up when she saw him made Marcus feel like he'd swallowed the sun.

"They left you all alone out here!" Quinn hurried

over, already rolling up her shirtsleeves. He loved the way she never hesitated to get in there, get her hands dirty, get involved.

"I don't mind. I like the quiet," he told her.

A shadow crossed her face, but her voice was light and playful as she teased, "Oh, is that so? I can go, if you want . . ."

She laughed when he snagged her by the elbow and reeled her in for a slick, sexy kiss that tasted like sweet tea. Marcus dropped the shovel to get both his hands on her hips, flexing his fingers against her firm curves and aching to drag them up, under her shirt and bra, to find the soft round globes of her breasts.

But they weren't in her bedroom. They were in her parents' yard, in full view of the house. So he reluctantly opened his hands and let her go.

"Mmm," Quinn said, touching her fingertips to her bottom lip as if it were still tingling. "I think you missed me."

That was more than Marcus could admit to aloud. He bent to pick up the shovel and get back to work.

Luckily, Quinn was getting better at reading his silences. "Yep, you missed me," she said with satisfaction, although it faded when he glanced at her.

"So, you were enjoying your quiet solitude when I came home." Quinn glanced over her shoulder toward the house. "Does that mean my parents were arguing again?"

"Apparently they both care—deeply—about whether the north stone is exactly parallel to the south stone at the bottom of the circle."

Quinn's mouth twisted unhappily. "I'm afraid this whole project is pushing them further apart instead of closer together."

Marcus couldn't disagree. It was ironic that the fake relationship they'd created to help the very real marriage was flourishing, while the marriage was halfway over the cliff now.

"You're doing everything you can," he finally said, because he could see that Quinn was working herself up into a fit of guilt.

"I guess. It's all Ron's fault, honestly. He's poison! I don't know why Mother can't see that."

Ron's presence definitely wasn't helping. Anytime it looked as if Paul and Ingrid might be making strides, Ron jumped in with another suggestion or criticism of their relationship, and Paul shut down like someone hit his kill switch.

"I wish we could get rid of him somehow," Quinn was saying, glaring fretfully at the house. "But Mother thinks he's some kind of genius. I don't understand it at all."

Marcus wasn't ready to set himself up as an expert in what unhappily married women found appealing, but he couldn't believe it was slimy, bloated Ron Burkey, with his florid face and blank, emotionless eyes.

"Speak of the devil," he muttered as Dr. Ron threw

open the back door and strode down the steps as if he owned the place.

Quinn wrinkled her nose. "What on earth does he think he's doing?"

Not appearing to have noticed his audience in the garden, Ron reached into his lavender sport coat pocket and produced a tape measure. As they watched, he walked to the back corner of the house and measured the short distance to the stand of maritime pine between the house and the tip of Lantern Point.

Shaking his head, Ron tucked the tape measure under one arm and made some notes on his phone.

"It looks like he's surveying your parents' property. Although I don't know what that could be about, in terms of marriage counseling."

"Hey, Ron. What are you doing?" Quinn called.

Subtle, Marcus thought, holding back a grin. *Subtle as a wrecking ball, that's my girl.*

Ron stiffened for a moment as if he'd been electrocuted, but in the next breath, his natural sleek poise seemed to reassert itself. "I'm taking measurements. For the stone circle."

Quinn raised her brows and gestured at the half-finished circle where she and Marcus were standing. "You're a little lost. The stone circle is over here."

Nobody did a patronizing smile like Ron Burkey, Marcus had to give him that. "Yes, exactly where I envisioned it. But I must double-check the measurements of the surrounding elements, like the house and the woods. All must be in the correct proportions, at the proper angles, for the best feng shui. Don't worry your head about it. It's very advanced metaphysics, but I'll take care of it."

Rolling his eyes hard enough to sprain a muscle, Marcus went back to shoveling. He could practically hear Quinn's back molars grinding down on her annoyance, so he was impressed with the calm, level pleasantness of her voice when she said, "By all means. I'd hate to do all this work and then find out the flow is wrong. But if you'd rather not take the measurements by hand, I think my father had the house and land appraised. All the exact measurements from the county surveyor's office should be on there."

The way Ron went still, he looked like a pointer dog scenting prey. "Why, thank you, that would be extremely helpful. I didn't realize your father had gotten that far with the plans to sell this place."

He was all but rubbing his hands together like a miser counting his gold. Marcus smoothed the shallow hole he'd dug to anchor the next stone and contemplated the marriage guru.

"I'll just go ask your father about it now, shall I?" Ron was already hurrying back into the house, and Quinn watched him walk away with a thoughtful expression on her face.

"Interesting," she commented, her eyes slitted with suspicion. "Do you buy into that mumbo jumbo about feng shui and flow?"

"No," Marcus said bluntly. "But I can't tell if Ron does. He might believe his own bull, or he might be using the latest New Age buzz words to mask some scam or other."

"I think he's scamming us." Quinn tapped her fingers on her chin. "I asked my mom about his fees, and while they're not tiny, they're not life-changing money, either. But it seems to be his way into their circle of trust, and once he gets them to sell their house, he's going to turn it into a big personal payday somehow."

Marcus leaned on his shovel. "Maybe it's time to dig a little deeper. When I was with the Secret Service, we worked with the FBI to investigate threats against the First Family and others under our protection. The first step is always to figure out what the perp is after. So what do we know about Ron Burkey, Relationship Expert?"

Taking a step closer, Quinn leaned into his side until Marcus had to drop the shovel and get his arm around her.

"Thanks for taking this seriously."

Her words were muffled in Marcus's chest, but he heard them. "I just asked the obvious question."

"I mean it." Quinn looked up, shaking her hair out of her eyes to pin him with a serious stare. "Thank you. For not treating me like a hysterical child who's imagining things and creating a villain so she doesn't have to face what's happening between her parents. I worry, sometimes, maybe that's what's going on."

"You know your family better than anyone," he told her. "If you think something strange is going on here,

I believe you. And if he's trying to fleece them, the sooner we nip it in the bud, the better. So come on, what do we know?"

Quinn seemed to be comfortable, nestled under Marcus's arm. She didn't stray as she started ticking off facts on her fingers. "Well, he's married. And he has a website. According to his bio, he's trained in the science of unraveling psychic blockages and resolving spiritual heartache. Apparently, Marcus, once we unlock our inner selves, doors in the outer world will open."

Her voice was heavy with a cynical contempt that Marcus was almost surprised to hear from her. Not that Quinn was New Agey at all, but generally she was a lot more upbeat and less critical. In the few sessions he'd joined in on at the barn since that first day when he'd spilled his guts while coaxing Captain in from pasture, Marcus had been very impressed with Quinn's seemingly endless reserves of patience. No matter how slowly things moved with her clients, or how long it took them to grasp what she was trying to show them, she stayed engaged and interested in every step of the process. And it was a process that felt almost as fuzzy to Marcus, at times, as the string of buzz words Quinn had rattled off from Ron Burkey's website.

The major difference, he thought, was in how much Quinn cared about helping people. No matter how much Ron smirked and simpered and smiled, he never seemed to genuinely care for anyone but himself.

"Oh," she said suddenly, as if something had just occurred to her. "His site also mentions that he requires payment up front. So he's already been paid for the work he's doing with my parents. Which makes it feel like the reason he's going above and beyond for them must be to take them for a lot more money."

Marcus considered that. "We need more information. Can we find out more about his practice in New Mexico?"

"I can call them up, pretending to be a prospective client!" Quinn pulled away, beaming up at him as if he'd come up with the final fix that enabled the moon landing. "That's brilliant. I can ask all kinds of questions that way. Maybe I can even get a few referrals to past clients, and talk to them about his business practices."

She was so excited about this little foray into espionage. Marcus didn't want to find it adorable, but he couldn't help it. To hide the no-doubt besotted look on his face, he walked over to the edge of the woods where Ron had been measuring. He didn't see anything particularly interesting over there . . . pine needles and pinecones and a lot of rough-barked trees.

But when he glanced back, across the field of cord grass separating the Harpers' property from his father's, Marcus froze.

There he was. Dr. William Beckett. Standing outside of the dilapidated, rundown house that used to be the home Marcus's mother had been so proud of.

Marcus stared across the expanse of time and distance between them, and his father stared back, motionless. He couldn't name what he was feeling, but whatever it was nearly choked the breath from his lungs. One of Marcus's arms twitched, unsure if he wanted to raise it to wave. Before he could decide, his father climbed the sagging stairs to the wraparound porch and vanished inside the house.

"I've seen him out there a few times in the last week," Quinn said softly, joining him under the trees. "He comes out to watch you work. I think . . . I think he misses you."

That broke Marcus out of his paralyzed indecision. He turned on his heel and headed blindly for the garden shed. "You don't know anything about it."

"I know I don't." Quinn dogged his steps all the way down the winding garden path. "Because you won't tell me anything about it."

"There's nothing to tell. I don't want to see him. End of story."

"Oh, Marcus, that's the middle of the story, if anything!"

He shot her an unimpressed look before throwing the shovel into the shed and slamming the door closed with more force than necessary. "Well, it's my story and it has nothing to do with you. Leave it alone."

Quinn drew back as if he'd struck her, and Marcus fought down a wince at the harsh tone of his voice still hanging in the air between them. But he didn't have time to figure out a way to walk it back.

"Sure," she said quietly, eyes shuttered. "Sorry. Of course I have no right to an opinion about your relationship with your father. You only know everything there is to know about my family, all the gory details. But I won't mention your father to you again."

"Don't be like that," Marcus said, guilt wrenching his voice tight and guttural.

She blinked. "Like what? You were right. It was my mistake. It won't happen again."

Marcus caught at her wrist when she turned to leave him standing there. He hated feeling this way, twisted up and jagged inside. He didn't know how to stop it, only that the feeling got worse when Quinn left him alone.

"I'm sorry," he said, the words punched out of him. "I know I keep hurting you. That's not what I want."

She wouldn't look at him. "For something you don't want, you're pretty damn good at it."

Marcus ground out a curse and let go of her wrist to run his hands through his hair. "This—all of this, being close to you. It's not easy for me. But I want it. I'm trying."

The thin, hard set of her mouth softened. "You are. I can tell. I wish it were easier for you. I wish I could help."

"You do help."

Marcus reached for her, and to his intense relief, she came into his arms easily and laid her head on his shoulder. It felt like the snick of a locked door behind the person you were guarding so you knew they were safely in for the night. Marcus closed his eyes in the waning light of evening and tried to hold on to that sensation as tightly as he held on to Quinn.

Chapter 14

Quinn clutched her plastic container of wineberries to her chest and carefully skirted around the broken boards in the steps up to the wraparound porch. It would be just her luck to fall through and break her stupid ankle when she wasn't even really supposed to be here.

I'm not doing anything wrong, she told herself firmly as she marched up to Dr. William Beckett's front door and reached for the knocker. *I'm being neighborly. That's all. And if I happen to find out anything that can help me mend fences between Marcus and his father, well, that's the icing on the cake.*

With that in mind, she gripped the dull brass knocker and rapped it smartly against the door.

Silence spread around her like a pool of water, broken only by the lopsided porch swing swaying on its rusty chains. Quinn knocked again and waited.

Just when she was about to give up, a thud from somewhere inside the house made her pause. "Hello? Dr. Beckett? Are you home?"

Of course he was home. He almost never left the house except to get groceries, ever since he retired a few years back. Quinn didn't know anyone who'd had an extended conversation with the man in almost a decade. Dr. William Beckett had gone from respected surgeon to basically a hermit, and no one really knew why.

Well. Other than the grief over his wife's death and the loss of contact with his son.

"Who's there?" said a creaky voice from the other side of the door.

Quinn's heart rate picked up. She leaned closer to the door and spoke as clearly as she could. "It's your next-door neighbor, Dr. Beckett. Quinn Harper? My mother's wineberry bushes got ahead of themselves and started producing so much fruit, we can't handle it all. I was hoping I could offload some on you."

There was a short pause. Quinn bit her lip. She was banking on the fact that everyone on Sanctuary Island loved wineberries. A smaller, sweeter relative of raspberries, wineberries grew thick and wild along the sunniest parts of the island all summer long. It was a surprise to see them this early, but that only made this crop more special. And hopefully, more tempting to Marcus's father.

"Dr. Beckett?" she wheedled.

The door opened a crack, showing nothing but

darkness inside the house. William Beckett peered out at her, overlong gray hair tufting out all over his head like the fuzz on a gosling. Quinn smiled encouragingly and did her best not to show how surprised she was to see the former surgeon looking so unkempt.

"Hi," she said brightly, holding out the plastic tub of wineberries like a peace offering. "I picked these myself, just this morning, before the birds could get them."

But to her surprise, Dr. Beckett didn't even glance at the plump, scarlet berries. Instead, he stared at her as if she were some sort of mythical creature. Quinn shifted her weight from foot to foot. Not for the first time, she wondered if this was a bad idea.

There was no way Marcus wouldn't be angry when he found out about this little visit. And if she hoped to hide it from him, then what was the point of doing it? Because ultimately, she wanted to help Marcus build a bridge back to his father.

She was gaining insight, Quinn told herself. Just like with her investigations into Ron Burkey. She needed information in order to understand the best way to give Marcus the help he'd practically asked for. Almost asked for. If she squinted.

Anyway, she'd get more info if she got inside the house. She wanted to assess the conditions enough to be able to let Marcus know how his father was living and how badly he needed assistance and care. Marcus might be angry with his father, but Quinn had never known anyone in her life with a stronger sense of duty than her fake fiancé. If his father was in trouble, Marcus should know.

Armed with that determination, Quinn beamed at Dr. Beckett. "Would you mind if I came in? I can put the berries in one of your bowls and bring the Tupperware home with me to my mother. How does that sound?"

Dr. Beckett blinked his red-rimmed eyes. They were the same silvery gray as Marcus's eyes, Quinn noticed with a pang.

He cleared his throat rustily, as if he weren't used to using it for speech. "You know him. Don't you."

Quinn didn't pretend not to know who he meant. "Yes. Your son is a wonderful man."

His jaw worked silently for a moment, as if he had more questions to ask but didn't know how to begin. Finally, he pushed the door open wider and disappeared into the depths of the dim hallway, leaving Quinn to waver on the doorstep.

Did he mean to invite her to follow him? Okay, he didn't slam the door in her face, but that wasn't exactly the same as an engraved invitation. But Quinn Harper wasn't the kind of woman who waited around to be asked to dance—she did the asking, if she wanted to get out on the dance floor. This wasn't any different.

Quinn shoved open the door and marched into the house after Marcus's father.

Whatever sort of messy or depressing living situation she found here, she promised herself, she wouldn't judge Dr. Beckett. He'd had a hard, sad life with a lot of tragedy. Quinn mentally prepared herself for towering stacks of old newspapers and magazines or flies buzzing around forgotten plates of half-eaten food. She was ready, she told herself.

But nothing could have prepared her for what she found in Marcus's father's house.

"I can't believe you went over there. You know how I feel about this, Quinn." Marcus's hands were shaking so he shoved them in his pockets. He felt as if he'd been standing on a rug that someone had come along and wrenched out from under him.

"I don't know how you feel about it," Quinn said, "as you so rightly pointed out last night, because you won't talk to me. That's why I went, to see if I could figure out a way to help you at least talk about it, if not do something about it. But I found so much more than that."

Marcus felt something jump into his throat. Maybe it was his heart. Maybe it was the instinctive urge to stop Quinn from saying anything else. He didn't want to hear how badly his father was doing on his own. He didn't want to feel obligated to help the man who had kept him from saying good-bye to his dying mother. But Marcus wasn't someone who could turn his back on his responsibilities.

For better or worse, his mother had raised him right.

"How bad is it?" he asked, sticking his hands under the faucet to wash the sandy dirt from his hands. The stone circle was almost finished, after a solid week of work. Marcus was looking forward to not having to scrub under his nails for half an hour every night.

"That's just it," Quinn said eagerly. "The house looks beautiful. Clean, tidy, you'd think he had a maid service three times a week or something, but it's just him."

The line of Marcus's spine went loose with relief. He shut off the water and dried his hands, turning to prop his hip against the lip of the kitchen sink. "That makes sense. He spent a lot of years as a surgeon—he always liked things clean."

Quinn nodded. "I was really glad to see it. I'd had some awful fantasies about him having turned into a hoarder or something. You hear about it with older people on their own. I think it gets hard to let go of things when you feel your life slipping away."

Reluctantly touched by the compassion in Quinn's soft voice, Marcus pulled out a chair and sat at the kitchen table. He folded his hands in front of him, stilling any possible fidgeting or telltale movement. "But his life isn't slipping away. He's fine."

"Well, I wouldn't say fine," Quinn hedged. "He's lonely, I could tell. But the way he's channeling that loneliness is . . . honestly, it's inspiring, Marcus. You'd be proud of him, I think."

Marcus snorted. "Not likely. Pride isn't a feeling we're used to having about each other anymore."

Not since Marcus rejected his father's life and hopes for his future by turning down medical school in favor of the army. Marcus knew exactly how much

Dr. William Beckett had wanted his son to follow in his footsteps. Refusing to take that path had been the only revenge Marcus could conceive of that would come close to paying his father back for stealing Marcus's last moments with his mother.

"It's not what you would expect." Quinn grabbed two tall glasses from the cupboard and filled them up with lemonade from the pitcher in the fridge before sitting down across from Marcus. She pushed one of the glasses over to him, and he accepted it gratefully.

"I don't expect anything," Marcus told her, completely truthfully. "I don't care what my father is up to or how he's coping. He made his choices, like everyone else in this life, and now he has to live with the consequences. He's the one who taught me that."

"He taught you other things, too, didn't he?"

Marcus had a sudden, vivid image of himself trying to get his father to play catch with him, like the other guys' dads did on the weekends. But not Marcus's dad. He had to take care of his hands, protect them from injury, because they were his most important surgical instruments. The disappointment had been crushing . . . but Dad had made it all go away by taking Marcus fishing instead.

He thrust away the memory of a lazy afternoon floating in a rowboat across the mirror-smooth surface of Lantern Lake. "I'm done talking about this."

"But there's so much more I could tell you, if you'd just listen . . ."

"Move on, Quinn. I mean it." Marcus stared her down.

Taking a frustrated sip of her lemonade, Quinn pursed her lips at the tartness of it. Or maybe she made a face at Marcus's stubbornness. He couldn't be sure.

"Fine. I get it. You don't care how your dad is doing emotionally. But let me at least tell you the main thing I found out!"

Marcus sat back in his chair, getting ready to stand, but Quinn reached across the table and stopped him with an urgent hand on his wrist. "What?" he asked shortly.

"Your father recently—like, in the last few weeks, recently—was approached about selling his house." Quinn paused, her gaze boring into Marcus. "By an out-of-state real estate developer."

Carefully controlling the muscle spasm that wanted Marcus to clench his hands into fists, he forced his brain out of shocked paralysis and back into working order. "That's quite a coincidence. The only other house on Lantern Point besides your parents' is sold, right around the time someone starts trying to get your parents to put their house on the market."

"Right?" Quinn released him, obviously aware that she'd succeeded in capturing Marcus's interest. "I thought it was too much coincidence to be believed, so I asked your dad more about it. He said he hadn't put the house up for sale and hadn't planned to move, but he was approached last month by a woman he'd never heard of. The offer she made him—it's well above market value for a residential home on this island, especially one this far out from the heart of downtown."

Marcus was glad Quinn had let go of his wrist. It enabled him to drop his hands under the table to his lap, to surreptitiously wipe his clammy palms on his dirty jeans. "He took the offer."

"He didn't." Quinn tilted her head, her eyes steady on his face. "But he's thinking about it."

The pang in Marcus's chest surprised him. He turned it into anger as quickly as he could. "Of course he is. He doesn't care about keeping my mother's home safe. So what if she loved it? She's dead now. It doesn't matter what she would have thought."

Quinn flinched from his harsh, biting words, nearly knocking over her lemonade glass. Marcus would have been lying if he said he got no satisfaction from that.

"I don't think that's fair," she said, sticking her pugnacious chin in the air. "Your father cares more than you might realize."

"He doesn't. He'll move on and he won't look back." Guilt and shame roughened Marcus's voice. Hadn't he done exactly that? Moved on and never looked back?

Like father, like son.

Temper snapped in Quinn's blue eyes. "Well, as the person who has spoken to the man in the last decade, I'm telling you that you're wrong about him. Not about what he'll do—I couldn't predict that. But if he accepts the deal, it'll be because he's finally ready for a fresh start . . . and I guarantee, even then, he will still treasure the past."

Marcus felt his lip curl mockingly. "That must have been some visit. Did he give you his whole life story or what?"

"We talked for an hour or so," Quinn said, tart as a green apple. "I asked questions and he answered them, openly and honestly. It's called a conversation. You should try it sometime."

Gritting his teeth, Marcus went doggedly back to the main point. "I hope you at least got the name of the woman who made the offer."

"I did." Quinn put her elbows on the table and leaned in, face flushed and eyes bright. "This is the part where we know for sure that it's no coincidence."

Marcus raised his brows, and Quinn nodded.

"Yep. The commercial real estate developer who made an offer on your father's house is based in Taos, New Mexico. Where my parents met Dr. Ron."

"What's her name?"

"Amber," Quinn said, with the slow satisfaction of someone dropping a bomb into the proceedings. "Amber Burkey."

Chapter 15

Quinn was so full of interesting information, she felt like a water balloon about to splatter over someone's head. Preferably Ron Burkey's.

She hadn't had the chance to speak to her parents yet about what she'd found out. Marcus thought they should hold off until they knew the whole story, to better convince her mother that Ron was a charlatan with ulterior motives. Quinn agreed, but even more than that, she wanted to go ahead with what they'd planned for that evening—the dedication of the now complete stone circle.

Quinn had big plans.

Mr. Marriage Guru, himself, stood at the edge of the completed circle of standing stones gazing around with a level of pride that seemed out of place for a man who hadn't lifted a finger during the building process.

"Wonderful," he cried, "simply wonderful. Exactly the way I pictured it."

Quinn wondered if he'd pictured her family this way, too. Ranged around the circle they'd worked so hard on, her mother was barely looking at her father as he held a match to the pyramid of kindling in the center of the circle. Things were even strained between Quinn and Marcus, although they'd moved past his anger over her visit to his dad by basically pretending it never happened.

Which was frustrating enough, considering what she'd found out about Dr. William Beckett, but Marcus had made it clear he wasn't ready, and goodness knew Quinn had enough of a challenge on her hands trying to cobble her own family back together. Marcus and his father would just have to wait their turn.

Unfortunately, it looked like they were in for a longer wait than she'd hoped. Her parents seemed more at odds than ever.

Maybe tonight would change that. Because tonight, they were blessing the stone circle by lighting the first fire in the center, a ritual Ron assured them was necessary to the proper functioning of the mystical energies.

The stones cast eerie shadows across the garden in the fading twilight. Ron's eyes seemed to glitter like shards of quartz as he intoned, "Come into the circle."

Holding back a shiver, Quinn stepped forward. She didn't want to be affected by any of Ron's silly nonsense, but there was truly something strange and powerful about this moment. Daddy stood up and joined them at the inner edge of the circle, standing between Mother and Marcus. Quinn met her father's eyes over the flickering flames and gave him a commiserating smile. She could see how miserable he was, and for a terrible moment, she wanted to shake her mother. Why couldn't Ingrid see her husband's unhappiness?

But the truth was that Ingrid was unhappy, too. And that unhappiness made her blind to the unhappiness of others.

Quinn did her best to summon up some empathy for her mother, even though Ingrid was the one who'd gotten them into this mess. If it weren't for Ron Burkey, they'd probably be drinking lemonade and playing cards like they used to in the evenings. This was all his fault.

She glared over at Ron, who didn't notice. He was too busy shrugging off his pin-striped suit coat and laying it fussily over the bench just beyond the circle. Stepping back to his place and clearing his throat importantly, Ron said, "Now, do you all have your release items?"

"We do." Quinn spoke up before anyone else could. "And I know your idea was that we should all bring something to burn that we could release into the universe—but we had some disagreement among ourselves about what things to release."

He frowned. "I was very clear."

Quinn blinked with all the innocent sweetness she

could muster. "I'm sure you were! The confusion is probably my fault. I just couldn't understand, from a therapeutic standpoint, why you would want us to bring something that represents an aspect of another person in the family that we'd like to get rid of. That sounds like a recipe for defensiveness and hurt feelings to me. So I thought you must mean that we should each be ready to burn an item from our pasts that represents an element that is currently blocking us from finding true happiness. That's what you meant, isn't it, Dr. Ron? Because I spoke to my teachers in the therapeutic riding program and they agreed that it sounded more likely. And more effective."

Ron's throat worked in silence for a long, heavy moment. Quinn hoped he got an ulcer from swallowing down all that impotent rage.

"Of course that's what I meant," he snapped, smoothing down his completely smooth hair with both hands. "Now, who wants to go first?"

Everyone turned simultaneously to look at Ingrid. Quinn was willing to bet her father and Marcus were going through the same thought process she was— namely, that this was Ingrid's show, and she could darn well be the opening act.

"Oh, all right," Quinn's mother said, her hands fluttering nervously. One of them was curled tight, clutching a small object Quinn couldn't make out in the leaping light of the bonfire.

Ingrid stepped forward, closer to the fire, and glanced at Ron for guidance.

"Well done, Ing," Ron said unctuously. "You're very brave. I know this is a highly charged and vulnerable moment, but all the greatest transitions in life and nature are made with difficulty. This is your chance to change what's inside of you, which will naturally lead to a change in your outer behavior and circumstances. Everyone else, your role is merely to bear witness to Ingrid's spiritual transformation. No words are needed from you at this time."

That sounded a little overly optimistic to Quinn— real change, as she knew from hard experience, was a lot of work over a lot of time. You didn't just decide things would be different and expect that to happen without any further effort on your part. But no real change was possible without that first moment of internal determination, so maybe this wouldn't be a complete waste of time.

Even if she was still convinced that whatever Ron was planning for the land at the tip of Lantern Point, he had no idea what he was doing when it came to psychology.

Ingrid closed her eyes for a moment, swaying in the breeze that snapped sparks from the burning pine boughs. Her loose dress of natural linen appeared white in the darkness, making her look like one of the long-stemmed lilies she'd planted in the protection of the landward side of the house.

"I'm glad to go first, to set the tone for this evening. And also to thank you all for taking part." She opened her eyes to look briefly into the eyes of each person around the fire. "I know it's not what most of you would choose to be doing with your Sunday night, but Ron says it's important. And goodness knows, it's hard to get started, so that makes me think Ron must be right. Anyway, here goes."

She took a deep breath and lifted her hands, opening them to show the item she'd brought to toss into the fire. It was a spool of hemp thread, dyed blue and coiled in the center of her palm.

Quinn remembered the period when her mother was obsessed with learning to weave her own clothes. She'd bought a loom and hundreds of pounds of wool and cotton and other natural fibers. She'd made one piece of clothing—an apron, if Quinn remembered correctly—and never made anything else. The loom sat in the living room corner now, unused and dusty, a monument to one of Ingrid's short-lived enthusiasms. If her mother bringing this thread to burn meant she was finally willing to give up on the idea that she might go back to weaving one day, Quinn was all for it.

"Quinn and Paul know what this is," Ingrid said with a wry smile. "But they don't know what it represents to me. This thread, and the loom and other things I bought to play with, represent a time in my life that lasted for years. To tell the truth, it's something I still struggle with. The idea that I need to do more, try harder, to make my life mean something. And I'm constantly failing, which is . . . disheartening."

Quinn swallowed hard around the lump in her throat. Her mother looked so defeated. She'd never realized what was behind Ingrid's mad passions and obsessive interests. Ron had told them all to be quiet and listen, but Quinn wanted so badly to ask her mother a ton of questions.

Why did she feel like a failure? How could she not know her life had meaning?

"I'm tired of it," Ingrid said, lifting her chin. "I want to know that I'm enough. Whether I can weave my own fabrics, go vegan, learn to hot-air balloon, or write the definitive study of dream imagery—or if I don't do anything more than grow the prettiest tulips on the island. I want to be enough, in and of myself. So I'm throwing away this prop, this external thing I thought would make me more than I am, because I don't need it. Or at least, I don't want to need it. Anymore."

With trembling fingers, she dropped the spool of thread into the heart of the fire, where it instantly flared and blackened. Bowing her head, Ingrid stepped back to the stones, away from the spotlight of the fire, and Quinn had to restrain herself from clapping and cheering. She only managed because she was afraid her mother would think Quinn was mocking her.

But she wasn't. That was beautiful, and Quinn felt she understood her mother better in that moment than she ever had before.

Quinn knew what it was like to worry about not making her mark—to feel sure that something more meaningful lay just around the next corner. She knew the disappointment, mostly in herself, of not finding that unknown something. She also knew she was lucky to have finally found what she'd been unconsciously searching for all her life, and it made her sad to know that her mother's search had been much longer and more heartbreaking.

To show solidarity, when Ron asked who wanted to go next, Quinn steadied herself and said, "I'll go."

The fire beckoned her near, hot against her front while the evening air chilled her back. She'd thought about this moment a lot, ever since she came up with the way to turn Ron's terrible idea on its head. She knew what she had to do, and she was ready. Quinn met Marcus's gaze briefly before dropping her stare to the leaping flames.

This was a message for Marcus. She hoped he got it.

"First, I want to say how impressed I am with you, Mother. What you shared was beautiful, and it taught me something—not just about you, but about myself. We're more alike than I ever thought." Quinn smiled at her mother, whose lips trembled as she smiled back.

"And second . . ." Quinn paused to marvel at how nervous she was. "Sorry, everyone. This is going to smell."

From the plastic bag at her feet, Quinn produced a battered pair of old sneakers and tossed them on the fire, one by one. The rubber soles smoked, the laces curling and twisting like snakes. Quinn was surprised by how much lighter she felt, all of a sudden.

"I'm through with running," she announced, looking up from the fire and straight into Marcus's shadowed silver eyes. "Not that I plan to stop moving forward or trying new things . . . but I'm ready to let myself be happy staying in one place for a while."

With the right person, she wanted to say, but she chickened out. Ducking her head, Quinn stared at her charred running shoes and slid back a pace to get away from the glare of the fire. Hopefully if Marcus could make out her blush in the darkness, he'd attribute it to the heat.

The back of her neck prickled, cold or embarrassment or relief at being done with her part, Quinn didn't know. Everything swirled together in a messy chaos of emotion. All she knew was that when she managed to glance up and meet Marcus's gaze, he was smiling at her. Actually smiling, the slight, almost-unconscious quirk of his lips that he seemed to reserve especially for her.

Quinn's heart lifted so much that she swore she felt her feet leave the ground for a moment. She clasped her hands behind her and rocked back on her heels with a grin.

Catching their silent exchange, Ron narrowed his eyes and said silkily, "Marcus, how about you? Are you ready to go next?"

Marcus didn't even look at Ron. He had to look away from Quinn, too, as he came forward.

Even though she'd clearly meant for Marcus to watch her fire blessing and know she was speaking directly to him, what he had planned was also a gift for Quinn, in a way. He was going to confess something he'd never told another living soul, including the shrink who tried to get him to stay in the Secret Service after it all went down.

Marcus was damn glad he hadn't had to go first. The intensely personal things Ingrid and Quinn shared had made it easier to open up.

In theory, anyway.

The fire popped and hissed, dry pine branches crackling inside the blaze while above their heads, the stars were starting to twinkle into sight as the last of the sunset faded. Marcus thought of another starlit night, one that had haunted him for more than a year.

Reaching into his jeans pocket, Marcus pulled out a small, hinged box made from a swirled seashell. The luminescent nacre of the shell's surface gleamed pale pink in the firelight. He fingered the antique brass clasp, poking it with his thumb in a way he knew wouldn't make it flip open. There was a trick to the thing, and he'd learned its secrets long ago.

For the briefest of moments, his fingers closed around the box too tightly, gripping almost hard enough to crack the fragile thing. He wasn't sure he'd be able to let it drop. But, with an effort of will, Marcus opened his hand and allowed the pillbox to fall into the hottest part of the fire.

It felt like a part of his heart was tearing loose to follow it, to burn and blacken in the embers. Grief welled up in Marcus's throat to sting at the backs of his eyes. Disbelief and horror clenched around his heart and he knew he couldn't do this after all.

Without a word, he turned on his heel and strode away from the fire and into the cold darkness beyond the stone circle. Quinn called out to him, the distress and concern in her voice ratcheting the vise around his chest even tighter, but he didn't stop. He couldn't. He had to get away.

Even though he knew, from bitter experience, that there was nowhere he could go. There was no place that was safe from the memories locked in Marcus's mind, or from the guilt that filled his soul.

Chapter 16

"No, no, let him go," Ron commanded, seeming pleased at this dramatic turn of events. "The fire-blessing ritual can be powerfully unsettling. Not everyone is ready to stretch their spirit in this way. Your fiancé's aura is very dark, Quinn. I'm sorry to be the one to tell you that."

"Say whatever you want about his aura," Quinn said impatiently, her eyes searching the shadowy garden for any sign of Marcus. "It couldn't matter less to me. I need to go after him."

But her mother stretched out an imploring hand. "Oh, sweetheart, I think he wanted some time alone! And your father hasn't done his blessing yet. Can't you please stay for that, and then go find Marcus, after he's had a few minutes to gather himself?"

Quinn wavered. She knew Marcus, and he wouldn't

want anyone to see him overcome with whatever emotion had driven him away from the stone circle, not even Quinn. Maybe especially not Quinn. But that only made her want to find him more, to help him.

By forcing your presence on him when he clearly wants to be alone? a skeptical voice from the back of Quinn's brain asked.

"Exactly," Ron put in, waving his arms as if to dispel whatever "dark" energy Marcus had left behind. "Just what I was going to suggest. You wouldn't want to miss your father's blessing, would you? I'm sure it will be very moving."

Three heads swiveled in Paul's direction. Quinn was surprised and dismayed to see the grimace on her father's face. He shuffled his feet a bit—he was all but tugging at the collar of his gray polo shirt. Quinn's stomach sank.

"That's okay, we can just call it a night," Paul suggested weakly. "Quinn wants to make sure Marcus is all right. I understand completely. Go ahead, honey."

Quinn didn't move. "No. I'm going to give him a moment to himself. So *you* go ahead, Daddy. What did you bring from your past that you'd like to let go of?"

"Well, the thing is . . ." Paul trailed off, not really looking at anyone. "The thing is that I don't really want to let go of the past. My memories are happy—I'm lucky, I've had a great life. As far as I'm concerned, if things went back to the way they used to be, everything would be perfect."

Worried, Quinn darted a look at her mother to see

how she was taking it. Next to Ingrid, Ron wore an expression of barely concealed delight, but the look on Quinn's mother's face . . . Quinn swallowed hard, fear piercing her chest like an arrow. Ingrid looked gutted.

"I don't understand," she said, her voice low but surprisingly steady. "There's nothing you would change— about your life, about our marriage, about yourself? You're perfectly content?"

Stubbornness firmed Paul's jaw. "Yes. I'm content."

"How can we both be in the same marriage?" Ingrid exploded. "You're content, and I've never been so unhappy."

The words billowed up into the night sky like the smoke from the fire, gone in an instant, but leaving behind the unmistakable residue of regret, sadness, and resentment. Quinn ached for her parents, both of them.

Even though she could cheerfully strangle her father in this moment.

"I don't understand what changed," Paul said, stubbornness giving way to helplessness. "I thought we were happy. Weren't we happy?"

Ingrid wrapped her arms around her midsection as if she suddenly felt the chill of the evening breeze. "Of course we were. But things change and we have to adapt. And I know you don't want to acknowledge it, but you *aren't* happy now, Paul. You say you're happy, but you're not, and I can feel it. Don't think you can fool me. You're not happy, but the reason you didn't bring anything to burn is because you don't take this process seriously. You think I'm stupid for buying into it, you think it's all a crock, but don't you see that I'd do anything to save our marriage? To save us? And don't you think it hurts to know that you . . . you won't?"

Her voice broke on a sob, and in a flurry of linen skirts, she was gone. Quinn's heart pounded in her ears, her eyes prickling and burning with unshed tears. She stared at her father, who had slumped against one of the standing stones, letting it support his sagging weight.

"I'm losing her," he gasped. "This can't be happening."

"Well, if you'd take my advice," Ron began, but he broke off at the murderous glare Quinn's father sent his way. "Ahem. In any case, I should check on Ingrid. Excuse me."

Quinn stared at her father, willing him to punch Ron's lights out or tackle him to the ground, or at the very least to insist that he be the one to see to his own wife. But instead, Paul let the marriage guru go, glowering at his retreating back before sliding down the stone pillar to sit in the dirt. He dropped his head into his hands, the picture of abject misery, and Quinn couldn't help it. Her heart wept for him.

Skirting the fire, she went to kneel down next to him. "Daddy, you need to snap out of this. I hate to say it, but you are going to lose Mother if you don't do something."

"I can't believe this is happening. I don't understand what changed between us. I really don't."

He sounded as lost and hurt as a child, which filled Quinn with a painful mixture of tender protectiveness and fear. It was awful to hear her father, the man she'd always looked up to and counted on as her own sturdy rock, sound as if he were on the verge of tears.

Should she mention what she'd found out about Ron? she wondered. A week ago, she wouldn't have hesitated. She would have assumed getting rid of Ron would drain all the poison out of her parents' relationship.

Now? Quinn wasn't so sure. She was very afraid their problems went deeper than an interfering marriage counselor. Whatever tensions Ron was exploiting, they'd existed long before he came on the scene. And Quinn was starting to worry that exposing Ron's schemes wouldn't automatically fix her parents' marriage.

"I know, Daddy. This is all so hard and confusing, and I'm sorry you and Mother are going through it. But you need to go through it together. You can't leave Mother hanging like this again. If you don't know what's changed or why, *talk to her.* Please."

"She's just so angry, and I don't understand why."

Quinn slapped her hands on her thighs and started to get up. "Well. There's only one way to fix that."

"It's not that easy . . ."

"I never said it would be easy." Quinn stared at her

father. She couldn't back down; this was too important. "It won't be easy. It'll be one of the hardest conversations of your life—but if it ends with you and Mother on the same page, vowing to fix whatever has gone wrong between you, won't it be worth it?"

Her father tipped his head back to rest it against the limestone pillar. Firelight played softly across his face, highlighting the creases and marks of age. He smiled up at her faintly. "When did you get to be so wise?"

"Don't act surprised! I'm going to school to help people learn to communicate better," Quinn pointed out. "Among other things."

"It sounds to me like that program is pretty good," Paul said gruffly. "I'd like to hear more about it sometime. I don't know how you're paying for it, but if you need any help—"

"The barn is paying for it," Quinn interrupted quickly. "I have no idea where they got the money, maybe a grant came through, but they offered and I took them up on it. So while I appreciate the offer, I don't need your help this time. It means a lot to me that I'm doing it on my own, actually."

Her father gazed at her fondly. "In case I haven't made it clear, I'm proud of you and what you're doing with your life, sweetheart."

Quinn's heart leaped like a startled deer. "Do you mean that?"

His eyes widened in surprise. "Of course I do. It may have taken you a while to find your path in life, but I think you're on the right track now. At the barn . . .

and with Marcus. Go easy on him about tonight, okay, kiddo? I don't think his issue was that he didn't take the thing seriously enough."

"No," Quinn agreed huskily, through a throat clogged with emotion. "Marcus cares deeply—but he doesn't like to show it."

"Don't give up on him," her father said, weary and solemn. He reached up to clasp Quinn's hand, and with a heave, she helped him to his feet.

"I won't," Quinn promised, feeling a little like a stand-in for her mother in that moment. She wasn't sure if they were still talking about her and Marcus . . . or if her father really wished he could get that promise from his wife.

A promise not to give up.

"Show Mother you're willing to fight for her," Quinn whispered, her voice a thread of sound, barely louder than the hiss of the fire. "And if you're not . . . then let her go."

That startled her father, badly. He dropped her hand and turned toward the house, as if he wanted to go racing off to find Ingrid immediately. But first, he looked back at Quinn. "I hear you. And thank you. It's . . . well, it's kind of wonderful to have an adult daughter to talk about these things with."

The knot in Quinn's throat broke, nearly choking her with a half sob, half laugh. "You know, I think that's the first time you've ever referred to me as an adult."

Her father put his hands on her shoulders and looked

into her face. "I'm sorry. Maybe we wanted you to stay our baby forever, on some level. But I can see you're all grown-up now. And I'm grateful for the chance to build an adult relationship with the woman my sweet little girl turned out to be."

That was it, Quinn was crying. She shrugged one shoulder high enough to rub her damp cheek on it. "Oh, Daddy. I'll always be your little girl. When I'm a hundred and two, I'll still be your little girl. Don't ever doubt it."

Paul gathered her in close for a hug, and Quinn took a deep, shuddering breath that smelled like the most comforting parts of her childhood.

"Thanks, sweetheart," her father said into her ear. "I needed to hear that. All of it. Now, I suggest we go find Marcus and your mother. It's time to have some difficult conversations."

Quinn nodded, but first—she had some research to do.

Marcus lay on Quinn's childhood bed, fully clothed and staring up at the ceiling. There was a crack in the plaster, directly above his head. He focused on it and tried to let everything else go.

He was getting so good at focusing on the crack in the plaster, he nearly missed the slow creak of the bedroom door opening and Quinn padding in on bare, quiet feet.

Almost, but not quite. Marcus felt every atom in his body come to attention the moment he sensed Quinn's nearness. He managed not to look at her, but it wasn't easy.

"How are you feeling?" she asked tentatively, coming to hover over the bed.

"Fine."

"Oh. I thought maybe you were sick. Or something."

"Nope."

She huffed. "Okay, then. Are you going to tell me what's wrong?"

"Nothing is wrong. I didn't want to be there anymore, so I left."

"That's fair. No one was holding you hostage. You're free to participate or not, as you choose."

Marcus arched a brow in her direction. "Who exactly are you trying to convince here?"

He saw Quinn throw up her hands in his peripheral vision. "I'm trying to be understanding, but you're not making it very easy! Do I wish you'd stayed and finished your blessing, since you said you'd do it? Of course. But if it turned out to be too much for you, I get that. Considering I nearly broke down in tears when I did mine."

Clenching his back teeth on a denial that he'd been anywhere close to tears, Marcus laced his fingers together on his stomach and settled his shoulders more firmly against the bed. "Okay. Thanks."

Quinn sighed, but didn't press him. Marcus was simultaneously grateful and guilty, a combination that swirled in his gut like he'd taken shots of tequila, rum, whisky, and vodka one right after the other.

She went to the bathroom and he heard the sound of running water and splashing. Marcus could clock her bedtime routine with his eyes closed at this point. First she would wash her face with plain white soap, then she'd brush her teeth and floss with the stoic concentration of a child with a dentist appointment in the morning. Then she'd undo her braid or pull her hair down from its ponytail and brush it out until it was smooth and gleaming in red-gold waves over her shoulders. She'd change into the soft cotton sleep shorts and skinny-strapped tank top she wore to bed, then she'd slip under the covers next to him and nudge close until her head was on his pillow, her gentle breaths tickling his ear.

Marcus breathed in deeply, envisioning each step until he heard the tread of her bare feet across the floor. "The bathroom is all yours, if you need it," she said neutrally as she sat on the edge of her side of the bed.

He stared at the straight line of her back and missed the brush of her warm breasts against his arm, the weight of her body snuggling closer under the covers. "I'll get ready for bed in a minute. Come here."

Quinn half turned to speak over her shoulder. "I'm thinking about taking the couch downstairs for the night."

Marcus felt his body turn to granite. "Why?"

"This isn't working," she said, eyes down. "You and me. If we can't even have one, simple conversation about your past, how can we expect to build a future together?"

He sat up, suddenly feeling at a disadvantage flat on his back. "So I didn't want to spill my guts in front of your parents and Ron freaking Burkey. Sue me."

"You don't have to spill your guts to anyone," Quinn said with a sigh. "You know, I thought about Googling you, to see if I could find any information on what happened to you when . . . that was something that belonged to the First Lady, that you threw in the fire, wasn't it? You were going to tell us something about your work with her, but fine—you decided not to. It's okay. I realized I don't want to know anything you don't want to tell me. It's entirely your choice—but the fact that you clearly don't want to tell me about an incident that has had a profound effect on you . . . it makes me feel like we're not as close as I thought. Not as connected. I don't want to emotionally black-mail you here, but that's a problem for me, Marcus. I hope you can understand why."

Marcus swung his legs off the bed to plant his feet firmly on the floor. A big part of him wanted to stand up and walk out of that room, out of that house, and away from Quinn and the terrifying weight of her expectations and needs.

But he forced himself to sit there, back-to-back with her, because he knew if he walked out the door he'd be cutting short his time with Quinn. And that, he couldn't do. Not when he already knew that their time together would be fleeting, no matter what he did.

Besides, Quinn deserved better than his silence. She

deserved the truth. As much of it as he could bear to give her.

"After I left the army," he said abruptly, feeling the mattress shudder under him as Quinn scrambled around to face him. But he stayed where he was, staring at the opposite wall. It was easier that way, somehow. "I was recruited to the Secret Service. I worked at the White House for a while, and my experience there made me the perfect addition to Buttercup's security team when she started receiving threats."

"Was . . . I didn't know she'd been threatened. It wasn't in the news." Quinn sounded tentative, as if she weren't sure she should interrupt with questions.

"They all get threats," Marcus told her. "Basically everyone in public office, in the public eye, has gotten as least one scary letter or threatening e-mail. We take the letters more seriously—it's more of a commitment to put actual pen to actual paper, write out an address, stamp and mail the envelope, than it is to dash off an angry message and send it into cyberspace—but most threats turn out to be nothing. Part of my training was to distinguish between the two. I'd also had some success at convincing the objects of those real threats that they were in danger. That was what they hoped I'd be able to do with Buttercup. She liked to slip her security detail and go out on her own, visit soup kitchens and inner-city after-school programs without the media circus that followed around after the Greatest First Lady of the Century. She used to snort when anyone called her that. God, she was a stubborn old battle-axe."

Marcus smiled, against his will, at the memory of her steel-gray curls like a helmet under her pillbox hats. She didn't like a lot of fuss and fanfare, but she did like a classic Chanel suit.

"You loved her," Quinn observed.

"It wasn't my job to love her," Marcus snapped. "It was my job to keep her safe."

"I'm sure you did the best you could. What happened?"

"What happened?" Marcus stood up from the bed in a rush, needing to move. He prowled the perimeter of the room like a caged animal, lashing his tail at the onslaught of memory. "I let her send me away. She wanted me to visit my father, after she found out we were estranged. I let her convince me she'd be fine with the other agents assigned to her detail. And an hour after I started the drive from D.C. to Sanctuary Island, I got the call that she'd snuck out behind her detail's backs and gotten shot on the street. Shot down like a dog, by someone who didn't think she should be wasting her time helping poverty-stricken children in rough neighborhoods."

"Oh, Marcus."

"Don't pity me." Marcus slashed a hand through the air, striking out at his own frustration. "I don't deserve it. I left my post, and the woman I was protecting—a woman who meant a great deal to the nation and to me, personally—was killed."

"It wasn't your fault," Quinn protested.

Marcus had heard that before, and intellectually, he

could even admit it was true. "But if I'd been there, I could have prevented it."

"Maybe not. Maybe you would've been killed instead."

He tightened his jaw. "I would've gladly taken a bullet for Buttercup. Beyond the fact that it's what I signed up for, to put my body between her and danger—she was an incredible woman. She would have done more for the world and the people in it in her few remaining years than I would manage if I had a hundred years."

"I don't doubt that Mrs. McCarty was an amazing person. I admired her my whole life." Quinn stilled his tense pacing by standing directly in his path and forcing him to either stop or crash into her. "But if you had been there and sacrificed yourself to save her . . . my life would be immeasurably worse. That's probably selfish. But I can't stand the thought that I might never have seen you again, that we might never have met as adults and had the chance to be together. Marcus, please."

He looked down into her serious, pleading eyes.

"What?" he rasped.

"Hold me." Quinn tucked her chin to her chest and knocked the crown of her head into his sternum, searching blindly for comfort from the cold reality of the life Marcus had once known.

He couldn't say no. He couldn't resist. His arms came up and around her, and he felt the shiver that wrenched through her before she lifted her own arms to encircle his waist tightly. "So now you know," Marcus said into her hair.

"I know you're riddled with guilt for something that wasn't your doing," Quinn replied doggedly. "Oh, Marcus. It must have been horrible, heartbreaking, to hear the news and wonder if you could have made a difference. All while dealing with your personal loss, which sounds like it was intense. The ex-First Lady almost sounds like a . . . like she was a mother figure to you."

Marcus stiffened slightly. "I had a mother. A great one."

"A great mother who you lost too early," Quinn agreed quietly, lifting her head to rest her chin on his collarbone. "I'm just saying. I'm sure you're still grieving, and that's perfectly natural. But I wish you could let go of your guilt over what happened to Buttercup. I never met her, but I bet she wouldn't appreciate you tying yourself in knots over this."

The laugh that forced its way from his chest surprised him. "No. She'd call me a fool and slap me upside the head, and probably accuse me of using her death as an excuse for not living."

Quinn's eyes crinkled at the corners. "She sounds like someone I would have liked."

"You would." Marcus pressed an absentminded kiss to Quinn's forehead. "And she would have loved you. God. I never would've had a moment's peace, once she met you, until she knew we were getting married and settling down to make her lots of godbabies."

A bright pink flush rose to Quinn's cheeks, but her grin was pleased. "Well. Gosh. Now I really wish I could've met her."

Marcus snapped back to the present from his bitter-sweet imaginings of Buttercup's reaction to Quinn. Quinn, who was in his arms, gazing up at him and implying . . . what? That she was ready to settle down? That she might want him . . . permanently? His heart kicked over and roared to life, making his pulse pound in his ears.

She didn't mean it, he told himself. But even still, just the vague implication of it turned him on like nothing ever had.

Quinn Harper. His. Forever.

Marcus slid his hands up the sides of her neck to shape her delicate jawline before he gave in to temp-tation and kissed her. The kiss went deep and wild immediately, teeth and tongues clashing, stroking, thrusting together in a heated simulation of sex.

She clutched at his back, her fingernails raking at him through the thin material of his shirt, and sud-denly Marcus needed to be skin to skin. He broke the kiss long enough to catch a breath and strip off both their tops before diving back in. He felt like he couldn't get enough of her, like he was drowning and needed Quinn's mouth to breathe. Except breathing was the last thing on his mind.

Quinn groaned when the tips of her breasts crushed into the mat of springy hair on his chest, and she twisted against him as if she liked the sensation. The sounds she made went to Marcus's head like strong drink. Since the very first time, he'd been addicted to the way Quinn loved sex. She was so responsive, so eager and natural in the way she enjoyed how their bodies came together. Maybe it was her youth and relative inexperience, or maybe it was a quality all Quinn's own either way, she made Marcus feel young again. She made him feel like every time was the first time, a discovery of what their bodies were made for— an exploration of how much pleasure their bodies could contain without exploding.

Hard and aching with it, Marcus walked Quinn backward to the bed. When it hit the backs of her knees, she tumbled onto it with a laugh and laid herself out for him. Her narrow waist and the curves of her hips were still hidden by those cotton drawstring shorts she wore—those shorts shouldn't be sexy, but damn, they were. Marcus's eyes devoured her like a feast for a starving man. The rounded softness of her breasts, tipped with pink and begging for his mouth. The line of her neck as she threw her head back and silently invited him closer, invited him to have her. And he would.

He did. And it was glorious.

Chapter 17

Quinn bounded down the stairs, full to the brim with energy and a determination to make the most of the day.

She'd woken up twined around Marcus Beckett like a very affectionate Virginia creeper vine, and they'd repeated last night's wonderful, sweaty, bed-shaking adventures before she'd leaped into the shower and gotten dressed.

Last night—even before the bed shaking, it was a pretty incredible night. Marcus had opened up. Maybe only a crack, and maybe what he'd shared had only made her more aware of the damage he carried around like a badge of honor, but still, it felt like progress.

As long as she ignored how hard she'd had to work to make him tell her anything.

Breezing into the kitchen, she found her father sitting alone at the table, nursing a cup of coffee. When he looked up, she frowned at the dark smudges under his puffy eyes.

"You look like you didn't get a wink of sleep. Did you and Mother talk for a long time last night?"

"Sorry to dash your hopes, but your mother was asleep when I got upstairs. Or at least, she pretended to be. I thought I'd talk to her this morning, and I hardly slept, thinking about what I'd say—but I guess I did eventually pass out, and she was gone before I woke up."

Disappointment wilted Quinn briefly, but she shook it off and grabbed a mug to pour herself some coffee. "I'm sorry, Daddy, that sounds like a rough night. But it's only a setback. Can't you go talk to her now? Marcus is in the shower and I can make myself scarce, give you some privacy."

"I would if I knew where she was. But the car is gone, and so is Ron. So they're off together doing God knows what."

"Daddy! You don't mean that." Quinn plopped down with her coffee and regarded her father across the table with concern. "Mother would never cheat on you."

He slumped over and put his forehead in his hand. "Honestly, I don't know what to think anymore. I don't know what to do. The problem is so much bigger than I even imagined. It's overwhelming."

"Well, I know one thing we're going to do." Quinn set her coffee cup down with a clack. "We're going to have an intervention. Mother is addicted to Ron Burkey and his breath work and astral healing and spiritual psychobabble. But I have a lead on some information that might help her kick the habit. Let Marcus and me dig into it a little more today, and then tonight we'll sit her down and talk it out, as a family. How does that sound?"

Paul smiled weakly. "It can't hurt. Do you really know something about Ron that will change your mother's mind?"

"It's more of a suspicion than a fact," Quinn hedged. "But Marcus and I have plans to get some confirmation, enough to convince Mother that we're right."

She thought he'd ask more about it, but instead, he only nodded and got up to refill his coffee. He moved slowly, shuffling across the linoleum like a much older man, and Quinn felt her heart crack in two. She wanted to promise him everything would be okay, but of course, she couldn't know that for sure.

For the first time since she hatched her crazy scheme to make Marcus into her fake boyfriend, Quinn faced the fact that there truly might be nothing she could do to save her parents' marriage.

The realization threatened to break her heart, but even as her throat ached and swelled with emotion, Quinn was conscious of a tiny seed of relief sprouting in her chest.

If she couldn't change the outcome for her parents . . . maybe their relationship wasn't actually her responsibility? Maybe even their problems . . . weren't her fault.

None of that meant that Quinn would stop fighting for her family. At the very least, she was going to get to the bottom of whatever Ron had planned for the land he and his wife wanted to buy up. Exposing the truth could only be a good thing. Then whatever choice her parents made would be based on having all the facts.

But even if this didn't go the way Quinn wanted, even if the worst happened and her parents split up—for the first time, Quinn thought she might survive it. She'd be okay, and so would Mother and Daddy. If they truly couldn't make each other happy anymore, then they would honestly be better off apart.

The way she felt about Marcus . . . that's what she wanted for her parents. And if they'd lost that, she couldn't fault them for wanting to end the marriage.

Quinn drained her coffee and took the mug to the sink. She hadn't had this many deep thoughts before breakfast since college. "Okay, Daddy, I'm going to make some calls about Ron. Will you keep an eye on the driveway and give me a shout if it looks like they're coming home?"

"Sure." Paul perked up, bending to pull out his frying pan. He always liked to have a plan, Quinn mused. "I'm going to start breakfast. How does Marcus feel about French toast?"

"I don't know. Let's find out!" Quinn knocked a kiss onto her dad's cheek before heading to the home office at the back of the house. A few quick internet searches later, she had the contact information she needed.

Quinn cracked her knuckles and picked up the phone. Holding her breath, she dialed in the number and waited while it rang.

"Burkey Commercial Real Estate," said a cool, collected female voice. "How can I help you realize your dreams today?"

Pitching her voice a little higher and more nasally than usual, Quinn said, "Yes, ma'am, hello. I'm calling from the offices of the Sanctuary Island Town Council. We understand you have a client looking into purchasing some land there, and I'm going to need a little information from you so I can get the zoning permits started . . ."

Paul had wondered how Quinn intended to get Dr. Ron out of their hair long enough to do an intervention for her mother, but in the end, Ron made it easy. When he and Ingrid came back to the house that afternoon, he said he'd made arrangements with a local who owned a boat to take him on a tour of the coves and inlets around the outskirts of the island.

"I'll be back for dinner," he assured Paul, who bared his teeth in a smile that felt more like a snarl.

"Can't wait," he replied flatly.

The minute Ron was gone, they all gathered in the living room. Ingrid was reluctant—he could tell she didn't want to talk about where she'd been with Ron all morning. And she didn't want to talk to her husband at all. She'd barely even look at him.

So it was Quinn who started things off, after sharing a glance with her fiancé that seemed to bolster her spirits.

"Mother, we need to talk to you about Ron."

Ingrid huffed and crossed her arms over her chest. "Must we have this conversation again? Believe me, I know how you all feel about him, but he's here to help. It's not his fault that the process is painful. That's how you know it's working!"

"It's true that productive therapy can be painful," Quinn said, obviously choosing her words with care. "Which is why it's all the more important to only undertake work like that with a trained, licensed professional who has your best interests at heart. Marcus? Tell her."

Raising both brows at Marcus, Ingrid sat up in the rose-upholstered armchair. "Yes?"

Marcus was perfect for this kind of thing, Paul thought. His serious, emotionless expression and matter-of-fact tone made Ingrid relax almost imperceptibly from her defensive stance. Until she heard what he was saying.

"Ron Burkey—'Dr.' Ron—" Marcus said, making the gesture for air quotes with his fingers, "is not a doctor. He doesn't even have a Ph.D., much less an M.D. He has no legal or ethical right to be running a psychology practice."

Ingrid didn't move. She didn't flinch. Paul, who was

watching her intently for any sign that she'd heard and understood, finally said, "Honey, you know what that means? Ron is a phony."

"Excuse me," Ingrid retorted. "But that's not what it means at all. Ron may not have the backing of the medical establishment, but that's hardly surprising considering how cutting-edge his theories are. Of course he doesn't have a degree—he's self-taught! More than that, he's one of the foremost thought leaders when it comes to spiritual psychology and intuitive healing. There's no one who's a bigger expert than he is, so that means there's no one higher up to give him that stamp of approval. So what?"

A chill spread from Paul's insides to the tips of his fingers. If even this didn't convince Ingrid to stop listening to Ron's poison, then what would?

"I hope you didn't drag me in here just for this," Ingrid said, gathering her long skirts up as if she were about to stand. "It's been a long morning and I'm tired. I was thinking of lying down for a nap before dinner."

"A long morning doing what?" The words popped out of Paul's mouth before he could stop them.

His wife glared at him across the coffee table. "Is this an intervention or an interrogation?"

"It's neither," Quinn soothed, leaning over to put a hand on her mother's arm. "Not really. But . . . can I make a guess about what you and Ron were doing?"

Ingrid stiffened visibly, but Quinn didn't wait for a response.

"Were you looking at apartments and smaller houses closer to downtown?"

Pulling away, Ingrid sank back into her chair. "How did you know that?"

The implications hit Paul like a sledgehammer between the eyes. "You went looking for a new place to live . . . without me?"

"Don't make such a thing of it." Ingrid's cheeks were red as the roses embroidered on her chair. "Ron only wanted me to see that there are options."

"In case you do decide to sell the house," Quinn clarified, glancing at Marcus again. He nodded encouragingly.

"After last night, we can't pretend this last-ditch effort to save our marriage is going well." Ingrid lifted her chin and spoke with the innate dignity that had always drawn Paul to her. There was a grace to Ingrid's movements, the straight line of her spine and her long neck, that stopped his eyes whenever they passed over her.

He couldn't believe how close he was to no longer seeing that graceful posture every day.

"Ingrid." His mouth was dry. "Honey, please."

She looked torn, her face screwing up for a moment as if she almost couldn't bear it—and that's when Quinn struck.

"I guessed that Ron had taken you house-hunting today, because I know the truth about why he wants you to sell this place," she said baldly. Only her tense fingers, white with pressure where they gripped her knees, gave away her inner turmoil. "He wants to buy it."

Paul stared as Ingrid's head reared back. "That's ridiculous. He never said one word about buying this house. He hasn't made us an offer! What makes you think—"

"He wouldn't make the offer himself," Marcus interrupted. "At least, that's not how he did it with my father."

"Your father?" Paul's gaze shot to the front window, where the ramshackle house up the lane was framed between the gently waving curtains. "Will sold his house?"

"Not yet," Marcus answered. "But he's thinking about it. He has received an offer . . . from Ron's wife, who is a commercial real estate developer."

Ingrid went absolutely rigid, as if all her bones and muscles had been replaced with steel rods buried in cement. "What."

Her voice was deadly soft, but Quinn didn't back down. Paul was proud of her.

"It's true," she said, calm and steady. "I spoke to Amber Burkey this morning. She confirmed that she and her husband think Lantern Point would make the perfect spot for a brand-new 'wellness spa.' They want our land, and Marcus's family's land, to build it on."

Without a flicker of an eyelash, Ingrid got up and crossed the living room to stand by the window. Looking out toward the Beckett house, she said, "Are you certain Ron knows about this plan?"

"I haven't confronted him about it," Quinn said, "but his wife used the word 'we' a lot. And she talked about the therapies her husband plans to offer. So I think it's safe to assume that Ron is in on it, Mother."

Wincing, Paul watched his wife carefully to see if she bridled at Quinn's accusatory words, but for the first time since Ron Burkey came into their lives, Ingrid didn't leap to his defense. Instead, she nodded once, as if she were confirming something to herself. And then she said, "Quinn, Marcus. Could you give us a moment alone?"

Quinn's hands twisted in her lap. "I . . . I know this is a lot to take in, Mother. I know how much you believed in Ron, but—"

"It wasn't how much I believed in Ron," Ingrid corrected her absently. "It was how much he believed in me. Or at least, he convinced me that he did. It doesn't matter now. I need to speak to your father in private. I appreciate the effort you put into finding the truth, sweetheart. You, too, Marcus. I'm sorry you had to get involved."

Paul saw from the way Quinn bit her lip that she was reluctant to leave without hearing some sort of acknowledgment that her mother renounced Ron Burkey and everything he stood for. But Paul knew his wife. She had something to say, and if she didn't say it, she was going to explode. "Go on, sweetheart, get out of here and let your mother and me talk. That's what you've wanted all along, remember?"

"I guess it is. And y'all deserve to have some privacy," Quinn said, standing up.

"Privacy's not easy to come by when we're all living on top of each other like this," Paul said with a smile, heart pounding with nerves. "But I'm glad we've had the chance to get to know you better, Marcus. And to see you and Quinn together—I can tell you're good for each other. Thanks for being here."

Marcus set his jaw as if he didn't know what to say, and Quinn jumped in to rescue him before it got unbearably awkward. "Okay, we'll leave you two in peace. Marcus, want to take me out to the Firefly for dinner? We can meet y'all here afterward and decide what to do next."

"Sounds good," Paul said, slapping his thighs and smiling for all he was worth. "That should give us plenty of time."

Plenty of time to figure out where they stood now that Ron Burkey wasn't standing between them.

But after Quinn and Marcus left the house, Paul and Ingrid spent the next few minutes in tense silence. Paul watched his wife, who was still standing at the window looking out. He used to be able to tell exactly what she was thinking just by looking at her. When did he lose that ability?

Finally, Ingrid turned around to face him. Dry-eyed and face set, she said, "You win. Ron is a fraud and I feel like a fool. I'll tell him to go."

She was shaking, Paul saw with a shock. He shot off the sofa and headed toward her, but she held up both hands to stop him from coming closer.

"Don't."

Taken aback by her sharp tone, Paul blinked. "But . . . please, Ingrid. Let me comfort you. I know you've been hurt by this news—"

"I'm not hurt," she interrupted. "I'm furious. And if you come any closer, it's possible I'll lose my grip on my emotions and lash out at the nearest convenient target. I know how much you hate it when I get overly emotional, so I'm giving you fair warning."

Paul frowned, but he stopped moving closer. "I don't hate it when you get emotional."

"Please. It embarrasses you, or you're made uncomfortable, or you wish I'd just be calm and rational like you. Mr. Logic." Ingrid smiled, but it didn't reach her eyes. "It's fine. I'm working on it. But it's probably better for everyone if I'm alone right now."

Everything inside Paul rebelled at that idea, but he didn't know how to say that to his wife. Ingrid had always been a full-blown rose, wild and carefree, her petals open to the sun. Now she seemed more like a rosebud, furled tightly closed against him. Paul wavered, unsure what to do, how to reach her.

And then he had an idea. A terrible, amazing, exhilarating idea.

"Okay, I'll give you some space," he finally said. "But we need to have that conversation we told Quinn we'd have. We can't keep putting it off. I'm going out to the garden. Come find me when you're ready."

Without waiting for a reply, Paul strode from the room and made for the stairs, taking them two at a time. He felt more energized than he had in years, since before he retired.

Half an hour later, in the waning light of the afternoon sun, Paul struck a match and watched the new bonfire blaze up from the ashes of last night's charred wood.

"Oh my goodness," breathed his wife from behind him. "What in the world are you doing?"

"Nothing rational or logical, I'll tell you that," Paul replied, feeling giddy. He glanced over his shoulder to where Ingrid hovered outside the stone circle. "And I have to say . . . I'm enjoying it."

Wide-eyed, Ingrid stared at the bonfire where a pile of shiny suits, loudly patterned ties, and bright pocket squares were smoldering merrily. "That's . . . that's all of Ron's clothes. You're burning Ron's clothes."

"Yep." Paul put his hands out toward the fire, enjoying the warmth. "I'd say it's the least he deserves, after what he tried to pull."

"He's going to call the police." Ingrid sounded more awed than worried. "He's going to sue you for destruction of property or something."

Paul scoffed. He might have gone outside his logical, rational comfort zone in an attempt to show his wife how much he cared—but he hadn't had a complete personality transplant in the last half hour. He'd thought it through. "Ron isn't going to call the police. If he threatens to, I'll make it very clear that he'll be facing charges of his own, for practicing psychology without a license, and misrepresenting himself to us."

"Still." Ingrid shook her head as if dazed. "I can't believe you'd take the risk."

"Any risk is worth it, to show you that you're not alone. Ron fooled us both—I didn't think he was a good marriage counselor, but I certainly never suspected him of using our troubles to gain some sort of advantage for a shady real estate deal. No one would expect something like that. It doesn't make you a fool, Ingrid."

She ducked her head, her long, silvery blond hair swinging forward to hide her face. Her hair was more silver than gold, these days, Paul realized with a start. Somehow, it suited her even better. "That's very kind. I appreciate hearing it, but you could've just said that. You didn't need to go to all this trouble."

"I think I did. Somewhere along the way, you stopped hearing me or believing me when I tell you I love you." Paul's throat was dry with nerves, but he swallowed with difficulty and went on. "I had to do something to show you, instead. I know you think I'm an old stick-in-the-mud, and you're not wrong. You've always been the free spirit in this marriage. But I wanted you to know that I can change. I can be more spontaneous. At least, I can work on it. Please don't give up on me. On us."

When Ingrid lifted her face, her eyes were shining

with unshed tears but she was beaming that beautiful sunshine smile at him, and Paul felt his nerves evaporate under that smile like morning dew off the grass.

"You really mean that?" she breathed, stepping forward to clasp his hands between her own smaller ones. "Oh, Paul. You think I don't hear you? I'm so sorry. But sweetheart, if I stopped hearing you at some point, I feel that you stopped seeing me years ago."

Paul wanted to deny it, to protest, but he clamped his jaw shut. They had to get everything out in the open between them, they had to listen to each other. Quinn had been right all along. Ingrid, who'd paused as if bracing for an argument, relaxed slightly and continued.

"The business consumed you for so many years. And I understood that, even if I didn't always like it. The shop was our livelihood, our legacy for Quinn, our future. But I hoped that when you retired, it would get better. Instead . . . it felt even more lonely to spend every moment side by side and still be invisible."

She blinked and the tears in her eyes overflowed to trickle down her cheeks. Paul's heart clenched. "My darling. I never stopped looking at you, I swear it. Retirement has been . . . hard. I can admit that. I think I defined myself by the business for so many years, judging myself and our life by how successful the shop was, that when I didn't have that as a guiding compass any longer, I was completely lost. I am lost. I don't know who I am anymore."

It was a difficult confession to make. Paul's fingers were tense and unmoving in Ingrid's warm grip, and the soft squeeze she gave him was a comfort. But not nearly as comforting as the surety in her voice when she said, "You are Paul Harper. You're Quinn's father. You're my husband and the love of my life. Everything else, we can figure out. Together."

Now it was Paul's turn to feel moisture prickle at the corners of his eyes. "I don't deserve you. I know I've reacted to all this uncertainty by retreating into myself, like a turtle pulling his head into his shell, and that left you on your own. That was unfair, and I'm sorry. I can't promise I'll never react that way again—it's an instinctive defense, I think. But please hear me now when I say that I don't mean to ignore you. Ever. You're the only thing I want to see every single day, the only thing I care about. I could look at you for hours and never get tired. You're more beautiful to me every single day, and I swear I'll devote the rest of my life to making you believe it, if you'll only promise not to leave me. Because I couldn't bear to be without you."

"Oh, Paul," she said brokenly, stumbling forward into his arms. He caught her gladly, bending his head to steal a sweetly familiar kiss from her perfect, trembling mouth. But he had one more thing to say before they left this chapter of their story behind and began writing a new one.

Breaking off the kiss, Paul pulled a checkbook out of his back pocket. It was warm and comforting in his hand, the weight of it like a tether to a time in his life when he'd understood his place in the world and been a productive part of it. For a moment, he wondered if he needed to make this final gesture after everything he and Ingrid had just talked through—but then it occurred to him that the time he remembered so wistfully had still been unhappy for Ingrid, in many ways, and he knew this was the right thing.

"Is that . . . the shop account checkbook?" she asked, confused.

"It is," Paul confirmed, thumbing at the pages one last time before he tossed it onto the fire to burn with Ron's fancy suits. "I don't know why I kept it, except to feel like maybe I still had some small connection to the shop. But I don't. I sold it, and it's time to move on. The only connection I care about is my connection with you, Ingrid. And to prove it, I want you to marry me. Again."

With her entire heart in her eyes, Ingrid took her husband's hand and brought it to her lips. "I would marry you a hundred times over, Paul Harper," she whispered to his palm, never breaking eye contact.

He had to kiss her again, that very second, and she met him eagerly, kiss for kiss. Love, excitement, and relief exploded in Paul's chest. He couldn't believe he'd come so close to losing this, through inattention and complacence. But things would be better from here on out.

Sure, there would be times when they'd fight. Two intelligent, strong-minded individuals in a relationship guaranteed some friction, here and there. But as Paul twirled his wife around and bent her laughing form back over his arm like a tango dancer, he swore to himself that he'd never again take his marriage, or the gorgeous, incomparable life force in his arms, for granted.

Chapter 18

After an early dinner at the Firefly Café, Marcus drove them over to the bar to set up for opening that evening.

"I can drop you at home, if you want," he offered when they pulled out of the Firefly parking lot, but Quinn shook her head.

"My parents really do need some privacy. They've got a lot to work out, but almost for the first time since we started this whole thing, I think they might have a real chance."

Marcus was surprised to realize he agreed. "You never gave up on them. Even when it seemed like nothing you were doing made a difference."

"They're my family." Quinn shrugged helplessly. "You don't turn your back on family."

Something in the region near Marcus's heart went solid and cold, like a block of ice. "That's what makes your family different from mine, I guess."

Quinn bit her lip, but if he'd expected her to leave it alone, he was doomed to disappointment. "We had other things to focus on, so I didn't push. But Marcus, you really need to go over and see what your father has been doing. It might make a difference to how you feel about things."

He tightened his grip on the wheel and took extra care with his speed and the safety of his turns. "If my father is in trouble, tell me straight out. No more dancing around."

"He's not in trouble." Quinn sighed, glancing out the window. "But he's lonely. And he's getting older. And he's the only father you've got."

The only parent you've got left. She didn't say it, but Marcus knew they were both thinking it. The trouble was, whenever he thought of the fact that his mother was gone, it only intensified his desire to never see his father again.

"I know you want to help," he finally said, with some difficulty in getting the words out. They kept wanting to be an angry growl instead of a calm, composed tone. "But it's too late for my dad and me."

"Is it? Or did you move back to Sanctuary Island at least partly because you wanted to reconcile with your father? I mean, Marcus, you could have gone anywhere. I know property is pretty cheap here if you can find a vacancy downtown, so maybe it was just about the money, but there are other inexpensive places to live."

Marcus pressed his lips together. She was persistent, he'd give her that. But she was also easily distracted. "It's not about the money. There's plenty of that, thanks to Buttercup."

As he'd hoped, that got Quinn's attention in a big way. She turned her whole body in the passenger seat until she was facing him, one leg drawn up on the cushion under her. "Oh my gosh. Buttercup gave you money?"

"She made a provision for me in her will," Marcus clarified, remembering the sharp shock and guilt of hearing that will read aloud. "She always told me I was her favorite, and I guess it was true. She left me enough to start the bar . . . to start a new life. I think she knew if and when she died, even if it had been of natural causes, I'd be done with the Secret Service. There are some assignments you never come back from, no matter how they end."

Quinn reached out to lay her hand atop Marcus's on the gear shift. "What an amazing friend she was to you. I'm so sad that I never got to meet her. But I'm so grateful to her for everything she did to push you back toward Sanctuary Island."

Clearing his throat, Marcus blinked away any mistiness as they pulled around to the back of the Buttercup Inn and parked. "Pretty sure opening a bar isn't what she had in mind for me to do."

"Oh, I don't know. She seemed like a lady who could appreciate a stiff drink," Quinn argued as she climbed down from the truck cab. "Didn't she have a bourbon on the rocks in her hand through that entire infamous interview?"

Marcus let out a bark of a laugh, rusty and hoarse, but real. He hadn't been able to laugh at any of his Buttercup memories yet, but that was a good one. "It was soda. Flat. She wanted it for a prop, and to make Barbara Walters feel like she was getting the whole story. But no one ever got the whole story from Colleen. She was too smart, and too skilled at diplomacy. Everybody got exactly the snippet they needed to get, and no more."

"And then she'd tell you all about it in the car on the way home," Quinn guessed.

Marcus let them into the cool, dim interior of the building. "Pretty much. God, what a woman."

"You must have loved her a lot."

There was something odd in Quinn's tone, a wistfulness without jealousy that made Marcus uncomfortably aware that he'd never told Quinn how he felt about her. Not in so many words. "Colleen McCarty changed my life. I'd be an entirely different person if I'd never met her. But she's not the only one who's done that to me."

Quinn dropped her purse on the bar stool at the end of the row, where she usually sat, and gave him a quizzical look. "Oh?"

It took a lot of effort not to roll his eyes like a surly

teenager. "Yeah," he said slowly, looking her up and down.

"Oh . . . oh!" Quinn went bright pink and pleased. Propping her elbows on the bar behind her, she leaned back casually. The pose let Marcus admire the slim, straight line of her body, the lithe muscles of her thighs in those jeans, and the tip-tilted swell of her breasts under her V-neck top. All of a sudden, he was awash in memories of the times they'd made love in this very room while they were fixing the bar up and getting it ready for business. Those older memories were overlaid with vivid sense memories of the night before— the rough, longing sounds Quinn made when he nipped at that certain place on her neck and the coiled strength of her legs closing around his hips and drawing him in.

"We're supposed to open up the bar in half an hour," he said, already reaching for her.

"I guess we'll have to be quick then, won't we?" Quinn murmured. Her smile tasted like strawberries and champagne. Her skin was smooth and hot and as hungry for touch as Marcus was. He could never resist her. He didn't even want to try.

An hour later, Marcus was pulling another pint and working at keeping a straight face when the bar stool they'd used for support was occupied by the crotchety, fussy old Dabney Leeds. The tyrannical head of Sanctuary Island's town council sipped at a small glass of sherry and glared around the bar as if suspicious of so many people in one place having a good time. Although he brightened up a bit when Miss Patty arrived to squeeze onto the bar stool next to his. Sanctuary Island's oldest residents put their heads together and seemed to have a pretty good time of their own, chatting and drinking.

The Buttercup Inn was packed to the rafters. Marcus was cautiously optimistic, when he had a moment to consider it between filling drink orders, washing glasses, and pouring pretzels into bowls.

Quinn whipped past the bar with a grin and a tray in one hand. She'd been pressed into service taking orders almost as soon as she'd come back downstairs after freshening herself up.

"You're a hit," she said gleefully, dropping off the empties from her tray and scooping up a bottle of cabernet and a trio of wine glasses for the table in the corner.

The next time Marcus had a chance to catch his breath and look up, it took him a minute to find Quinn in the crowded bar. She was at the front door with her arms around someone—it was her mother, Marcus saw with some surprise. Ingrid laughed and threw back the shot Quinn offered her, straight off her tray, with a celebratory air.

While Ingrid coughed and wiped her streaming eyes, Quinn hugged her again. Beaming brightly enough to light up the bar, Quinn linked her arms through her parents' elbows and turned to face the room with her mother and father flanking her.

"Can we have your attention for a moment?" Ingrid called, her high, clear voice carrying over the bustle and laughter of the crowd. "We have an announcement to make."

"This is too good a chance to miss," Marcus heard Paul say as the bar quieted down. "It looks like everyone in town is here tonight."

"Just about," Quinn agreed. She was flushed with more than the exertion of running around the bar and chatting with customers. Marcus allowed himself to hope for some good news.

"Get on with it," Dabney Leeds shouted grouchily from his bar stool. "What's so important you need to interrupt our evening?"

But no amount of grumpiness could put a damper on Ingrid's expression. She looked happy enough to float up and fly around the ceiling. "This Saturday, Paul and I will have been married thirty years."

The bar erupted in applause as Paul leaned over Quinn to kiss his wife enthusiastically. When the cheers died down, he took over. "We've decided to renew our vows at a ceremony in our back garden—and you're all invited!"

That got an even bigger explosion of happy cheering and clapping. Some people stamped their feet under their tables, others pounded their empty beer steins on the bar. Even Marcus joined in with the shouting. He could see Quinn's shining eyes from across the bar. She radiated happiness. It was his favorite look on her.

Ingrid, too, appeared almost drunk with joy—or maybe it was that shot of Jack kicking in. Right in the middle of accepting congratulations and good wishes from the people at the tables closest to them, her eyes went huge and she went up onto her tiptoes, her hands fluttering like wings. "Oh! I've just had the most marvelous idea! Quinn, darling—why don't we make it a double ceremony?"

The bar went hushed and quiet as heads jerked back and forth between Marcus and Quinn as if the viewers were at a tennis match. But all of Marcus's focus was on Quinn, who'd gone salt white and stiff.

"Wow, okay. That came out of nowhere!" Quinn tried to laugh, but it came out sounding wrong.

"Not at all," Ingrid said, apparently oblivious to her daughter's sudden nerves. "You're engaged, and no one could say you rushed into it—you've known each other all your lives! It would mean so much to me, at least tell me you'll consider it, sweetheart."

With effort, Marcus kept his face impassive even though he could feel the eyes of his customers searching for some hint of his reaction when Quinn said, "Mother, that's really kind of you. Maybe we could discuss it some other time, in private."

"Nonsense, these people are all our friends!" Still high on life, Ingrid actually did a twirl, her long skirts flying out around her. "They all want to be there to wish you well on your big day!"

Quinn darted an anxious look at Marcus, her eyes pleading for something. He wasn't sure what. He couldn't think clearly.

"Mother," she said sharply. "There isn't going to be a big day!"

Through the static buzzing in his ears, Marcus heard a few gasps. He kept his gaze locked on Quinn, who all of a sudden wouldn't look back at him.

"What do you mean?" Paul asked, a frown line appearing between his eyes.

Her mouth turned down unhappily. "Do we have to get into this right now?"

Ingrid swayed toward her, grabbing onto her daughter's shoulders for balance. "Sweetheart, is something wrong? Are you breaking off your engagement?"

Red splotches appeared on Quinn's white cheeks. "Yes, okay! Yes, the engagement is off. Now can we please get back to talking about your vow renewal?"

That was it. It was over.

Marcus laid down the cloth he'd been wiping the bar with and carefully closed out the cash register. He didn't even raise his voice. He didn't have to. Everyone in the bar was already looking at him.

"Show's over," he said. "Bar's closed. If you haven't settled up yet, your drinks are on me. Now get out."

Horrified, Quinn hurried over to the bar. This was all spinning out of control faster than she could keep up. "Marcus, wait, no, that's not what I meant, it's not what you think . . ."

"No?" Dabney Leeds slid off his bar stool with the help of his cane. "This young man thinks you're dumping him after he went to the trouble of paying for your schooling so you could get the job at the barn. I'd throw your cute little butt out, too."

"Oh, Dabney." Miss Patty, Marcus's older lady friend, clapped her hand over his mouth as if she could put the cat back in the bag. "I told you that in strictest confidence! Catch me ever telling you one of my secrets again."

"A secret is just something you tell one person at a time." Dabney cackled and let himself be led away by an apologetic Miss Patty. Everyone else in the bar slowly followed suit, gathering up their jackets and scarves and heading for the door while Quinn tried to make sense of what was happening.

"Is it true?" she asked Marcus.

He wouldn't even meet her gaze. Just kept tidying up behind the bar as if she meant nothing to him. "You weren't supposed to know."

Shame burned up the back of her throat—or maybe that was acid, because suddenly Quinn thought she might throw up. "So that's what was going on when you broke up with me the first time. You paid for me to have a new start and a new job to salve your conscience when you kicked me to the curb."

"I anticipated the inevitable." Marcus shrugged. "We weren't going to last, so I made sure you had somewhere soft to land, and I let you go. Just like I'm doing this time."

Quinn wanted to pull her hair out. She hadn't been breaking up with Marcus this time! On the contrary, she'd been terrified that being put on the spot and talking about setting a date for their fake wedding—a date that happened to be about four days from now!—

would make Marcus run for the hills. All she'd wanted to do was slow things down a bit, to give them time to be together as a real couple and find out where their relationship was heading.

But as of this moment, she was so angry, she wasn't sure their relationship was heading anywhere at all. "You lied to me. Don't give me any crap about how you just didn't tell me everything—a lie of omission is still a lie. Oh my God, all the time we spent together at the barn, talking about my program, and you never said one word."

"What does it matter now?" Marcus finished counting out the night's take and slammed the drawer shut on the register. "We're through. We both got what we wanted. It's time to end it."

"Sweetheart," her father called softly from the door. Quinn looked around, realizing her parents and she were the only people left in the bar. "Maybe you should come on home with us."

"No. You guys go on without me." Quinn planted her feet. "I'm staying right here and having it out with Marcus."

"Go home, Quinn." He rounded the corner of the bar to flick off the neon beer signs while her parents reluctantly left. "It's over."

"It's not over until you tell me why you never came clean about the money!"

"Screw the money," Marcus growled. "I don't give a crap about the money. I didn't make that donation to insult you, I did it to help you."

Quinn's stomach clenched and lurched. "So I should be grateful? You think old man Leeds is right, I owe you something now? Because I never asked for your help! I wanted to make it on my own, Marcus, and you knew that. You, of all people."

"Damn it, Quinn, don't be an idiot." Marcus's eyes blazed in his still, grim face. "Of course you don't owe me anything. We're square. Which means I don't owe you anything, either—including, I don't owe you the chance to tear a strip off me in my own damn bar."

She lifted her chin, swallowing hard to stave off the tears that threatened to burst free in an angry sob. "Tough, because I'm not leaving."

His mouth worked silently for a long moment before he grabbed his leather jacket off the peg by the door and said, "Fine. If you won't leave, I will."

Frustrated and furious, she spat, "If you leave now, don't expect me to stick around, waiting for you to come back."

Marcus paused at the door. Without turning around, he said, "I never expected you to stick around, Quinn. And see? I was right."

With that, he stalked out and slammed the door behind him, leaving Quinn alone in the dark, empty bar.

Chapter 19

Despite her angry threats, Quinn waited at the Buttercup Inn for hours. Tired down to her bones, aching with unspent emotion, she halfheartedly tidied up before going upstairs and using her old key to get into the room she'd rented across from Marcus's apartment.

She curled up by the window and sat there, staring out at the alleyway, all night long.

But Marcus never came back.

When dawn broke, gray and misty with the onset of a spring storm, Quinn slowly picked herself up off the window seat. She felt old and stiff, her body cramped from spending too long in one position. Before she turned away, she caught a glimpse of her hazy reflection in the glass of the window. Her hair was a mess, her face a pale oval with dark smudges for eyes.

She looked exactly how she felt . . . like the ghost of herself.

The ghost of a woman who had tasted happiness for the briefest of moments, and lost it almost as quickly as she found it.

Shaking her head to clear the morose thoughts, Quinn dragged herself down the stairs and out to her car, still parked next to Marcus's truck in the back alley. The whole drive to her parents' house, she was conscious of a tiny, flickering flame of very foolish hope that she'd find him there.

But of course when she pulled up and ran inside, all she found were her parents necking on the sofa like a couple of teenagers.

"You guys," she said, covering her eyes with her hand. "Get a room! You have one right upstairs, in fact!"

Her parents didn't spring apart like they'd been caught doing something naughty. In fact, going by the sounds, they exchanged one last, lingering kiss before Ingrid said, "Oh, sweetheart, you're home. Are you all right? We were worried about you."

Quinn dropped her hand and arched a brow. "Yes. I can see you've been up all night . . . worrying about me."

Coloring delicately, Ingrid said, "What did you want us to do? Follow you around wringing our hands? Call you and demand you come home because you missed your curfew? You're a grown woman, Quinn. You have every right to stay out all night, and to make your own decisions. Like calling off your engagement in public, in front of the entire town."

Quinn flinched at the mild disapproval in her mother's tone. "I didn't mean to. You put us on the spot, and I panicked. And then Marcus got the wrong idea and then I got mad and made things worse . . ."

"I'm going to make some breakfast," her father said, standing up. "How do cornmeal waffles sound? Quinn, you sit here and tell your mother all about it."

"Wait, first I want to know—where's Guru Ron?"

Her parents exchanged a speaking glance before her mother said primly, "We asked him to leave, and he did. He made a bit of a fuss, but we were firm. I think we've seen the last of Ron Burkey, Relationship Expert."

"Then I guess it was all worth it," Quinn said, with a shuddering breath.

Ingrid's face went soft and worried. "Oh, my darling. Come here."

As Quinn sank onto the couch and let her mother enfold her in those graceful, patchouli-scented arms, she took a moment to be so, so thankful that she had her parents back and happy. Without these people in her life, in her corner, and in her heart, Quinn didn't know what she'd do.

Which made her think of Marcus, who was so alone, it made her throat close up. His mother and his mother figure, both gone. No relationship with his father. Who did Marcus have to comfort him, when his whole world fell apart? She'd hoped she could be that person for him, someday.

Now, as she dropped her head onto her mother's shoulder and finally let the tears come, Quinn couldn't imagine how she'd ever been so stupid as to think Marcus Beckett would ever need her the way she needed him.

When Marcus grabbed his jacket and escaped the Buttercup Inn and the wreckage of his relationship with Quinn, he hadn't had a clear plan in mind. With his hands in his pockets and his head down against the wind, he'd walked for hours in the dark, following Sanctuary's winding one-lane roads and skirting the shoreline.

There were no stars, no moonlight to guide his steps, but it didn't matter. Marcus didn't have a desti-nation. He didn't care where he ended up.

Until he found himself at the familiar turnoff for Lantern Point.

He almost kept walking. There was nothing for him down that road. But stopping, even for a moment, had forced him to confront the fact that he was literally going nowhere. And though the sky was still as dark as midnight, a glance at his watch told him the sun would be up in an hour. He needed a place to stop and gather his thoughts, make a plan. But he couldn't stand to see Quinn again, not yet. He needed a place she'd never think to look for him.

He stared down the road, glad it was too dark out to see much of the tidy little house at the very end of the lane, where Quinn was no doubt sleeping peacefully. He could have been there at her side, if he wasn't so messed up. And whose fault was that?

Inexorably drawn, Marcus turned his focus onto the ramshackle place where he grew up. The way the shutters hung at angles and the paint peeled in ugly strips from the porch railing made Marcus's stomach knot.

His mother had loved this house. He couldn't believe his father had let it fall to ruin like this.

Actually, he could believe it, he reflected grimly as he strode up to the doorstep and contemplated whether to knock or simply walk in. His father had never cared about what happened at home, with his family. Dr. William Beckett had been an important surgeon, too busy saving lives to spend time with his kid.

He'd been too busy to make time to call his kid to come home in time to say good-bye to his dying mother. He'd started Marcus on this path, years ago, and until Marcus confronted him, he'd never be able to chart a new course.

Marcus's hand curled into a fist and rapped loudly on the door.

For a long moment, there was only silence from inside the house. Then, with a loud creak, the door opened a crack.

"Marcus?" said his father's voice, rough with disuse. "Is that you?"

The gap widened and Marcus faced his father for

the first time since the day of his mother's funeral. Dr. William Beckett looked . . . old.

Well, of course he did. It had been years, and from the state of the house, they seemed to have been hard years. But somehow, Marcus hadn't expected the stooped shoulders and the wispy, wild shock of gray hair. He also hadn't expected the sharp, completely aware and intelligent glint in his father's heavy-lidded eyes.

"Hello, Dad." Marcus fought the urge to stand at parade rest. This man wasn't his commanding officer. He was barely Marcus's father. "I have some things to say to you."

"I didn't expect you to come see me," his father said thoughtfully. The hungry, avid way he stared made Marcus almost uncomfortable.

He wasn't about to apologize for how long it had taken him to show up on his father's porch. "Well, I'm here now. Are you going to let me in?"

The dad Marcus remembered would have glowered at that tone. But the older version only blinked and pushed the door wider to invite Marcus into the house.

"No luggage?" Will asked mildly.

"I'm not staying long."

"Where's that nice neighbor girl? Quinn? She said you were staying with her."

"That's over." Marcus made sure his tone conveyed how final it was. "And it's not what I'm here to talk about, so lay off."

His father's eyes flickered with interest, but he didn't

comment. Instead, he gestured up the dim staircase. "You remember where your bedroom is. It's late. We can talk in the morning, if you want to get some sleep."

Marcus knew he should be tired. And on some level, he was—exhausted right down to his bones. But he was grimly certain that if he lay down and closed his eyes, he'd do nothing but replay every moment he'd spent with Quinn on endless repeat. He couldn't take that yet.

He'd put off this showdown with his father for long enough.

"I'm fine." As he steeled himself to tear into his father, Marcus's gaze caught on a photo of his mother propped atop the entryway table. He swallowed, imagining her soft, disappointed voice saying she'd raised him better than this. It made him waver as nothing else could have. "You go on up, if you want to catch a few more hours."

"I don't sleep much." Will shrugged, still staring at Marcus as if he thought his son might disappear at any moment. "I have some work to do, actually. If you're not ready to talk."

Marcus's lip wanted to curl. "Of course you do," he said harshly. "Don't worry, I'll be fine without you. I always was."

"Oh," Will replied quietly. "I was going to ask if you wanted to see what I'm working on, but you don't need to feel obligated."

Guilt prickled at Marcus, and he hated it. This confrontation wasn't going the way he'd imagined it. "You don't need to entertain me. This isn't a social call."

"You said you wanted to talk . . ."

"Well, maybe I changed my mind," Marcus said, too loudly.

Damn it. I can't do this.

"I should go. Leave you to your work."

His father seemed to shrink a little before his very eyes. "Okay. If you want to. But I wish you'd stay."

Marcus gritted his teeth down on the words "You can't make me." He'd made that point a long time ago, when he was barely more than a kid. He was an adult now. He didn't have to lash out, just because being back in this house made him feel as out of control as that kid had been.

Besides. Maybe the sight of his father, old and stooped and thinner than he remembered, had taken the edge off Marcus's righteous anger. But that didn't mean he had to ditch the man so soon. Marcus was tired of walking aimlessly, trying to outpace his own grim thoughts. He needed a place to rest, and this was as good a place as any.

"Fine," he finally said, "I'll stay. For a while."

The sheer joy that brightened his father's eyes took Marcus aback. "Wonderful, wonderful. I have something to show you. I've been waiting to show you . . ."

Rubbing his hands in happy anticipation, Dr. William Beckett faded quietly down the hall toward the nook, a glassed-in porch off the kitchen where Marcus's mother had spent much of her time.

Quinn had been right, Marcus found as he followed his father slowly through the downstairs rooms. The striped wallpaper in the dining room was peeling at the corners. The air in the living room felt stale, as if it were hardly ever disturbed by anyone walking through it, but it wasn't obviously dusty or dirty.

Marcus lingered over the photos arranged on top of the closed upright piano his mother used to play carols on at Christmas. In the cluster of pictures of his mother, by herself and smiling, holding a serious-faced baby Marcus, with her arm around her much taller high-school-graduate son, there were a number of empty frames.

Frowning, Marcus picked up a filigreed silver frame and tried to remember what photo used to fill it. But he couldn't. All he could do was stare at the images of his mother, captured moments in time, and let grief seep into his heart.

It was an old grief, worn around the edges like a well-read book. Less intense, in some ways, than his fresh, spiky grief over Buttercup's senseless death. But this was his mother, the woman who gave him life and taught him everything he knew about what it meant to be a good person in the world. About how to love.

And he couldn't help worrying, along with the deep and ever-present sadness of missing her, that she wouldn't be any too impressed with how he was acting. Either with Quinn or with his father.

"I know, Mama," he murmured, reaching out a fingertip to touch the bloom of her cheek beneath the glass. "I'm trying. But it's harder than I thought it would be, this life stuff. I wish you were here."

"I say that to her at least twice a day," said his father from behind him.

Startled and angry at being observed, Marcus bumped the piano with his hip when he turned, and some of the frames fell over. Cursing, he bent to pick them up.

"Sorry," Will apologized, taking a step into the room but then pausing to hover on the threshold. "I just came to ask if you'd drink some coffee. I was going to make it anyway."

"I don't want any coffee," Marcus snarled.

"I know. You want your mother back," Will said, voice shaking. "I want that too, son. But she's gone."

Marcus exploded to his feet, all the anger that had propelled him down the lane and into this house burning to life in his chest. "I know she's gone. I've known since you called me up at college and told me she was dead, and I'd missed it. Missed my chance to see her one last time, to say good-bye, to tell her I loved her . . . you robbed me of that memory."

"And you'll never forgive me for it." Will nodded, resigned. "I understand. I don't blame you."

Breath coming fast and furious, Marcus clenched and released his fists. "You never even said you were sorry."

For the first time, Will looked surprised. "Because I'm not sorry."

That was it. Flames. But before Marcus could deto-
nate and blow his father, this house, this entire island
to smithereens, his dad went on.

"It was what your mother wanted. She made me
swear not to call you home. I carried out her last wish,
even knowing you'd hate me for it, and I can't regret
that choice."

Marcus's legs shook, his knees going watery. He sat
down on the piano bench with a thud. "Mama wanted
me to stay away."

"She wanted you to finish your exams," Will explained. "It was all she could talk about, in those final
days. Her son, the doctor. Imagining your future enabled her to let go of her own."

Marcus wanted to deny it, to argue and rage and tell
his father he was wrong. But through the dim clouds
of memory, a moment surfaced where a little girl on a
bike told him something very similar mere moments
after he'd shouted at his father that he never wanted to
see him again. As much as Marcus didn't want to believe it now, he hadn't been ready to hear it then at all.

"It was still wrong," he rasped. "I should have been
here."

"I agree," Will surprised him by saying. "And I am
sorry for the way it hurt you, not to be here. That's not
what your mother or I wanted."

Complicated feelings cascaded through Marcus, re-
arranging everything he thought he knew about his
family. His past. His life. "Mama wouldn't have wanted

me to fight with you after her funeral, either. And she definitely wouldn't have wanted me to storm off and join the army instead of becoming a doctor."

Will looked away. "Maybe not. But she wanted you to be happy more than anything else. Are you happy, son?"

The question threw Marcus off balance. "Happiness is for children. Or people who don't know how fragile life is. I'm not sure it's meant for people like me."

Sinking down into an armchair, Will bowed his head over his knees. "You sound so much like me after a bad day at the hospital. After losing a patient at the end of a ten-hour surgery or fighting with insurance companies for the chance to try a lifesaving operation. I know I wasn't much fun to be around, on those days. I know I wasn't much of a father to you."

Marcus felt like he was supposed to deny it, to tell his father he'd been great, but the words stuck in his throat. And as he stared at the remote figure who'd been so distant and untouchable for most of his childhood, he didn't believe his father expected a denial. "I had Mama," Marcus said hoarsely. "She made up for a lot."

A slight smile creased Will's cheeks. "Your mother was the ultimate proof that happiness exists, and it's meant for everyone. I could come home at the end of one of those days and look into her eyes, and I knew happiness was real. And it was right there, for me."

"I miss her all the time," Marcus said, the words

falling out of his mouth like they'd been dying to escape. "It's been how many years? And part of me still expects to be able to pick up the phone and call her."

"Sometimes I get mad about it," Will said, with a broken laugh. "She's been gone too long. It's time for her to come home. But she is home. We're the ones who still have a ways to go. Longer for you than for me, I hope."

Marcus felt a thread of connection wind around his heart and extend to wrap around his father, pulling taut and strong between them. "Christmas is hard. And my birthday."

"She had a way of making those days special."

"It's dumb. I'm a grown man, not a little kid."

"Everyone is a little kid when they're missing their mother," his father said matter-of-factly. "I miss her most in the mornings, the early hours we spent together with coffee and the newspaper and making plans for the day."

This was exactly the conversation they should have had at the funeral, Marcus was realizing. Years late, but better late than never. Every word lanced a wound he hadn't realized was still infected. "I miss her most at night. Right before I turn out the light. I always get the urge to beg for one more story."

His mother had been a wonderful natural storyteller, insightful about people and what made them tick, with an instinctive grasp on the kinds of things that made stories magical for kids. Her stories were full of dinosaurs and dragons, moon landings and ancient cursed pyramids, and dogs who talked and solved crimes. Marcus had told her for years that she ought to write them down and try to turn them into books, but she'd always laughed him off.

A strange expression had come over his father's face. "I'm retired," he said out of nowhere.

"I heard," Marcus said shortly, not seeing the connection and not quite ready to stop talking about Mama.

His father fidgeted a bit with the untucked hem of his slightly wrinkled button-down shirt. "I meant . . . did Quinn tell you what I'm doing with myself these days?"

"She was mysterious about it," Marcus admitted, suddenly curious despite himself.

"Come with me," his dad said, rushing from the room.

Marcus followed more slowly, his mind racing. He felt as if he'd been sipping a cup of poison, every day another sip for years and years, and he'd finally managed to put it aside. His vision was still clouded with the residue of a decade of resentment, but it was clearing.

It wasn't only that Marcus had resented being kept away from his mother's deathbed. He'd blamed his father for his mother's death, on some deep, irrational level. It wasn't fair. She'd had cancer; she'd decided when she no longer wanted to pursue treatment. She'd made the choice to go home to die. At the time, Marcus had wanted his mother to fight to live, but with the benefit of age and experience, he understood better how tired of hospitals she must have been, how point-less another round of painful, unsuccessful treatments would have seemed. And how much she longed to spend what time she had left in a place that she loved.

It wasn't fair to blame his father for any of that. He couldn't quite blame his father for carrying out his mother's last wishes, either. Maybe it was time to for-give his father and move on.

He couldn't imagine they'd ever be close, but there didn't have to be an ocean of pain, regret, and anger between them, either.

Marcus tracked his father through the kitchen to the nook, where the old, wooden table they'd used to eat breakfast at was covered in paper. Large pages filled with pencil-scratched writing were spread across the scarred surface, mingling with line drawings shaded gray and rolling up at the edges.

Will had dragged the lamp down from their bed-room, Marcus saw, to cast its buttery yellow light over the table. And instead of the ladder-back dining chairs they used to sit in, there was a cushy armchair piled high with extra pillows. This was clearly where his father spent most of his time. But doing what? Marcus still didn't get it.

Chapter 20

"What is all this stuff?" Marcus asked.

Will shuffled through the papers eagerly. "My work! You could call it a retirement project, I suppose, but really, I think it's the most important work I've ever done."

Marcus, who'd never imagined his father caring more about anything than he did about being a surgeon, felt his jaw drop open in shock. Clamping it shut again, he held out his hand to receive the paper his father wanted to show him.

It was a story, he realized with a sense of wonder. A story that tugged at the softest and sweetest of Marcus's memories. There was the dog, Mr. Meander, *yes, of course*, confronting a suspicious-looking young bird about the theft of a dinosaur fossil from the Natural History Museum.

"I remember this one," he said slowly, his eyes scanning to the end of the page. "It turns out there's a witch who brought the dinosaur back to life, so he stole his own bones."

"Because he needed them," Will agreed, smiling broadly. "And really, they belonged to him already, when you think about it."

Against his will, Marcus felt the corners of his mouth stretching into a smile. He didn't know why, since his eyes and nose were burning with tears at the same time, but the urge to smile won out.

"You're writing down Mama's stories?"

Will sat down in his chair and pulled another pile of papers closer to him. He ran his fingers over the pages lovingly. "I can almost hear her voice in my ear, sometimes. The way she'd do the different voices for the characters to make you laugh."

"I didn't know you ever heard us," Marcus said blankly, staring down at a drawing of the intrepid Mr. Meander's furry, bearded face and expressive eyebrows. "I thought you were always reading medical journals in your room."

"Sometimes. But a lot of the time, I sat outside your room and waited for your mother to kiss you goodnight."

"Why didn't you come in?" Marcus's voice broke at the end, but he didn't even care.

"You and your mother—what you had was so special." There was a wistfulness to his father's smile, but a sort of pride, too. "You were everything to her, Marcus. And vice versa. I was happy to live on the edges of that. Just to hear you whispering together, and laughing—that was enough for me."

The fault line down the middle of Marcus's chest cracked open. "Dad."

"But then she was gone," his father continued, still staring down at the clever, quick drawings that somehow perfectly evoked the characters as Marcus had always imagined them. "And I didn't know how to talk to you. I didn't know how to be the one who made you laugh, who held you and comforted you. And I'm sorry for that, son."

Marcus dropped the pages on the table and went to stand next to his father's chair. He looked down at the man whose absence had colored every memory from his childhood. His father was smaller than he ever realized.

Will Beckett was his father. But he was also a man, a man who had expected a long life with the woman he loved, and who'd had to say good-bye to her much too soon. He was a man who hadn't always known how to be a father—but looking at the drawings and stories Will had so laboriously created, Marcus realized that his father was a man who knew how to love.

"Dad, I forgive you. And I hope you can forgive me, for lashing out at you, for staying away for so long, for never even trying to understand what you were going through."

"My boy." Will blinked up at him, his cheeks damp and his hair a mess. "You're my son. If I had never seen you again in this life, I would still have loved you every day. Every minute."

Marcus crumpled down to hug him tight, painfully aware of the brittleness of his father's bones.

Maybe he still had a few things to learn from his old man, after all.

So Marcus spent the next couple of days trying to do just that. He found out how his father had coped with his mother's death—mainly by burying himself in work until he had a cardiac episode that scared him into stopping. And by then, he'd removed himself so completely from the social life of Sanctuary Island that even when he retired, it was hard to get back into the habit of seeing other people. It became easier to close his door and retreat to his nest . . . retreat into his memories.

It worried Marcus, because being completely on his own wasn't good for his dad. He didn't need medical training to see that. But on a deeper level, it freaked Marcus out because he could envision himself reacting exactly the same way. It had always been one of Marcus's deepest fears—that he might be more like his father than he wanted to admit. Like father, like son. And the more he got to know the man his father had become, the more Marcus had to admit the truth of that old adage. He and his father were a lot alike.

One area where they were not in sync? Will Beckett had turned into a man who loved asking personal questions. That would be a reason for Marcus to dislike his father's total isolation, if nothing else.

"Tell me again why you aren't staying with that sweet Quinn girl?" Dad asked while bent over the sketch he was working on.

Marcus listened to the fast, fluid strokes of his father's pencil while he scrambled eggs and popped some bread in the toaster.

"Because we broke up," he explained, as patiently as he could manage, given the rawness of the wound. "It's over. She doesn't want to see me anymore."

"Did she say that? Because I got the impression when she visited me that she liked being around you. Quite a bit."

How to explain to this man who had loved one person in his life, so entirely that he felt as married to her now when she was long dead as he had when she was alive—how could Marcus tell his father that sometimes love wasn't enough? Sometimes people were too far apart, too different, to make it work.

"Quinn has her whole life ahead of her," he finally said, scraping the eggs onto a pair of plates. "I know she had feelings for me, an infatuation, but she came to her senses and she's better off."

"I don't believe that." His father blinked up at him reproachfully as he approached the kitchen table. "No one could be better off without you."

Castigating himself for the years he'd wasted being pointlessly angry at his father did no one any good. But Marcus couldn't help wishing he'd gotten his head out of his ass earlier. It wasn't easy to ignore the role Quinn had tried to play in this reconciliation, but he managed it.

"Thanks, Dad. But it's more complicated than that."

"More complicated than you wanting to be with her and her wanting to be with you?" Dad accepted his eggs, and Marcus could feel his questioning gaze on his back when he went to get the toast.

"Yes," Marcus said, aware that he sounded stubborn but unwilling to soften the blow. He couldn't take too many more versions of this same conversation without cracking. "In fact, I'm thinking about taking a break from Sanctuary Island for a while."

"What do you mean?"

Marcus shrugged, setting down the plate piled with golden-brown toast. "I could close the Buttercup Inn for a while, and we could take a trip. You and me. Maybe someplace you went with Mama. Would you like that?"

"No!"

Surprised and a little hurt, Marcus looked up from buttering his toast to see his father wince and wave his hands. "No, I mean, yes, I would like to spend time with you. I don't care where, here or somewhere else, it makes no difference to me. But you can't run away from Sanctuary Island now!"

"It's not running away," Marcus snapped, although maybe it was, a little. So he didn't want to be around to see it when Quinn moved on and found someone more age-appropriate to lavish her smiles and kisses on. That didn't make Marcus a coward, it made him smart enough to be aware of what he could and couldn't handle.

"Look, son." Dad scraped his fork through his eggs, moving them around on the plate without eating them. "It's been a long time since we sat at this table, talking this way. Maybe we never did, when your mom was alive, because she was there to be the linchpin of our family. But you're all the family I have left, now, and I'm all you've got, too. So maybe it's a bad idea for me to rock the boat. Maybe I risk sending you out of here, mad as hell and not wanting to talk to me for another ten years. I'd hate that, but I have to take the chance. Because, Marcus, my boy. You're making a mistake."

The food in his mouth turned to sawdust. Marcus hadn't heard this solemn tone from his father in more than a decade—since the phone call that informed him his mother was gone. That tone made him want to get up from the table and head for the door, as fast as his legs would take him.

But the sorrow and determination on his father's face kept Marcus in his chair.

"Dad, I want to build a relationship with you," he said, attempting to halt this runaway train before it crushed them both. "But I don't want to talk about this. My love life is off-limits."

"I'm not talking about your love life," Dad argued. "Where you take some date for dinner or whether you've kissed yet. This is your *life* I'm talking about.

You can't separate the love out of this equation and still have a life."

"I don't even know what that means."

Dad dropped his fork with an impatient clatter. "It means . . . look. You wanted to be there when your mother was dying. You wanted to be around not only for the good parts of her life, but the hard parts, too. That's love."

"Yeah, but I wasn't there." Marcus felt his throat close.

"Only because I prevented it. That was my fault, not yours. You were brave enough for love, back then. Your mother taught you that. I don't know what's happened in your life since then, but it was something that made you afraid. Of love. The hard parts, and the good parts, too. But I know you're strong enough to face it all, to let it all in. I want that for you, Marcus. Very badly. And your mother would have wanted it, too."

Marcus pushed back from the kitchen table so quickly, his chair skidded across the floor with a loud noise. He gathered up his still full plate without even looking at it and carried it over to the sink.

He needed to move, he couldn't just sit there and listen to that garbage.

"You want to know what happened to me?" Marcus flipped on the hot water and grabbed the dish soap. "I grew up. I stopped expecting love to mean anything except pain. I learned that some people are bad at being there in the ways that matter, when it counts, and I'm one of those people."

"Marcus, that simply isn't true."

Infuriated, Marcus scrubbed harder at the plate with the sponge, as if he were trying to take off the enamel. "It is true, Dad. You don't know anything about me. But you, of all people, you know that the worst part is . . . when you love someone, they leave. The people you love leave. And it sucks."

His mother, Buttercup, now Quinn. All gone.

Except. His hands stilled in the soapy water, the plate slipping through his fingers to clink gently against the bottom of the sink. He knew what his father was going to say before the man even opened his mouth.

"Except you're the one who's leaving this time. Aren't you? Not Quinn."

The truth blazed down over Marcus like a searchlight, leaving him nowhere to run and nowhere to hide. He braced his hands on the edge of the sink and hung his head, trying to catch his breath. It was like sucking oxygen after a body blow.

A tentative hand touched his back, settling between his shoulder blades. Paradoxically, the solid weight of it seemed to lift some of the pressure from his chest.

"People do leave," Dad said quietly. "But that's why you have to grab onto love with both hands. Because life is uncertain. Happiness isn't so common that you can afford to let it go without a fight."

"But . . . I've pushed Quinn away so many times," Marcus realized, his stomach roiling with tension. "She'll never be willing to take a chance on me again."

"I don't know her well," Dad said thoughtfully, "but she doesn't strike me as the type who's afraid to take a chance. Maybe she'll surprise you. Maybe you'll surprise each other."

Marcus straightened, determination filling him. This might not work, but Dad was right, he needed to fight. And if he failed, he'd go down swinging.

"Maybe what I need . . . is a plan."

Quinn woke on the morning of her parents' vow-renewal ceremony and stared up at the ceiling of her girlhood bedroom.

She felt flattened. By life, by the weight of her own dashed hopes and dreams. By her own melodrama.

It seemed ridiculous to be heartbroken over a man who had clearly never been very serious about her. Looking back, Quinn couldn't believe she'd let herself get in so deep, when you only had to glance at Marcus Beckett to see the NO TRESPASSING signs posted all over him. The serious ones that said things like BEWARE OF DOG and TRESPASSERS WILL BE SHOT and NO, SERIOUSLY, QUINN, KEEP OUT.

But she couldn't deny it, even to herself. Her heart was in a million sharp, jagged pieces, and she wasn't sure how she was ever going to put it back together again on her own.

The knock on her door reminded her that she wasn't on her own, not entirely, and today wasn't about her broken heart. It was going to be a celebration of enduring love, which lasted through the years, bridged all distance, healed all pain, and made unicorns fly on rainbow wings through starry, cloudless skies. Or whatever.

Mentally slapping herself, Quinn hauled her butt out of bed and opened her door to peer out at her mother's radiant face.

"I'm up!"

"About time," Ingrid scolded breathlessly, her smile never fading. "I'm ready to start getting dressed and I want your help with my hair."

Quinn, who never did anything more complicated than a braid with her own hair, wasn't sure how much help she could be. But again, it wasn't about her. And looking at her mother's sparkling eyes and excitement-flushed cheeks, Quinn had no trouble working up a smile of her own.

"I'll do my best," she promised. "Just let me throw on my dress and I'll come straight to your room. Or should I wait until the last minute to get changed? I'd hate for anything to happen to the dress while I'm setting up chairs in the garden or whatever last-minute things are bound to come up."

"You don't need to do any heavy lifting! We hired the Hackley boys to do all that." Ingrid reached out and clasped her daughter's hand between both of her own. "I want you to enjoy yourself today, as much as you can."

Quinn bit her lip. "I'm sorry if I've been carrying

around my own personal raincloud, the last few days. I promise, I'll come out from under it soon. It's just taking a little time."

"Of course it is! You don't need to apologize to me," her mother said sincerely. "Breaking off your engagement and your relationship, your ex-fiancé disappearing before you can get anything settled or even say good-bye properly—of course you're in a funk. It's only natural, and when I see Marcus Beckett again, I intend to slap him silly for making you suffer like this."

Quinn laughed, the sound as bitter as lemon rind on the back of her tongue. "Don't worry, you won't be seeing Marcus again."

Her mother's hands squeezed supportively. "Oh, sweetheart. Really? You think Marcus is gone for good?"

It was hard to talk about it when the words wanted to stick in her throat, but Quinn forced them out. "I think he's gone. For better or worse. But honestly, I'm not sure he ever believed we had a future at all, and if that's true . . . then it *is* good that he's gone. If you and Daddy have taught me anything, it's that both partners in a relationship need to believe the relationship is worth saving."

Ingrid was quiet for a long moment, her gaze searching. "Well. Sweetheart. I don't claim to be a quote unquote relationship expert, like some. But I'm not sure I agree with you."

"What? Really?"

"Maybe it depends on the relationship," Ingrid said

slowly. "Not every single one works the same way. But when you're talking about an extended relationship, over many years . . . well, the truth is that you and your partner won't always be on the same page. Sometimes you may not even be reading from the same book! Marriage is long, or at least you hope it is when you start out. And I think the ones that last—the lucky ones!—are the ones where even in the out-of-sync times, at least one of the spouses believes in the relationship strongly enough to hold on . . . until the other spouse can find his or her place in the story again."

"That sounds hard," Quinn whispered, her fingers curled in her mother's gentle grasp.

"Well, frankly, it is. Marriage isn't a recipe for an easy life." Ingrid reached out to cup Quinn's cheek in her palm. "I would've thought that's what your father and I taught you, if nothing else."

Heart swelling until it pressed at her rib cage, Quinn struggled to hold back tears. "Then why do people do it, if it's so hard? Wouldn't it be easier to be alone and free? Wouldn't that keep your heart safe?"

Ingrid looked thoughtful. "Marriage certainly isn't the only path to happiness. Plenty of people are happy being alone and free, although I think if your motivation for staying single is to never be hurt, that might not be the healthiest way to live. Or the smartest—everyone gets hurt, sometimes. But when you find the right person, the person you want to hold on to even when everything is falling apart around you—then getting married is a way to show your commitment, to that person and to the world. If I got to *choose* what you learned from your father and me, it would be this: that marriage is hard work, but when it's the right person, it's worth it."

"But what if you find the person you want to hold onto . . . and they let you go at the first sign of trouble?"

"Oh, my dearest girl." Ingrid's eyes filled with the tears Quinn wouldn't allow to fall. "I wish that Marcus had held strong, no matter what. I want that for you, of course. But sweetheart, you did break off the engagement. Is it possible he thought you were the one letting go?"

Frustrated, Quinn pressed her lips together. She wanted to tell her mother about the fake engagement but the words wouldn't come. Quinn didn't know what difference it could make now—as Marcus had pointed out, they'd both gotten what they wanted from the charade. But this was almost the first deep, open conversation she'd ever had with her mother. Quinn had always been a bit of a daddy's girl, and that tendency had turned into a habit that had turned into the way things were in their family.

But these past few weeks had shown Quinn a new side of her mother. Or, to be more accurate, Ingrid hadn't changed—but Quinn had learned to see her mother in a new way. She'd found that her vague, easily distracted mother could focus like a laser when it was important.

And Quinn had learned that she was very important to her mother.

Even so, Quinn felt too shaky at the moment to test the limits of her fragile, new connection with her mother. Besides, what could she say? Even if the engagement hadn't been real, the breakup definitely was, and Ingrid was right. Quinn had started it. From her mother's perspective, Quinn could see how it looked.

"Mother," she said with difficulty. "I know it's taken me a long time to . . . well, to grow up, sort of."

"Growing up is overrated. That's a phrase people use when they want to stifle your spirit and squash your free, creative impulses."

Quinn grinned. "Thanks, but that's not what I mean. I'm talking about the fact that I've never been in a serious relationship before Marcus."

"That doesn't mean you aren't serious about Marcus," Ingrid protested.

"I know, but it *does* mean I don't have much to compare it to. Maybe he's right," Quinn worried, smile fading. "Maybe I'm not mature enough to settle down. Maybe I'd only screw it up. It's not like I've had any practice."

"There are never any guarantees that you won't screw it up—either of you! If that's what Marcus is waiting for, or what you're waiting for, it's going to be a very long wait, my darling. But if you're not sure of your feelings . . ." Ingrid studied her face, and Quinn wondered what she saw there. "Well, dear. Only you can decide if your feelings are real. Now come on. Those rosebuds aren't going to weave themselves through my hair."

Quinn returned her mother's hug and followed her down the hall. But all through brushing out her mother's long silver-blond hair and laughing over how to fix the flowers to it without resorting to Super Glue, Quinn wondered.

Could a relationship that started as a fake have a real future?

Chapter 21

Paul Harper gazed out over the backyard that he and his wife had made beautiful with their own two hands. He stood in the shadow of the henge they'd built, surrounded by the stones that were supposed to smash their marriage to dust, but instead had lifted them up to a new place. A stronger place. Together.

That was pretty good, he thought. He'd have to remember to tell Ingrid that bit later, about the stones lifting them up. She'd like that.

If he weren't standing here in front of all their friends and neighbors, he might take out his pencil and add that line to the vows he'd written. But it was too late for that, he reflected with satisfaction. The music was starting, the throbbing strings of a quartet of acoustic guitars wafting over the spring garden.

The whole town had turned out, it seemed like.

Standing room only, people were clustered around and throughout the winding garden pathways, some perched on folding chairs, some sitting on blankets they'd brought along to spread on the grass. So many people, Paul couldn't really register them all—they were a bright blur of happy faces among the flowers.

Daffodils bobbed their white and yellow heads while the wild cherry and plum trees bordering the yard released a shower of pink petals to float over Quinn and Ingrid as they stepped out of the house and started the long walk down the center aisle. Paul's heart seized with a quick spasm of love. Quinn looked so beautiful in that lavender dress with the soft, flowy skirt rippling in the breeze and her red-gold hair waving around her shoulders.

She held out her arm to her mother, to walk her down the aisle, and Paul finally let his gaze fall on the woman he loved. Ingrid was a vision in royal purple, as bright and vivid as her personality . . . but no match for the dazzling brilliance of her smile.

She was happy. He'd made this incredible, endlessly fascinating and complicated woman happy.

Chest swelling with pride and pleasure, Paul kept his head up and his gaze steady as he watched his wife and daughter's progress down the aisle. When they reached him, Ingrid and Quinn hugged, then Quinn stepped up and kissed her father on the cheek before taking her mother's bouquet in hand and moving to stand behind them, looking out over the assembled guests.

They'd talked about keeping Quinn with them as part of the renewal vows and the rededication of their family as a loving unit, but Quinn had insisted that this moment wasn't about her. It was about them, the years they'd spent as husband and wife, and the years they hoped were yet to come. Quinn was a part of it, she'd said, but she wasn't all of it.

And though Paul had come up with a way to include her as much as possible, he thought now that his daughter was wise beyond her years. She'd understood more than Paul had—in this moment, as heart-glad as he was to have his beloved daughter nearby, all he wanted was to take his wife's hands and gaze down into her eyes as if they were the only two people on earth.

"You're here," Paul said, softly enough that only Ingrid could hear him.

"There's nowhere else I'd rather be," she assured him. Her luminous smile was both familiar and new, like coming home after a long, long journey.

"Friends and neighbors and loved ones," Quinn said clearly, her voice like a bell. "Thank you for being with us today as my parents, Paul and Ingrid Harper, recommit their lives, hearts, and souls to one another."

The crowd clapped, loudly enough to send the sprays of daisies and hyacinths dancing along the aisle. Ingrid grinned up at him, impishly delighted to have gotten their skeptical, pragmatic daughter to talk about their souls in public.

Paul loved them both so much, it nearly stopped his breath.

"If this were a traditional ceremony, I'd be calling you 'Dearly Beloved,'" Quinn joked. "But since this is the Harpers we're talking about, I'll just say, hey, y'all. I can't believe how many of you showed up to witness this moment that is so worth honoring. Thank you for being here, and we love you. And now it's time to turn things over to the man and woman of the hour, my beautiful mother and sweet daddy. I love you guys."

Quinn's voice broke a little on the last part, and Paul noticed for the first time that a tear was tracking down her cheek. She smiled tremulously at him and stepped aside, giving them the floor.

Paul drew in a deep breath and raised his and Ingrid's joined hands to press a kiss to her knuckles. In a way, they'd already said their vows right here in this very spot, a few days before. But Ingrid believed, and Paul agreed, that there was meaning and power in proclaiming those same vows in front of their community.

He opened his mouth, his mind full of the words he planned to say, words he'd thought about and written down and worked over until he basically had them memorized. But before he could speak, a commotion in the crowd of guests drew his attention.

Stomping through the flower beds like a human wrecking ball was their erstwhile marriage guru, Ron Burkey. And he looked *pissed*.

"What the hell are you doing here?" Paul demanded, muscles tensing.

He dropped Ingrid's hands and faced off with Ron, who puffed up like he was about to explode. There was a crazed look in his bulging eyes. A vein throbbed visibly in his forehead. "I'm here because you people have ruined everything! You're not supposed to renew your vows, you're supposed to break up! This whole ceremony is a sham!"

"You're the sham," Ingrid said sharply, eyes flashing. Paul had never been more proud of her. "Get off our property, Ron. Yes, our property, which will remain our property because we're not selling it! To you or anyone!"

"What a waste," Ron groaned, his hand clenched so tightly around his phone that his knuckles were white with strain. "And I just found . . . it's not important. You've ruined me. I had a lot riding on this deal, and all you had to do was break up, the way you were already planning when I found you. It was perfect. Until she came along."

His eyes narrowed on Quinn, and Paul's head whipped around to see her chin lifting defiantly. "I have zero regrets, Mr. Burkey. Now, I think you should leave."

Paul quite agreed. He stepped forward to assist Ron out of his backyard, by force if necessary, but Ron shrugged off his restraining hand with surprising strength.

Sneering, Ron replied, "Oh, I'm sure you do wish I'd leave. Preferably before I tell your parents and all your friends here that you've been lying to them for weeks."

"Quinn?" Ingrid sounded confused. "What does he mean?"

"He's a liar," Paul growled, grabbing hold of the slick collar of Ron's shiny sport coat. "We don't need to listen to anything he has to say."

"Oh no?" Ron struggled, clearly out of his mind with fury. "Then you don't want to hear about how your daughter perpetrated a fraud on this entire town by pretending to be engaged to that overgrown lunk Marcus Beckett!"

"But they were engaged," Ingrid said blankly. "We were there. We saw him ask her."

Paul couldn't take another second of this. "Ron, you're just mad at Quinn and Marcus for discovering your underhanded scheme to turn our property into a spa for people with more money than sense. It's time for you to leave. Now."

He started hauling Ron backward by his coat collar, working against the resistance put up by the bigger, meatier man, who was also shouting red-faced craziness as he went.

"They were never even involved! It was all a lie, a fake, and you fell for it. I heard them talking about it! They pretended to be in love and ready to settle down so you'd stay here and she could have time to ruin everything for me, the *little bitch*."

Flames licked up the sides of Paul's face and his vision went black for a moment. Then he blinked, and Ron was on the ground, moaning about his nose. Which was gushing blood. Paul's knuckles were throbbing.

"Paul, darling!" Ingrid flew toward him through the crowd to throw her arms around his neck. "My hero! This is the best vow renewal anyone ever had!"

"I hit him," Paul said stupidly. "I've never hit anyone before in my life."

"If you ask me," said a man beside him. "Ron Burkey was a good place to start."

"Marcus!" Quinn gasped, her hand coming up to cover her mouth. "You're back."

Watching with interest while Ingrid laid her head on his chest contentedly, Paul saw Marcus make an aborted motion as though he wanted nothing in the world more than to go to Quinn. But instead, he glared down at Ron. "I never left. And I'm ready to haul this guy out of here and put him on the first ferry off this island."

"No, let me," said another man whom Paul recognized as another newish transplant to the island, Johnny Alexander. Johnny hauled Ron up by the scruff of his neck, like a disobedient terrier.

"He broke my nose," Ron whined, staring around at the onlookers as if hoping for sympathy. His eyes lit on the khaki-clad figure of the sheriff. "I want to press charges!"

Sheriff Shepard gave him a flinty look. "I'm afraid I didn't see a thing. Except this homeowner asking you to leave his property, more than once. Which means you're currently trespassing. Mr. Alexander, do you need any help? I can call in one of my deputies, if you'd like."

"Or I can go with you," Marcus offered.

When Ron visibly deflated at the sheriff's stern tone, Johnny Alexander grinned and clapped Marcus on the back with his free hand. "Nah, I've got this. And you, my friend, have other things to take care of here."

With that, he frog-marched the unfortunate and still bleeding relationship expert away. They disappeared around the side of the house and were gone, leaving behind a shell-shocked crowd staring at the Harper family and wondering what the heck was going to happen next.

As Paul held his wife securely in his arms, he had to admit, he had no idea.

From her vantage point by the stone circle, Quinn looked out over the assembled crowd of well-wishers and wished, with all her heart, that they would leave. This day she'd fought so hard to give to her parents, this day she'd planned and hoped for—it was ruined. And it was all her fault.

But maybe it was time to face the music. Marcus was here, after all. He hadn't left. Maybe that meant he'd listen to what she had to say.

First order of business . . . no more lying.

"It's true," she said into the quiet that settled after Ron was finally out of their yard and their lives, hopefully for good. "I mean, Ron was a liar and a schemer, but he was also telling the truth. About Marcus and me."

She met Marcus's gaze across the crowd and was startled to see pain and uncertainty flicker across his handsome features. Replaying exactly what Ron had accused them of, Quinn felt her own eyes widen.

"I mean about the engagement! That wasn't real."

Her parents gazed up at her, shock all over their faces, and Quinn's cheeks burned with shame. "I'm sorry for deceiving you. All of you. This town deserved better from me, after all you've given me throughout my life. But I was worried about my parents' marriage, and I would've done anything I could to help them."

Most people around the garden were nodding, clearly understanding her motives, although a few looked disappointed in her. Quinn bore up under it; she'd done wrong and she knew it, but if the end result was her parents once again happily married? She couldn't regret her choices.

Especially since those choices had led her here to this second chance with Marcus. Or was this her third chance? Fourth? She wasn't keeping track, but maybe she should be. No one had an infinite number of chances to get it right.

Part of her wished she and Marcus could have worked things out alone, just the two of them—but a bigger part of Quinn understood what her parents had been trying to accomplish with this vow-renewal ceremony. There was something about saying it out loud, witnessed by family and friends and everyone who was dear to her. Something that brought home to Quinn exactly how real, and important, this moment was.

If she said it now, here in front of everyone, that was it. No take-backs. And if it didn't end happily ever after, that was it, too. No more chances.

But at least she'd know that she'd put everything on the line and committed herself all the way, holding nothing back. She could live with that, even if she didn't get to live with Marcus. Maybe she wouldn't be happy, or as happy as she could have been, but she could move on.

Holding her head high, Quinn Harper, free spirit (or flibbertigibbet, depending on who you asked) said the words that would tie her to one man, one life, for the rest of her days.

She hoped.

"Not everything between Marcus and me was a lie," Quinn announced, scanning his face for any reaction. "The first time we were together, and broke up—that was all real. The second time around, it started out as a plan to get my parents back together, and to convince all of you that Marcus wasn't Satan incarnate so you'd try his bar. You should keep going there, by the way, no matter how this turns out. I appreciate the loyalty, so much, but I don't deserve it. I've made mistakes, more than my share."

She paused to swallow down her fears. Marcus was a statue, unmoving and unblinking. She'd never been able to tell what he was thinking, and today wasn't going to be the day she cracked the code. With a deep breath in, she shoved herself over the cliff.

"But the biggest mistake I made was to break off my fake engagement. See, over the weeks of our little arrangement, we'd started to grow closer again. I was falling for Marcus all over again, or maybe I never stopped falling. One or the other. But I was terrified that being forced into setting a date for our fake wedding would push Marcus to run in the other direction. So I ran first. I panicked. And I'm sorry for that, Marcus."

Every head swiveled to catch Marcus's reaction. And for the first time since he'd arrived, ready to kick Ron Burkey's butt out of town, Marcus showed a reaction.

He crossed the garden in long, ground-eating strides, the breadth of his shoulders stretching the cotton of his dark gray shirt and parting the people between them like Moses parting the waters of the Red Sea. Quinn watched him come for her with her heart in her throat and her entire future in his hands, but she still didn't know whether he was more likely to kiss her or throttle her.

When he was a foot away from her, he stopped as if he'd hit a wall. "Don't apologize," he said, his voice as roughly hewn as the limestones they'd used to build the standing stone circle. "Not about that. I overreacted and misinterpreted what you were saying. And maybe I did a little running away, myself. That wasn't fair to you, and it wasn't the mature way to handle things."

Quinn's mouth trembled with the urge to smile, but she wasn't sure where they stood yet. "So maybe we're not so badly matched, after all. I mean, even with our ten-year age difference."

To her immense surprise, Marcus threw back his head and actually laughed. When he caught his breath, he looked right at her and said, "God, I love you. There's no one like you in the entire world. You deserve better than a cranky old bastard like me, but I'm starting to think you might be a better judge of what you want and need out of life than I am."

"Well, amen to that. And it's about damn time!" Hope and gladness lit Quinn up from the inside, warming her chest and fizzing through her blood. "So what are you going to do about it?"

She expected him to swoop her up and kiss her, maybe, and she was looking forward to it. Looking forward to him twirling her around in the sunlit splendor of her mother's garden, and showing all their friends and neighbors that this relationship and their feelings for each other were as real as real could be.

She didn't expect him to kneel down.

So of course, that's exactly what he did.

Quinn's hands flew to cover her mouth as Marcus sank gracefully to one knee, his eyes never leaving hers. He reached into his pocket and pulled out a box. Her heart battered at the inside of her rib cage like it was trying to get out and leap across the space that separated her from Marcus.

"We never managed to buy a fake engagement ring," he said quietly. "But even then, I thought of this one. I just never thought I'd be able to offer it to you—or that you would, or should, accept."

He flicked open the worn black velvet box with his thumb and gazed at its contents for a moment before he turned the box around and showed it to Quinn. The slender, white gold band branched to cup a single, brilliantly faceted emerald. The shock of recognition ran from the top of her head to the tips of her fingers. She knew that ring.

As a little girl, she'd been fascinated by the fact that Mrs. Beckett wore her engagement ring on a chain around her neck instead of on her finger. She'd asked to see it almost every time she saw Mrs. Beckett, who would laugh and fish the chain out from the neckline of her nursing scrubs to dangle, flashing green fire, above Quinn's entranced eyes.

"Your mother's ring," she whispered through her fingers. "Oh, Marcus. You went home."

He blinked, like that wasn't what he thought she'd take away from this moment, but it was all Quinn could think of. "I did. Finally. I should have listened to you."

Quinn had a thousand questions—had Marcus seen his father's drawings and stories? Had he talked to him about the real estate deal? Did they finally make up?

Although, looking at the beautiful emerald winking up at her from Marcus's outstretched palm, Quinn knew father and son must have reconciled. That ring had to be one of Dr. Will Beckett's most cherished mementos of the woman he had loved and lost.

For him to give it to Marcus, to give to Quinn, meant more than Quinn could begin to express. Although she realized in that moment that she had yet to actually take the ring.

"What's it going to be?" Marcus asked. "Let's make this thing real, Quinn. Marry me, and I'll spend the rest of my life working to deserve you."

Quinn grabbed for the ring with one hand and slung the other one around the back of Marcus's neck, her fingers sliding on warm skin. She bent down to kiss him, unable to wait another second to have her mouth on his. That kiss felt like coming home, like the first day of the rest of her life.

"You deserve to be happy, Marcus Beckett." She pulled back just far enough to speak the words against his cheek while their assembled audience sent up a deafening round of applause and cheers. "And if you truly think I can help to make you happy, I'll marry you."

His gaze searched hers, as if he couldn't believe what he was hearing. "But are you ready to settle down? I can wait, Quinn. God knows, I'm not going anywhere. I can wait for you to finish your certification and start full-time at the therapy riding center, or however long. I'd wait for you for as long as it takes."

Heart brimming so full, it nearly overflowed in

happy tears, Quinn perched herself on Marcus's bent knee to try on the emerald ring. It slipped onto her finger as smoothly as if it had been designed for her, and she sent up a quick, silent prayer of thanks and love to Elizabeth Beckett.

"Marcus, you told me once not to let love tie me up in knots. You said the world was full of people who thought that because they loved you, they knew what was best for you. You told me to make my own choices—and this is my choice. I choose you. I choose a life of love and laughter and fighting and amazing sex and happiness and sadness and whatever else comes our way. Love isn't going to tie me up in knots, Marcus. I've never felt more free."

The last lines of worry smoothed from Marcus's strong forehead, and with a burst of pleasure, Quinn realized that she could read his mood better than she'd thought.

"I don't want to hold you back," he said gruffly, his broad palms settling on her back and making her feel as if she could fly. "You can go far, do whatever you want. Your life can be what you make it."

"And I want to make that life with you," Quinn said, looping her arms around his neck in a way that allowed her to still admire the sparkle of green on her ring finger. "We won't tie each other down or hold each other back, if we're determined not to. With you at my side, I feel like I can do anything. You give me the confidence to try things I never thought I could do. Like the new job, and the certification—which, thank you for that, by the way—and, I don't know. Growing up, maybe."

Marcus shifted and hooked an arm under her legs. He rose to standing with Quinn cradled against his chest, as if she weighed no more than an armful of her mother's roses. "I can't wait to see what we do with this life of ours."

Across the crowd, Quinn met her mother's tear-filled, happy eyes, and nodded once. "We'll hold on to it, and we'll hold on to each other. No matter what happens."

"I want to be here for you. For everything that matters, all the important moments." Marcus was fierce with it, his voice low and throbbing with emotion. "But I'm not going to change overnight and turn into some modern touchy-feely guy who wants to talk about his emotions all the time."

Quinn laughed. "I don't want you to change. Not a thing. I love you exactly the way you are. You might be a cranky old bastard, but you're my cranky old bastard."

"And you're the light of my life."

All the breath left Quinn's lungs in a whoosh. "You're not so bad at the touchy-feely stuff, tough guy."

Marcus grinned, a wickedly appealing expression she'd never seen on him before. Quinn hoped to see it many more times in the course of their long, happy life together. "Only with you. Don't tell anyone."

Around them, their friends were still talking and cheering and celebrating. The whole thing had turned into an impromptu party.

"Your secret is safe with me," Quinn said into his ear, and smiled when he laughed.

Like the rest of their secrets, she had a feeling that this one was public knowledge already. But that was okay. No couple was an island, after all, even if they were lucky enough to live on one.

Blushing and beaming, Quinn waved at their friends and thought about how lucky they all were, to have this place and each other. To know that they lived in a place where their neighbors were their friends and family—and to know that no matter what life threw at them, they'd be able to face it, together.

Thank you, Sanctuary Island. Thank you for bringing him back to me, Quinn thought, leaning in to steal another kiss as the spring sun struck sparks from her new ring and warmed the smiling faces of everyone she cared about, all gathered together in this beautiful place.

Thank you.

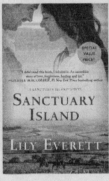